For my lovely mum, one of my biggest fans.

# MURDER IN THE VILLAGE

*DI Hillary Greene Book 4*

## FAITH MARTIN

Published in paperback 2020 by Joffe Books, London
Revised edition 2017

www.joffebooks.com

First published by Robert Hale in 2006
as *By A Narrow Majority*.

ISBN 978-1-78931-281-2

# CHAPTER ONE

Detective Inspector Hillary Greene watched Sergeant Duncan Baines check his .38 revolver and was glad it was him and not her. It was a cold and still March morning, and she shivered inside her long black coat, reflecting that frost and nerves never did make for a good combination.

Two other members of the Tactical Firearms Unit stood off to one side of her, watching the innocuous office unit without blinking. Neither appeared overtly nervous, which was reassuring, though Hillary for one was not totally convinced by their calm. Behind the bland faces, tension had to be high. Even on a low-risk offensive like this one.

'Hill.' A voice behind her had her turning and smiling. DI Robbie 'Dobbin' Dobson was an old friend of hers from way back, when she was still at her old Headington nick, and she'd been relieved when told that he was to be in charge of the arrests today. 'Still think it'll be a good one?' he asked her flatly. He was a tall man, with silver hair and pale blue eyes, and a quiet voice that always reminded her of a priest.

Hillary nodded. 'I don't think we're dealing with a bunch of desperadoes if that's what you mean. My snitch was adamant they're first-timers.'

1

Dobbin grunted, but wasn't appeased. 'They can be the worst of the lot,' he grumbled. 'No experience, see. Guys who tool up regularly, they tend to know the odds when they're surrounded, and give up without a fight. Amateurs think guns make them supermen. Then there's always the "if you got it, flaunt it" factor. Why have a gun if you're not going to fire the damn thing? Give even the mildest-mannered villain a gun in his hand and he thinks he's Jesse James.'

Hillary sighed. There was always something. 'My snitch is Gary Verney's wife, as you know. He's been a strictly petty B&E merchant until now; you know the sort — not too bright, but in no way vicious either. I just can't see him giving you any trouble. He spends more time inside than out, and Mavis, his wife, seems to prefer it that way. Word is she's got a stand-in ready whenever he's locked up, so she's never been a player until now.'

Dobbin grunted. 'But?'

'But she's been scared out of her wits ever since her nearest and dearest bragged about this new mate of his getting him some real hardware.' Hillary went over it again, even though she knew that he'd already been fully briefed by DCI Mallow. 'She doesn't know much about this new mate, or says she doesn't, but I got the distinct feeling from her attitude and reading between the lines that he's about as hard as last night's leftover fish and chips as well,' she carried on. 'So I'm really not expecting fireworks.' Even as she said it, she felt a moment of shame. It was easy to be sanguine when she wasn't going to go through the door until everything had been sorted.

Before she could say so, however, Dobbin nodded and sighed. 'It's a sign of the times when even the bottom feeders start tooling up.' He sounded as tired and dispirited as she'd ever heard him, making her wonder why he still did the job. He could have retired by now if he'd wanted to, and was a granddad twice over, and yet here he was, carrying a loaded gun and maybe about to get shot at. Still, he'd been doing it for years, so perhaps he was addicted.

Regular coppers could apply for firearms training at any point in their careers, of course, but surprisingly few did so. Perhaps it was the rigorous psychological evaluation that put them off. Others, like herself, had no fantasies of locking and loading and going down in a haze of bullets. Or, in this case, of raiding a rather dreary office unit in the outskirts of Bicester on a cold Monday morning.

Dobbin's earpiece stuttered and he listened intently, nodded and glanced at the other two armed men. Both looked way too young, to Hillary, to be carrying firearms. 'Team two are in position. Ready?'

Hillary felt the sudden and urgent need to go to the loo. She looked around nervously, but the business park was reassuringly deserted.

According to her snitch, the gun dealer in question was a previously unknown character by the name of Adam Fairway. Background checks had confirmed that he ran a legitimate garden equipment supply business from one of Bicester's many business parks, and the fact that he had no criminal record and hadn't even crossed the radar of any of Oxfordshire's police forces meant nothing. Nowadays, with gun crime on the rise, every Tom, Dick and Harry seemed to want in on the act.

She watched as the two officers, Baines and Dobbin, approached unit 62, using parked cars as cover. A second team, she knew, was in position at the back of the premises. It was barely ten o'clock, and most workers had long since settled in to their office routines. She hoped the sound of gunfire wouldn't interrupt their morning coffee. She hoped nobody would even know arrests had been made until gossip did the rounds at lunchtime.

She glanced over her shoulder once more and sighed. Where was Frank Ross, that worthless waste of space? As one of the sergeants on her team, and the longest serving member, he was supposed to be here to provide logistical support. Ha! She'd be better off with a trained poodle.

She rubbed her hands nervously across her dark blue skirt and tried to breathe normally. Sergeant Baines reached the door first, waited for a signal from his team leader, then tried the handle. It was open. Good. No need for the battering ram then, which meant one less hurdle and one less thing that could go wrong.

Hillary watched as first Duncan Baines, then her old friend entered the building, followed by the younger two. She glanced at her watch. 10:02. No shouting. No shots. She glanced behind her and saw two uniformed constables crouched down out of sight behind a furniture lorry. One of the business units housed the local depot of a large-scale sofa manufacturer. She looked down at her watch — thirty seconds had passed. Still no sounds. A door further down the avenue of block-like buildings opened and Hillary tensed. An office worker stepped outside and lit up a fag. Of all the times she could have chosen, Hillary thought grimly. She was dressed in a blue suit very similar to her own — skirt, jacket, white blouse. Only the secretary's skirt reached up to her bum, while Hillary's fell modestly down to her knees.

Hillary grimaced, feeling suddenly old. Forty-four was probably not old, but it wasn't exactly young either. Would she still be working long past the time when she could have retired, like Dobbin? Too scared of boredom or loneliness to quit while she still could? It was a depressing thought.

She glanced at her watch again, wishing the secretary would go back inside. It wasn't always feasible to evacuate an area when armed arrests were being made, and the woman's presence outside was making her antsy. Another thirty seconds had gone by. Then a whole minute. Her radio remained stubbornly silent.

What if she was wrong? What if her snitch had got it wrong, or, worse yet, had been leading her up the garden path? It wouldn't be the first time the wife of some old lag had decided to have a laugh and pull a copper's leg. But she didn't think so. Mavis Verney had struck her as genuine — in her own way, genuinely fond of her no-hoper of a husband, and almost comically indignant about the worthlessness of his newest buddy and his plan to get her husband tooled up.

Her radio suddenly squawked her designated number and she lifted it quickly to her ear. She wasn't aware that she'd been holding her breath until she released it on a long, relieved sigh when she finally heard Dobbin's voice. 'Eight-one, this is two-six. All clear.'

Hillary acknowledged the call with a dry raspy voice, and nodded across to the two uniforms to accompany her. She knew the call had also gone through to another team of constables, parked well out of sight up the road, who would now come in and help her do the scutwork.

Hillary walked the short space across the car park, glad that, at last, the office worker had gone back inside. Someone should tell her that smoking could seriously damage your health.

In unit 62, someone had gone nuts with cans of beige paint and had plastered it everywhere — the plywood walls, the artexed ceilings, the window frames and doors. Even the heavy-duty matting was beige coloured. A straight and simple corridor gave way to rows of doors, but Hillary could hear the murmuring of voices far down and to the left. She walked cautiously and very slowly forward, even though she trusted Dobbin's judgement completely, and knew that his team would have made a quick but thorough search before giving the all-clear. Still, it never hurt to be careful.

Just then, Duncan Baines opened one of the doors a bit wider, and grinned out at her. He was dressed, as were all the Tactical Firearms Unit team, in dark blue Kevlar. 'In here, Inspector Greene.'

Hillary walked into an office with posters of beautiful landscaped gardens plastered on every wall. A big box of newly published brochures, featuring that year's leaf rake and garden extension hose deal of the century, sat on a table. A young girl, obviously a secretary, was seated behind a computer screen in a little Plexiglas cubicle, not sure whether she was shocked, scared, fascinated or indignant.

Sitting behind a big desk in the main office, and looking distinctly shame-faced, was a man who could have posed for

Daddy Warbucks in the musical *Annie*. He was dressed in a very smart blue pinstriped suit, was almost completely bald, and had the florid complexion of a farmer. He was twisting a wedding ring nervously around and around on his finger. Looking tense and miserable on the other side of the desk from him was Gary Verney and a man Hillary didn't know.

'Are you in charge here?' Daddy Warbucks asked, trying to sound outraged. He couldn't quite bring it off.

'Mr Fairway?' Hillary asked, coming forward and opening out her ID card and rattling off her name, rank, and the fact that she worked out of Thames Valley's headquarters in Kidlington. As she did this, she glanced at Dobbin, who merely shrugged. Things had gone easy.

There were no guns laid out on the table — but then, with a secretary present, she hardly thought there would be. More likely the two men and the gun supplier had simply been negotiating a price. She sighed, and reached for the radio. 'Bring in the dogs.'

She glanced around and grimaced as Detective Sergeant Frank Ross sauntered in through the doorway. At least he hadn't turned up in the middle of the raid, just when he could do the most damage. Even so, it wasn't like him to miss the show. Frank considered himself to be an old-fashioned copper; harder than the actors in the seventies cop show *The Sweeney* and twice as streetwise. She knew for a fact that he'd applied for firearms training early on in his career, and she was sure that she could still hear them chuckling about it, even now. Needless to say, he'd been turned down. Frank Ross had to be the least liked cop at Kidlington nick, and when she thought about the serious competition he had, that was saying something.

'Frank,' she said dryly. 'So nice of you to join us.' Frank had never been her number one fan, and since she'd saved his life a few months ago, he positively hated her guts. She suspected his late showing was just another way of pissing her off.

'I demand to know what's going on,' Daddy Warbucks said nervously, rising from behind his desk on legs that even

Hillary could see were shaking. Just then, a uniformed constable came in with a beautiful liver-and-white spaniel. She saw Gary Verney's eyes widen as he saw it. No doubt he was expecting a slavering Alsatian that looked ready to rip the head off anything that moved. Most people did. But the fact was, spaniels, and many other assorted breeds, were regularly used by the police to sniff out drugs, firearms, and other assorted goodies.

Hillary handed over the search warrant for Adam Fairway to read, and nodded to Frank. 'Since you're here, you can help Tactical to oversee the search. Mr Fairway, you have separate premises in the rear of the lot, I understand?' She knew he had. They'd done their homework carefully before going in.

Adam Fairway went rather green as Hillary gave the trainer with the dog the order to start there. For a man who was into gardening, she supposed it was a good colour for him. Behind her, in her little Plexiglas cubicle, the secretary began to cry. Perhaps it was genuine shock, or perhaps she simply wanted one of the big, handsome, armed policemen to notice her. Which they did, of course, the youngest one going over to her at once and offering her a shoulder to cry on.

Hillary turned her attention to the two men sitting opposite the desk. 'Hello, Gary, remember me?' she asked, moving forward and nodding to Dobbin to take a seat opposite.

'Er, yeah. DI, er . . .' Verney was a little sparrow of a man; small, brown-haired, eyed and skinned, and fragile-looking.

'Greene,' Hillary prompted. 'I arrested you last, let me see, nearly ten years ago now, wasn't it? When I was still in uniform. Who's your friend?' She turned and glanced at the other man and smiled. He was slightly younger than the thief, a bit flashier, but probably no smarter. He wore an earring and a spider tattoo on the back of his left hand. He went a trifle pale with the sudden attention she was giving him.

'Eh? Don't know him,' Gary Verney said promptly. 'I was just here to order a lawnmower, like. This bloke came in just after I did. After a lawnmower too, I 'spect. Mr Fairway here was just telling me that he was doing this great deal on the latest hover mower. Weren't you?'

Adam Fairway nodded, but his sickly green colour intensified as the sound of excited barking reached them through the open back door.

'Gary, Gary,' Hillary said softly, shaking her head, 'you don't have a garden. You live in a block of flats, remember?'

The young officer not consoling the pretty secretary suddenly laughed. As did Dobbin. And so, after a short, startled pause, did Gary Verney. Hillary caught Dobbin's eye and shook her head slightly. Sometimes the job gave up a moment of farce so absurd that no theatre producer would touch it with a bargepole.

The stranger beside Gary, probably unnerved by the sudden levity, stood up. 'Look, all I was after was a hedge trimmer. I don't know nothing about this, so I'll be off.' He even pushed back his chair ready to move. Frank Ross strode forward and pushed him back down in his seat. As he did so, Dobbin's radio crackled.

Everyone froze. Dobbin listened, then nodded, then glanced at Hillary. 'They found weapons. At least eight. Want me to . . .' he paused and turned as Adam Fairway gave a little sigh and slid majestically from his chair towards the floor. His feet rocked the table a little as they came to rest up against the right-hand corner leg. All four of them stared down at the prostrate figure.

'Crikey,' Gary Verney said.

Hillary read the two their rights and had the uniforms cuff them and take them back to Kidlington for questioning. She called out the police doctor for Fairway, who she was sure had simply fainted, and then had him look at the secretary too, who seemed to be working up to a case of genuine hysterics.

By lunchtime, the Tactical Firearms Unit were gone, having recovered, recorded, photographed and packed eleven firearms — mostly fairly old but serviceable revolvers. 'I doubt he was getting rich on this lot,' had been Dobbin's final words, but he'd been pleased to get them out of circulation nevertheless. She supposed that, by now, the team would have changed out of their gear and be in the nearest pub, celebrating. She'd already phoned Mel, her immediate superior officer, back at HQ to tell him the raid had gone off without a hitch, and that several arrests had been made. She was just having a word with the evidence officer, a uniformed WPC who was even older than Dobbin and just as reluctant to retire, when one of the constables sorting through bags of fertilizer suddenly gave a shout.

It brought Frank, who'd been back in the main office drinking coffee and trying to flirt with the still weepy secretary, outside to see what all the fuss was about. Hillary got there first, and looked down to where the excited youngster was pointing.

'Oh shit,' she sighed. 'Another one.' The revolver, which like the others had been wrapped in a piece of old towel, looked smaller than the rest to her. Why it hadn't been stashed in the locked filing cabinet along with all the others, she had no idea. Perhaps this was the gun Adam Fairway had intended to sell to Verney? It would make sense for him to keep the hiding place of all the other guns a secret from his customers. Unlike popular belief, there was no such thing as honour among thieves. 'Take some pictures,' she said curtly to the uniform who'd found it. I'm not calling Tactical back again just for this. Frank, you can take it back to the evidence locker. Make sure you sign it straight in and give DI Dobson a call. He might want to keep the haul together.'

Frank gave her a two-fingered salute behind her back. She knew he'd done it by the look one of the young coppers gave him. She shook her head wearily. There was no point reporting Frank Ross for insubordination. He'd only deny it, and she was not about to ask a uniform to back her up at a disciplinary hearing. It would blight his career for years to come.

No, thanks to her late hubby Ronnie Greene, she was stuck with Frank. Her husband had died before he could be brought up on corruption charges, but everyone and their granny knew that Frank Ross had been in the mire up to his neck too.

She made her way back to Greenfingers Inc. offices and noticed the secretary had gone missing — probably headed for home and a stiff gin. She hoped the constable questioning her had made sure of her address before he'd let her go.

She turned on Fairway's computer and stared at it glumly for a few moments, then reached for her phone and called Detective Constable Tommy Lynch back at HQ. 'Tommy, it's me. I need you in Bicester,' she said cheerfully. One day she was going to have to take an advanced computer course. One day she was going to have to do a lot of things.

* * *

Back in Kidlington, DC Tommy Lynch took a deep breath and wished she wouldn't say things like that to him, especially without warning. 'On my way, guv,' he responded calmly, then glanced across at DS Janine Tyler, sitting at the desk opposite, and shrugged.

Everyone on Hillary's team knew about the raid, and Janine Tyler in particular had been furious to be left out in the cold. But it had been DCI Mallow's call that only Hillary and Frank Ross need be present. After all, it had been the TFU's show, and they didn't need everyone else there as well.

Tommy Lynch whistled as he drove to the small market town in the north of Oxfordshire. He was getting married in June, and didn't think it was a good idea to be thinking so much about his governor, but since there didn't seem to be a damn thing he could do about it, he supposed there was no point in tying himself up in knots about it either.

Hillary and the evidence officer were still poring over the inevitable paperwork when he arrived. Hillary pointed him in the direction of the perp's computer and told him she wanted its every secret. 'And see if he's got a safe hidden anywhere, will you, Tommy,' she added.

She had a gut feeling that Adam Fairway was the sort to keep records. Detailed records. And she wasn't wrong. But even she was amazed when Tommy called her over about an hour later to show her what he'd found. Hidden in a file under a separate password were records that would make Dobbin's mouth water. A list of weapons bought and sold going back nearly seven years.

A lot of people were going to be very happy about this — and it always paid to keep the brass happy. And the press liaison officer would be ecstatic. More than that, it was yet another good collar that would liven up her CV no end when a chief inspectorship came up for grabs. And all because Mavis Verney hadn't liked the thought of her Gary going out tooled up when he went out to nick CD players from the local Curry's.

Some days Hillary really liked her job.

* * *

Back at HQ, Hillary parked up and sighed. It was nearly three o'clock but she had hours of work ahead of her yet, and since it had turned overcast, it wouldn't be long before it got dark. She'd be glad when the clocks went on next week. Another hour of daylight at the end of her shift would come in handy.

She made her way through the lobby, where somebody had placed a tub of flowering daffodils, and accepted the good-natured congratulations and ribbing from the desk sergeant. News of the gun haul had gone before her, of course, and it was always nice to come back to the nest a conquering hero. At her desk, she slumped down in her chair and ignored her rumbling stomach. She'd missed lunch, but doubted that her middle-aged spread would notice. That was another thing she'd have to do one day — join a gym.

Yeah, right.

Frank Ross walked in, a suspiciously heavy bulge in his overcoat pocket. Hillary opened her mouth, about to blast him about not checking the gun into the evidence locker the moment he arrived, then got distracted as DCI Philip 'Mel' Mallow came out of his office and walked across the open-plan office towards her.

Mel was an old friend of nearly twenty years standing, and her immediate superior officer. The fact that he was nearly a year into a sexual relationship with her pretty blonde DS, Janine Tyler, was still something of a matter of contention between them. Still, she was grateful he'd kept Janine out of her hair this morning. Although a good cop who would no doubt go far, Janine tended to be too hungry for promotion and too ambitious for good sense to always reign supreme. She also suspected that Janine had applied for firearms training and had been turned down. Hillary could well imagine that her sergeant had come across as too gung-ho to be a serious contender. Still, a lot of cops saw weapons training as a way to get ahead, and Janine had certainly been keen to be in on the raid, even though the chance of any gunfire being exchanged had been judged as very low.

Mel Mallow glanced across at Frank as he spoke, reluctantly including him in the equation. 'The super wants us in his office for the latest update,' he said flatly.

Hillary groaned. 'The Fletcher thing again?'

Luke Fletcher was Thames Valley's biggest thorn in the side, and had been for many years. He ran both prostitution and drug rackets, and was suspected to be behind at least three murders, though nothing had ever been pinned on him. Last year, Superintendent Marcus Donleavy had been kicked upstairs, and a man from the Met, Jerome Raleigh, had been brought in. And the new broom seemed determined to sweep up Luke Fletcher.

Frank Ross grinned. 'About time.' For some reason, Frank, who could be guaranteed to hate the top brass simply as a matter of principle, had become a big fan of the new super, and that alone was enough to make Hillary uneasy. And the fact that Raleigh was insisting on keeping Frank in the loop made her uneasier still. The Met man must know of

Frank's reputation, so why was he keeping the oily little oik so close to the superintendent bosom?

Still, as she gathered up her bag and notebook and followed the other two out of the room, she had to admit that, lately, the super's intelligence on Fletcher had been impressive. It also made her wonder how a man from London had managed to get so many fingers into so many of Fletcher's pies, so soon. And was this the reason why the Met man had got the job? Had he been gathering evidence against Fletcher for far longer than just a few months?

Mel led the little cavalcade up the stairs to the super's office, but let Frank get ahead as they reached the landing. He laid a quiet hand on Hillary's arm, holding her back. 'You have any idea who his source could be?' he murmured quietly as the super's civilian secretary buzzed them through.

'Nope,' she murmured back. Like herself, Mel was intrigued, not to mention narked, at the new super's impressive dedication to nailing Fletcher. It was no secret that Mel had secretly been hoping to get Marcus Donleavy's old job, and that his nose had been well and truly put out of joint at being pipped at the post by an outsider was understandable. She only hoped her old friend's jealousy wouldn't make him do anything stupid. Nailing Fletcher, no matter who got the credit for it, would be many a copper's dream come true. Including her own.

Inside his office, Jerome Raleigh got to his feet as they trooped in. There were two men from Vice, DI Mike Regis and Sergeant Colin Tanner, already present. Mike Regis's eyes went straight to Hillary, and she felt her pulse rate thump, just a little. A while ago, she'd thought that she and Mike Regis might just have things to talk about. But that was before she'd found out he was married. Now, or so she'd heard, his divorce was imminent.

Would they have things to talk about then? She hoped so. 'Philip.' Superintendent Raleigh held out his hand to the man who'd hoped to have his job, nodded blankly at Frank, and smiled at Hillary. 'You know DI Regis and Sergeant Tanner, of course. Sit down, please. Help yourself to coffee.'

Hillary did the honours, without making a fuss. She never turned down good caffeine, and certainly not in the name of sexual equality. The only one she didn't hand a cup to was Frank.

Well, there were limits.

Raleigh hid a smile as Frank Ross heaved his bulk out of his chair to get his own. After that bit of entertainment, the meeting passed swiftly, and it was clear that the intelligence on Fletcher was building. Hillary could tell that Mike Regis, for one, was delighted. For the first time in what seemed like a long, long wait, it appeared as if Fletcher might actually be touchable after all. As a Vice man, Regis harboured a particular animosity towards Fletcher. Mel too was impressed, but careful not to show it, and asked several clever and cautionary questions. Hillary listened carefully and said nothing.

A small-time dealer, one of Fletcher's minnows, had been caught with enough dope on him to merit a five-year stretch. According to Raleigh he might be persuaded to talk. There were also rumours that Fletcher was about to take possession of a big and experimental shipment of drugs. Nobody knew if that was true, or just rumour. Twice Raleigh led them over to a board on the far side of the room to check out the latest intel posted up there. Twice Hillary wondered how the Met man had got so close, so quickly, to Oxford's kingpin.

It was already gone five, and was dark and raining, by the time Raleigh let them go. Hillary watched Frank Ross retrieve his overcoat and hurry away. Ross, a deceivingly benign-looking man with rounded cheeks and a chubby figure, never did overtime if he could help it. For herself, she'd be lucky to get off by nine.

'So what do you think?' Regis's voice behind her out on the landing made her turn and smile briefly.

'About what?' she asked. Us?

'Getting Fletcher. We're close to it this time. I can feel it. You must be glad to have a super so hellbent on it.'

'Marcus Donleavy was never slack either,' she said sharply, then bit her lip as Regis gave her a quick look.

Damn. The truth was, she missed having Marcus Donleavy in charge. She both liked and trusted him — as opposed to the man from the Met, whom she simply couldn't get a handle on. She'd have to be careful not to let her loyalties show though. Not that she was worried Mike Regis would shaft her. Still. Office politics was like dynamite. It needed to be handled carefully. 'Long day,' she excused herself briefly.

'Fancy a drink?' he asked quickly.

'Sorry, not tonight. Still got a lot to do.' She briefly told him about the raid — all cops liked to hear a success story — and by the time she'd finished, she noticed that Frank Ross was coming back up the stairs. Odd, she'd have thought he would be well on his way by now. He practically supported his local boozer single-handedly. 'Another time, maybe?' She turned back to Regis, trying not to sound too eager. Or too pathetic.

Mike shrugged. 'Sure, why not.'

Hillary watched him go and sighed. She wasn't sure why she was so attracted to him. He was nearing fifty and had thinning dark hair but very attractive green eyes. Perhaps it was because he thought the same way she did, and she liked the way he was at ease in his own skin. But then again perhaps she was fooling herself. After slapping him down in no uncertain terms just a few months ago, he'd probably already found someone else.

\* \* \*

Frank Ross waited until Raleigh's secretary had gone, then slipped quietly into the super's outer office. He went straight to the coat rack and squatted down. Shit. No sign of it. He crouched down and looked under the heating unit. He was sweating, but that had nothing to do with the hot air blasting from the painted radiator.

'Lost something, DS Ross?'

Frank jumped, inwardly swore, then got up with as much dignity as his well-padded frame would allow.

'No problem, guv. Just lost my car keys. Thought they might have fallen out of my pocket up here.'

Detective Superintendent Jerome Raleigh looked at Ross and smiled thinly. 'I can hear them jangling in your back trouser pocket from over here, Frank,' he said flatly. And opened the door behind him. 'Come on through.'

Frank gulped and followed, frantically thinking up a good lie. One thing was for sure: no matter what, he was not about to tell the super that he'd misplaced a gun.

* * *

Hillary filled in the last form and shook her aching fingers. Her only consolation was that, somewhere, Dobbin was suffering from the same plight. Paperwork was the bane of every copper's life. She glanced across the open-plan office and saw that the light was still on in Mel's cubicle. She wondered if Janine was in there with him, or if she'd gone home. Word had it she was almost living permanently now at Mel's des res in 'The Moors', Kidlington's answer to Belgravia.

She'd just slipped into her coat when she heard the phone ring in Mel's cubicle, then his voice answering. She grabbed her bag and was walking fast to the door when she heard him call her name.

Damn. Not fast enough.

She turned and tried to look interested. Mel smiled wearily, hardly fooled. 'We got a call from a village called Lower Heyford. Know it?'

Hillary did, vaguely. She'd visited it once on a previous case.

'Looks like a suspicious death — almost certainly murder. A local would-be politician. Want it?' Mel asked, this time with a genuine grin. Hillary nodded, all sense of tiredness abruptly gone. In truth, it had been a stupid question.

She always wanted murder.

# CHAPTER TWO

DCI Mel Mallow watched Hillary head for the door and smiled grimly before turning back into his office and reaching for the phone. He called his own number first, and waited. As he did so, his eye fell on one particular photograph standing on his desk. It was not of his ex-wife, or even of his son, but a picture of himself and Detective Chief Superintendent Marcus Donleavy. It had been taken many years ago now, right after a police rugby match, after their division had just knocked seven bells out of those gits from St Aldates nick.

His fingers tightened around the telephone receiver as Janine Tyler's voice suddenly sounded in his ear. 'Hello?'

'Janine, it's me. I've just sent Hillary off to Lower Heyford — Tangent Hall. There's been a suspicious death — almost certainly murder. Can you reach Tommy for me and get on over there right away?'

'Sure, lover, consider it done.' She hung up abruptly, and Mel winced. No loving words for him tonight, it seemed. He put the receiver down and walked restlessly to the window. Orange-coloured streetlights reflected the large car park and the surrounding environs of Kidlington. In the big pane of glass, his reflection showed him a handsome man, dressed in an impeccable suit. A man who should be superintendent himself by now.

Marcus Donleavy had made no bones about why the man from the Met had been chosen over him to get the job Donleavy's promotion had left vacant. Oh, the brass had made all the usual noises about wanting a fresh eye to look things over, and how new blood brought in from outside could only benefit them all, yada, yada, yada. But the truth was, they were uneasy about a DCI being shacked up with a DS in his own team. How could it not affect his decisions when assignments were being meted out, they wondered. And did it really show good judgement on his part to get tangled up with a woman a good ten years his junior in the first place, especially with two divorces already behind him. What did it say for his professional conduct when his private life was such a mess?

Mel sighed and leaned back against his desk. The simple truth was, if he'd known getting involved with Janine would have blighted his chances for promotion so damned effectively, he'd never have taken that first step and invited her out. But he also knew that he'd been lonely, and that Janine had filled a dull gap in his life. And yet another hard, ugly truth which had to be faced was the fact that he was going to have to dump her. And soon. With Jerome Raleigh proving to be so popular, it was almost a certainty that he'd never get promoted now, if he stayed at Thames Valley. Especially if the high-flying bastard actually succeeded in nailing Fletcher. He'd be the golden boy for now and evermore.

No, he was going to have to move on — maybe down south somewhere. Sod going north. Devon was nice, or so he'd been told. Hampshire too was possible; Dorset maybe. But wherever it was, he couldn't arrive at a new nick with a liability like Janine in tow. Not that she'd want to move anyway.

Mel reached up and pulled off his tie. He didn't particularly want to go home to an empty house, so he might as well make himself comfortable here. Besides, Hillary would be calling in with a preliminary report soon. He poured himself a coffee, and sat down wearily in his chair.

He didn't really want to move, and he resented having to. Thanks to the divorce from his wealthy second wife, he had a beautiful house in an upmarket area in town, and was well liked and well respected where he was. He felt settled, and until recently, well on the way to climbing the career ladder.

His chief investigator, Hillary Greene, was a good friend as well as a gem to work with — her success rate was second to none, and he knew for a fact that Marcus had always rated her too. He could leave her to handle this latest murder investigation without a worry, even if the political angle turned it into a hot potato. An old pro, she also knew not to make any office goofs that might land him, Mel, in the shit. Hell, he could even foist that pain in the arse Frank Ross on her and know she'd cope. But who could say who he'd end up with if he moved?

Still, if he wanted to get ahead, he had no choice. And he wasn't ready to stagnate just yet.

But he'd miss all this.

Of course, Janine would give him grief. He knew her too well to expect that she'd go quietly. Donleavy would probably call him all kinds of a fool for getting himself into this situation in the first place, but he knew his old mentor would keep an ear out for a good position, then would put a good word in for him wherever he ended up. And, if there was any justice at all, Hillary Greene would get his old job as DCI. After all the hassle she'd had with that loser of a husband of hers, she was due some good luck for a change. He'd have to have a word with Marcus, when the time was right, and see if they could swing it for her.

He pulled the folder for that month's budget out of the drawer and reached glumly for the calculator.

* * *

Hillary turned off the main Oxford-to-Banbury road at Hopcrofts Holt and headed past the large hotel and down the hill into the valley proper. At the bottom of the hill she sat waiting at a set of traffic lights that spanned a long water bridge, and then found herself heading up and over the combined railway and canal bridge.

Over on her left, shut up and dark now, was the narrow boat yard where she'd gone to interview a witness on her first murder case. She slowed down as she approached a small turn-off into a road simply called The Lane and found herself facing a beautiful village square, lit up from the lights spilling out of The Bell pub. A huge oak tree stood in pride of place, watching over thatched cottages and what had once been the village school.

Dispatch had given her directions to the crime scene, however, so she followed the road around the bend, then past an old-fashioned red-painted telephone box and round another steep curve. She peered ahead, looking for Mill Lane, which should be off to her left, found it, and turned down the narrow lane. Off to her right was a converted chapel, gleaming pale in the bright moonlight. The sky had cleared again, and once more a frost was in the air. At the bottom of the lane, Hillary found herself facing a metal drawbridge, and she drove over it gingerly, looking out of her window to the flat, dark expanse of the Oxford canal below. Right in front of her were a set of wooden gates belonging to Mill House, but leading off to her left was a muddy stone-paved road that followed the course of the River Cherwell. A few yards down, another set of gates, sandwiched between the two water courses, signalled that she'd arrived at her destination.

She parked behind an empty patrol car and climbed out. She didn't need a torch to read the words 'Tangent Hall' glittering in gold-painted letters on a slate-grey sign. She could hear the river gurgling away under a flat wooden bridge, and for a moment took in the quiet, dark night. Tangent Hall was not so much a hall as a big, fairly modern-looking bungalow. Worth what, half a million, given today's market prices? As a woman about to sell a house, she supposed she should be pleased that properties in the area were worth such small fortunes. But she couldn't help but feel sorry for the families of the native villagers who were being priced out of their own homes.

She sighed and straightened her shoulders as a figure at the entrance to the large wooden gates suddenly stepped out and a torch beam found her face. Hillary instinctively held up a hand to ward off the intrusive beam of light.

'Police, madam. Can I help you?' The uniformed constable stepped closer as Hillary got out her ID.

'DI Greene. I'm the senior investigating officer,' she said simply, as he lowered the torch. 'I take it I'm the first to arrive?'

'Yes, ma'am.' He was young but didn't seem all that overawed. 'The doc's on his way. Forensics too.'

Hillary nodded and got out her notebook as he made his preliminary report. It was concise but left out no relevant facts, and after five minutes of rapid shorthand, she had the beginnings of the Murder Book.

The Murder Book was usually assigned to one particular officer who kept it updated with all the relevant information, so that any member of the investigation could consult it to check on facts and keep up to date. It was usually Janine Tyler who took on this task, but Hillary thought it was time that Tommy Lynch had the responsibility and made a mental note to give it to him when he arrived.

'So, the victim is a Mr Malcolm Dale, resident here, who was found by his secretary, Marcia Brock, at roughly nine o'clock tonight,' she recapped, just to make sure she'd got it right. Mistakes made at the very beginning of a murder investigation could bugger it up for weeks to come. 'Mr Dale's wife, Valerie, is absent, believed to be playing bridge at a friend's place, a regular Monday night occurrence. Mrs Brock called 999 and remained on the premises. After a brief search to ascertain there was no one else in the house, you called it in.' Hillary glanced up at the dark figure in front of her. 'Where's Mrs Brock now?'

'In the living room, ma'am, with my partner.'

'And the body was found in the kitchen?'

'Yes, ma'am.'

'And he's definitely dead?' she asked quickly. She could still remember being called out, as a DS, to a 'murder' scene where her governor had taken one look at the so-called corpse and radioed for an ambulance. The victim had later died in hospital, as it turned out, but it just went to show that it wasn't always easy for an inexperienced person to tell the difference between dead and alive. And it always paid to make sure. Especially when the families of victims could sue you and the department if you didn't.

'No pulse, ma'am.'

'And you only touched his wrist?'

'Yes, ma'am. Didn't want to touch anything else. He's a bit messy. Looks to me as if he's been hit over the head a fair few times.'

In the darkness she heard him gulp. Obviously, he was not quite so hard-headed as he sounded. 'If you want to be sick, Constable, please go over there and do it in the grass.'

'I'm fine, ma'am.'

Hillary nodded, and looked up as another car rattled over the metal drawbridge, the sound echoing hollowly and eerily in the night. She recognised Doc Partridge's nifty little MG at once. 'All right, Constable. Stay out here and direct personnel as they come in. You've started a checklist?' It was standard procedure for everyone's arrival and departure to be noted down. 'Yes, ma'am. I've already got you in.'

'Fine. This is Doctor Steven Partridge,' she added, as the police pathologist walked gingerly across the muddy road to meet her. His shoes, she guessed, would have cost her at least a month's salary. Married to an ex-opera singer, Doc Partridge's sartorial elegance was well known to the cops at HQ.

'Hillary, glad to see you as always. Got something interesting for me?' he greeted her, cheerfully enough.

'Don't know; haven't been in yet.' As a general rule, she tried not to contaminate the scene too much before the men in white overalls arrived. It tended to piss them off.

'Well, you'll have to let the dog see the rabbit,' he murmured, and Hillary hid a smile as she followed the doc inside.

Tangent Hall was as modern inside as out, decorated in minimalist style, in muted, neutral colours. She saw Steven grimace as he looked around. With all the instincts of a peacock, she doubted it would appeal to him. For herself, she hardly paid the decor a second glance. Since living in a narrowboat, things like tiles and fireplaces weren't something that particularly mattered in her world.

'In the kitchen,' she said, glancing around for signs of disturbance. There were none. She could hear the voices of a man and a woman, off to the left — obviously the second uniform and the finder of the body. She nodded to a door that, logically, should lead to either a dining room or kitchen, and followed the medical man through.

The kitchen, unsurprisingly, was big, open-plan, and had the latest in gizmos and gadgets. But as well as a hanging set of expensive woks, an Aga, electric oven, microwave and genuine Welsh dresser complete with blue-and-white plates, there was a man's body stretched out on the terracotta-tiled floor. Darker patches of red at his head oozed between the cracks in the tiles. That was going to be a bugger to get clean.

Doc Partridge stepped gingerly around the prone figure and knelt down carefully. She was sure this had more to do with keeping the soles of his shoes and the knees of his trousers clean than it did his desire not to disturb the forensic evidence. Still, Hillary had a lot of respect for the small, dapper man. He knew his business, and she knew she wouldn't have to wait long for his report. Most pathologists liked to hum and haw for days. At least Doc Partridge was more sensitive to a copper's need to get started with at least a well-informed guess as to cause and time of death.

The victim, she knew from the constable's initial report, was thirty-five years old. He was thickly built, but not yet running to fat, although his dark hair seemed to be already thinning. He was dressed casually in designer jeans and a chunky-knit cream-coloured sweater that was stained with his blood at the shoulder, where it was pressed down on to the floor. From what she could see from where she was standing, there were no obvious defensive wounds or bruising on his hands. Probably hit from behind then, in situ, which probably indicated that he knew his attacker, although that was not necessarily so.

'Well, he's dead,' Doc Partridge said flatly, making a note of the time and writing it down in his own notebook. 'Not more than two hours, I should say. And, strictly as a preliminary finding, death occurred due to a blow or blows to the head, delivered with what appears to be a smooth, probably rounded object.'

Hillary nodded, looking around. There was no obvious sign of the murder weapon left behind. Smooth and rounded. If she was in one of those American cop shows, she'd immediately say 'baseball bat.' And, sure enough, she knew some villains who, lacking an imagination of their own, had taken to using baseball bats as their weapon of choice. So could Mr Dale have surprised a burglar? But it was a bit early for thieves, surely? Or was he usually out on a Monday night as well? Did he usually join his wife at her bridge game? Already she could feel the need to gather information itching away at her.

She watched Steven get carefully to his feet and peel back the thin rubber gloves he was wearing. 'I'll see if I can post him tomorrow — but I doubt it. Probably won't get around to him until the day after.'

'From what I hear, he was a politician — or about to become one or something. You might get pressure to do it fast.'

Steven grunted, unimpressed. 'Well, I must get back. My better half was beating me at billiards when I got called out.'

Hillary blinked at the mental image this conjured up and followed him out. Outside she told the constable at the gate to keep everyone but forensics out of the kitchen, and to make sure that her team, as they arrived, stayed on the rolls of polythene sheeting that he'd already put down.

Just then she saw Janine Tyler's car, a classic Mini, arrive, with Tommy Lynch not far behind her. Of Frank Ross there was no sign, so at least she was having some luck tonight.

'Constable, has anyone contacted Mrs Dale yet?'

'No, ma'am. I wasn't sure that that was advisable.'

Hillary nodded. It was good thinking. Sad fact though it undoubtedly was, whenever a spouse was found dead, the remaining spouse was firmly in the frame until eliminated. And she herself wanted to see Valerie Dale's face when she was informed of her husband's death.

'You have the address of this friend where she's playing bridge?'

He didn't. He radioed his friend inside, who asked the secretary, and then relayed the information back with an address in Adderbury, a large village not far from Banbury.

Hillary nodded and started back towards her car. Normally she wouldn't leave a crime scene so early, but until forensics had been and gone, there was little she could do here but hang around and get impatient. She greeted Tommy and Janine, who crowded round her, and filled them in.

'Right, Tommy, I want you to keep the Murder Book on this one. Janine, you can appoint the evidence officer. Doc's been and gone, so you can get the body removed when all the photographs have been taken and SOCO give the all-clear. Janine, get a preliminary report from this secretary, Marcia Brock. What was she doing here at this time of night, whether there was any argy-bargy going on — you know the drill. I'm off to inform the wife.'

'Boss,' Janine said briefly. Unlike most coppers, she balked at calling anyone 'guv' and had come up with her own title for Hillary, who didn't seem to mind. Janine walked up to the uniform and had a few words, then disappeared inside. Tommy Lynch watched Hillary climb into her car, an ancient Volkswagen Golf that she'd nicknamed 'Puff the Tragic Wagon,' and watched her back up towards the draw-bridge. He wished he was going with her.

He sighed and headed towards the house. 'Has a DS Frank Ross checked in yet?' he asked the constable at the gate, who shook his head. 'Good,' Tommy said succinctly, making the younger man smile. Frank's fame tended to go before him.

* * *

Valerie Dale's bridge-playing friends lived in a large property across the village green from the pub, which looked to Hillary as if it had once been two or maybe even three terraced cottages, now converted into one. It had an uneven grey slate roof, and had been newly whitewashed. Even in the dark she could see latticed woodwork climbing the walls, and suspected that in the summer it was awash with climbing roses, clematis and maybe even wisteria. Very nice. She appreciated gardens — mostly because her own efforts in the horticultural department stopped and ended with a few tubs of pansies slung on to her roof.

She knocked on the door and waited. The curtains were all closed, but light glowed behind most of them, and when the door was finally opened, she could hear the muted voices of several people coming from inside. The woman facing her looked to be about forty, with a neat pageboy blonde cut and carefully treated wrinkles at the sides of her eyes and mouth. 'Yes?'

Her pale grey eyes widened as Hillary held out her ID. 'Is there a Mrs Valerie Dale here, Mrs Babcock? It is Mrs Babcock?'

'No, I'm Celia. Celia Dee. Gale's inside. I'm dummy.'

Hillary, who knew a little about bridge, wasn't too disconcerted by this somewhat candid revelation. If she remembered right, Celia Dee wasn't commentating on her own intellectual shortcomings, but referring to the fact that she wasn't playing the card game for this particular rubber.

'Please, come inside.' Although she wasn't the hostess, she was too polite to leave her standing on the doorstep.

Besides, if Hillary knew people — and Hillary did — Mrs Dee was too busy wondering if her tax disc on the car was up to date or if any of her tyres were bald to worry about upsetting any of her fellow bridge players with her usurped hospitality.

Inside, the country cottage theme was being done to death, with the owner even going so far as to hang bunches of dried flowers from the genuine wooden beams. Brass wall clocks ticked ponderously from thick and bulging lime-washed walls, and Laura Ashley was being worshipped wherever the eye settled. She was led to a large, knocked-through lounge, where a real log fire was roaring away in the fireplace, surrounded by horse brasses, naturally. Sets of four people, seated at two individual round tables, turned to look at her.

'Four no trumps,' a small, grey-haired woman said in the sudden silence, then looked up and blinked, wondering why nobody was paying attention to her. At another table, a tall, dark-haired woman dressed in black slacks and a black silk blouse with a Chinese collar, slowly stood up. She looked not to Hillary, but to the woman standing beside her, an obvious question in her eyes.

'Oh, Gale, this is . . . er . . .'

'Detective Inspector Hillary Greene, Mrs Babcock,' Hillary said, walking forward. Although the house and company screamed ultra-respectable upper middle-class, Hillary didn't feel one whit intimidated. She'd taken an English literature degree from Radcliffe College, and although it wasn't one of Oxford University's affiliated colleges, hardly anyone knew that, and back at HQ she was known to be an OEC — an Oxford Educated Cop. Her own upbringing had been as middle-class as anyone's here. OK, her suit was probably the cheapest article of clothing in the room, and she worked for a living because she had to and not because she needed a hobby, but who the hell cared? She had a badge. That trumped even a Range Rover.

She smiled to reassure everyone, and said firmly, 'I'm looking for a Mrs Valerie Dale? I was told by Marcia Brock that I might find her here?' As she spoke she glanced around, instantly dismissing all the men, and the grey-haired woman. That left two possible contenders — an elfin-faced redhead, and a tall skinny blonde. It was the tall skinny blonde, looking nonplussed, who rose hesitantly from the table.

'Yes? I'm Valerie Dale. Is anything wrong? The children?' Her voice rose sharply.

Hillary mentally cursed. This was the first she'd heard about children. She took a step forward and smiled. 'I'm sure your children are fine, Mrs Dale,' she lied. The truth was, she had no idea whether they were or not. 'They're back at your home, Tangent Hall?'

'No, no. Jeremy's at boarding school and Portia's with my mother for the night.'

Hillary nodded, relieved. Not at the house then. That explained why no one had mentioned them. Children at a murder scene were a nightmare scenario.

'But what's wrong? Why are you here?' Valerie Dale suddenly demanded, her voice rising just an octave. Either she was a very good actress or she was genuinely alarmed. Naturally pale, her thin face seemed to go a milky colour and the pinched look that tightened her cheekbones couldn't be faked.

'I'm sorry, Mrs Dale, but I'm afraid I do have bad news. Would you prefer to talk outside?'

Even before she'd finished speaking, she noticed Gale Babcock take a step closer, and from her position beside her, Celia Dee also moved forward, coming to stand the other side of the distressed woman. Obviously Valerie Dale had friends. Protective friends. And she was going to need them in the months to come.

'What? No, no, just tell me what it is. Is it Mother?' Valerie asked. 'I know she's not been well, but I thought she was over it. It was only a tummy bug, wasn't it?'

Hillary took a deep breath. There was never a right way of going about this, and after years of having to deliver bad news, she'd never found any way that was easy. In the end she chose simply to state the truth as clearly and calmly as possible.

'I'm afraid your husband, Malcolm Dale, has been found dead at your home, Mrs Dale.' She was sure she was safe in stating this so certainly, because Marcia Brock had formally identified him as such. 'We've launched a murder enquiry,' she added quietly, and saw a blank dullness suddenly darken Valerie Dale's pale eyes. What colour were they exactly? Not blue. Green, perhaps.

She opened her mouth to say something, but no sound came out. Celia Dee said sharply, 'Bloody hell!' and grabbed Valerie Dale's wrist. But it was Gale Babcock who took control.

'Come on, Val, sit down. Jim, get a glass of brandy, will you?' One of the men peeled off obediently from the table and went to a drinks cabinet. Hillary said nothing as her witness was led to one of the black leather sofas grouped around the fireplace, and was pushed down. The man returned with a snifter glass and pushed it into Valerie Dale's shaking hand. She took it, and raised it automatically to her lips. Hillary wondered if she was even aware of what she'd done.

But all this show of shock and grief meant nothing, of course. She'd had a case once, while still in uniform, when a man had murdered his wife. On being informed of her death, he'd looked and reacted very much as Valerie Dale was doing now, and she'd been convinced because of it that he must be innocent. But her governor at the time, far more experienced and wily, had instantly liked him for it. And the evidence and an eventual confession had proved him right. See, he'd explained to her a little while later, some people could kill in a moment of rage or 'temporary insanity' then go off and manage to forget about it so completely that, when informed of their loved one's death, they were genuinely shocked. Other killers felt genuine remorse, too, and when it was brought home to them the reality of their deeds, were genuinely distraught. Just because someone was physically shocked or genuinely upset it didn't make them automatically innocent. It just meant they weren't cold-blooded.

Or were bloody good actors.

Hillary had come across some of those, too, in her time. Men and women who could make Olivier look like a ham.

Hillary sighed, and slowly walked over to an empty seat and sat down. It was going to take some time, and a lot of gentle persuasion, to ease Valerie Dale away from her friends.

In the meantime, now was as good a time as any to see how strong Valerie Dale's alibi might be. She turned to the man now sitting opposite her — the man who'd brought the brandy — and lifted out her notebook.

'If I could just have your name, sir, and the time you arrived here?' she asked quietly. After a startled pause, the man complied. Hillary wrote it down then asked as casually as she could, 'And what time would you say it was when Mrs Dale arrived here tonight?'

# CHAPTER THREE

Nearly half an hour later, Hillary was driving back to Lower Heyford, a silent and shocked Valerie Dale sitting in the passenger seat beside her, Celia Dee having promised to drive Valerie's own car back to her door tomorrow morning.

Hillary didn't question the new widow on the drive back, only asking her if she was warm enough, and then turning up the heater (with little hope of coaxing more heat out of the ancient car) when Valerie had said that she wasn't.

Back at Tangent Hall she could feel the tension emanating from her passenger ratchet up a notch at the sight of all the squad cars' flashing blue lights, and the rather eerie sight of men and women walking around encased from head to toe in ghostly white. It almost looked like a scene from a low-budget alien abduction movie.

'If you'll wait here a minute, I'll see if it's all right for us to go inside,' Hillary murmured. She got out and nodded to a constable, who instantly trotted over. 'This is the wife,' Hillary said, all but whispering. 'Stay with her — tell her she can call her mother's, if she wants, to break the news and see if her daughter's all right, but make a note of what she says.'

According to the bridge players, Valerie had arrived a little late, citing a flat tyre and the need to change it as an excuse. She'd have to set Tommy the task of trying to prove or disprove her story. Until he did, she wasn't going to give Valerie Dale any breaks.

'Guv,' the constable said in acknowledgement, then slipped in behind the steering wheel. She could hear his low voice rumbling a greeting as she walked away. The mortuary van was parked near the wooden plank bridge spanning the river, and two men stood quietly beside it, one of them smoking, awaiting the all-clear to remove the body. Just then, Janine came through the garden gate and beckoned them over. Obviously SOCO had finished. Her DS spotted her and began to meet her halfway up the track. As they walked back into the garden, Hillary gave her a quick update.

Even though it was now approaching midnight, in the bright moonlight Hillary could make out light patches of daffodils, and larger bushes of what would probably turn out to be forsythia in the morning light. It was a simple, low-maintenance garden, with plenty of paving and large tubs filled with the usual spring assortments. The landscaping alone must have cost a good bit. Hillary wondered how much the Dales were worth. Surely enough to make money a viable motive? Did the house and trappings belong to Malcolm Dale? And if so, had a divorce been in the offing? She would have to talk to the Dale solicitor soon and find out about the will. Plus any life insurance policies the dead man might have taken out.

It was Hillary's belief that the would-be Tory politicians of this world knew how to handle money. Had he had his wife sign some sort of pre-nup that would leave her too poorly off to consider divorce a viable option? Had murder seemed the only way out? All of these questions and more would have to be answered in the next twenty-four hours. She knew a detailed background report on both the victim and his spouse would be ready for her sometime tomorrow. While others might despise it, Hillary had always thought that there was a lot to be said for basic routines.

'Don't forget to keep Tommy updated. It's his first time holding the Murder Book.'

'Boss,' Janine said, unimpressed. Hillary sighed. When would Janine learn that, if she wanted to get on and earn her promotion, people management was as necessary a skill as knowing any of the technical questions that she might be asked at her Boards?

'Janine, I want you to escort Mrs Dale to her bedroom, then bag and tag her clothes.' It was almost beyond the realms of probability that the killer wouldn't have some splashes of the victim's blood on his or her clothing, as well as other forensic evidence. Besides, if Valerie Dale really had changed a car tyre that night, there'd be proof of that on her clothes and hands too. 'And give her hands a swab while you're at it. Ask the lab to check for traces of grease, motor oil, that sort of thing. And when we take Marcia Brock back, the same for her.' Hillary sighed. 'But with her finding the body, any forensics we get on her might not indicate much one way or another. Unless she's got a splatter pattern on her that gets the lab team excited.'

Whenever a victim was coshed, shot or stabbed, blood patterns on walls, floors and on the clothes of the killer could often testify to the what, where, how and when of it.

Janine nodded, wishing Hillary Greene wouldn't keep trying to teach her granny how to suck eggs. She could do this sort of routine work in her sleep. 'SOCO are almost done. Do you really like the wife for it?'

Hillary waved her hand in the air in a rocking motion. 'So so. Anything earth-shattering come up here?'

'No. Forensics took away a lot of possible murder weapons, but nothing that looks very likely. The fireplace poker, the wooden broom handle, stuff like that. They're dusting for fingerprints now, then they'll be finished.'

Hillary grimaced. That explained why Janine had come outside. The grey powder SOCO used to highlight dabs got everywhere — in the folds of your clothes, your hair, on your lips, you name it. 'You've taken a preliminary statement from Marcia Brock?'

'Yes, boss, just the basics. She got here about eight fifty, found the door shut but unlocked, and when nobody answered the bell, pushed her way in. Found him, palpitated a bit, swears she didn't touch him or anything else, and came out into the hall and used her mobile to phone us. Says she didn't go back in, but waited outside. Oh, and by the way, she's his campaign secretary, not his work secretary. She said she'd come tonight in order to go over an interview he was due to give on Radio Oxford tomorrow. You know, do some last-minute coaching. It all sounded legit enough to me.'

Janine didn't like to go into her own take on the witness too much, knowing that Hillary preferred to form her own opinions of people during interview. And Janine was well aware that her superior could often bring things out during an interview that she herself would never even have thought of. This ability her superior officer had to see things she'd missed, or think of things that had passed her by, both annoyed her and aroused envy and respect in equal measure.

'OK, they're coming out,' Hillary said abruptly. 'Mrs Dale's in my car.'

Janine nodded and moved away, and Hillary stepped to one side as the two mortuary assistants came out with the body bag on a stretcher. She hoped Valerie Dale wasn't watching, but couldn't see how the poor woman could possibly avoid it. Hillary always had it in mind that if the spouse wasn't the killer then he or she was a grieving victim as well, and deserved any consideration that could be given. The trouble was, an investigating officer very often didn't know which scenario was true until all the evidence was in.

She found Tommy in the kitchen, watching the last of the SOCO team leave. 'Tommy. Mrs Dale was late arriving at her bridge meeting. She says she had a flat tyre and had to change it. First thing tomorrow, see if you can get an exact location from her where this took place, and see if you can get any corroboration. If it happened on the open road, we'll have to do a newspaper and radio appeal for witnesses to come forward. If she was near some houses, we might get lucky straight away.'

'Wouldn't someone stop and offer to help?' Tommy asked thoughtfully. 'A pretty blonde woman all alone at night?'

Hillary shrugged. 'Maybe. Maybe not.' Nowadays, it wasn't always easy to tell. Many men who would have been gallant, say, ten years ago, might now think twice. And many women, too, would probably feel safer changing their own tyre rather than looking for help.

'I'd better phone Mel with an update. When things are finished here you can get off. I want us all fresh first thing in the morning.'

'Guv.'

* * *

Marcia Brock drove herself home, with a convoy of two following. She lived on the outskirts of Witney, in what had once been a council estate, but had long since been gentrified by first-time buyers and hopeful families.

She parked her six-year-old Toyota half on the pavement and locked it; Hillary pulled up behind her, and Janine Tyler overshot and parked up in front. Without a word, she turned and walked up a crazy-paved path to a front door with an afterthought of a porch. There she waited for them to catch up, still without speaking, then stepped inside and flicked on the hall light.

'Kitchen's through there.' She nodded towards a door that stood ajar. 'Don't mind the cat.'

She slipped off her overcoat and reached for a small thermostat, turning it up a notch. Hillary thought the house needed it. It felt distinctly chilly. As if noticing, Marcia Brock smiled grimly. 'Sorry, Inspector. I'm doing a master's at Reading — I'm in a gap year — and student habits die hard. I never waste electricity, or anything else, if I can help it,' she added ruefully.

'Really? What are you studying?'

'Political science with a slant towards sociology. What else?'

Hillary smiled an answer and walked on through to a small, functional kitchen. Sitting on one of the cheerfully yellow Formica worktops was a black and white tom, with battered ears and baleful green eyes. Janine, spotting it, sidled around it carefully, and pulled out one of the plain wooden chairs set against a small square table.

'Tea?' Marcia asked, picking up a kettle. 'Or something stronger?'

From Janine's preliminary interview, Hillary knew that Marcia Brock was thirty-one and unmarried. Janine had wryly twisted her lips as she recounted the lecture she'd been given when she'd mistakenly referred to her as 'Mrs.' 'A closet lezzie if you ask me,' Janine had added, making Hillary wince. Sometimes Frank Ross's malevolent influence reared its ugly head in unexpected places.

Now Hillary shook her head. 'Tea will be fine. I just need to go over a few things with you, Ms Brock. As you can appreciate, I know next to nothing about the victim, which is where I need your help. What can you tell me about him?'

Marcia Brock sighed and rolled her eyes. 'Where to start? OK, facts first. He's a little old to be going into serious politics, but then again, he's still just about young enough to make the real veterans sit up and take notice. I reckon somewhere down the line he had some pretty good advice, because he seemed to be relatively savvy. He's been a lifelong member of the party, of course, and knew how to walk the walk and talk the talk long before he hired me, which was just as well. He married well; his wife — I expect you've met her — is the only daughter of a local property developer. Very upmarket real estate, that sort of thing. So he knows a lot of very useful people, and his father-in-law is behind him one hundred per cent. Fancies seeing his daughter as the wife of a cabinet minister, I expect,' she added dryly.

The kettle boiled and Marcia broke off to pour the tea into three thick mugs.

She was small and rather chunky, with short black hair and rather startling clear blue eyes that didn't seem to miss much. As she handed over the steaming mugs, she dished out spoons. 'You'll have to fish out your own tea bags.'

Hillary smiled and did so, wondering why this woman was working for a wannabe Tory politician. If she'd had to guess she would have thought Marcia Brock would be a strictly New Labour girl. At a push a Lib Dem. And if she'd had to bet money, she'd have put her down for a Green.

'So you think he would have made it then? You know, got elected as MP?' she asked, and Marcia Brock snorted.

'Hardly! What do you know about local politics, Inspector?'

Hillary gave an inward groan and admitted it was next to nothing, in the sure and certain knowledge that, in the next hour or so, she'd learn far more than she'd ever want to know. Beside her, she could sense Janine's shoulders slumping, and knew that her sergeant was anticipating the worst too.

And Marcia Brock didn't disappoint. By the time she'd finished giving her the rundown on in-party fighting, the desperation that surrounded soliciting support, and the general back-biting and at times almost hysterical argy-bargy that went on when an MP's constituency became unexpectedly available, Hillary was glad that she never bothered to vote.

'So, basically, leaving out the by-rules and exemptions, it boils down to this. It's the Tory party members, not the members of the public, who get to put forward nominations for those who want to run as MPs?' Janine said, clarifying her shorthand. 'And the current MP for this area suddenly announced that he is retiring next year, and Malcolm Dale managed to win enough votes to put him in the running?'

'Right, along with two others,' Marcia said firmly. 'But one's a sop to the left, so the only real competition he had was George McNamara.'

Hillary could feel her eyelids drooping. What was it about politics that put her right to sleep? She forced herself to sit up and pay more attention. 'Was this Mr McNamara considered a real threat?' she asked quickly.

'In my opinion, yes,' Marcia Brock said. 'But Mr Dale was confident he'd win, if only by a narrow majority.'

'Which would mean he would stand as this region's Tory MP at the next general election?'

'Next by-election,' Marcia Brock corrected. Then launched into a truly bewildering narrative about the rules and regulations concerning the difference. When she'd finished, Janine looked ready to spit tin tacks.

'OK. Let's shift emphasis a minute,' Hillary said hastily, knowing her sergeant would probably kill her if she didn't. They could always trawl the internet later to build up a more solid idea of what happened in local Tory politics. 'What kind of man was he? Did you like him?'

Marcia shrugged. 'He was all right,' she said, then flushed, as if aware that she didn't sound all that enthusiastic. 'What I mean is, he ran his own business, so at least he knew more than most of them when he talked about economics and the plight of the small businessman.'

'Really? What was his business?'

'He owns, or owned, rather, I suppose I should say, Sporting Chance. You might know it — it's in that new shopping centre they built by the canal in Banbury.' Hillary didn't know it, but had no doubt that she would before long.

'Basically, he sells high-end sporting equipment to the country set. Fishing rods that can tell you the weight of the fish before you've even caught it. Purdey shotguns, handmade and decorated with real silver that can set you back sixty grand. Bespoke jodhpurs, Argentinian polo mallets, tooled leather riding boots from Spain. You get the idea — if you've got more money than sense and want to spend it on an afternoon's grouse shoot, Sporting Chance is where you go. He did very well at it. Course, round this area, he couldn't really miss. If you're not shooting it, chasing it, ripping it apart, hooking it out of water or sending terriers down holes after it, you're trying to be seen as if you are.'

Hillary watched the other woman slump back in her chair and take a deep, much-needed breath. Then she smiled wryly. 'I get the feeling you're not a blood sports aficionado, Ms Brock?'

Marcia had the grace to grin. 'Sorry. Can't say as I am. I'm a vegetarian, for a start,' she added, then, as if aware of how absurd that sounded, gave a sharp bark of laughter and leaned forward in her chair. 'Look, I didn't particularly like the man, OK?' she said earnestly. 'But I needed the experience, and being a campaign secretary for a politician — any politician — is going to look good on my CV once I get my master's.' She shrugged a little helplessly. 'A while ago a friend of mine told me about Malcolm Dale, and when I checked him out, I thought that his chance of at least making a good showing was too good for me to pass up. My friend put in a good word, and Malcolm hired me. Now, I suppose . . . Oh shit, I don't know what I'm going to do now,' she said, as the reality of her situation began to sink in. 'I'll be out of a job for a start, and I really needed that pay cheque even if it was peanuts. He was a tight bastard, you know. But then, that's the rich for you. They never give anything away, do they?'

'Was he rich?' Hillary asked casually.

'Oh yeah. Well, by my lights he was,' Marcia corrected with a brief grin. 'The shop was a goldmine, and his wife, of course, had her own private income from Daddy. The kids are already down to go to Eton and Cheltenham Ladies College. Can you imagine it? Having your life all mapped out for you before you're even out of nappies? Yeah, they're rich all right.'

'Did the Dales have a good marriage, do you think?' Hillary asked flatly.

On the way over here, she'd wondered if Marcia and the victim might have been having an affair, but that idea she now more or less scotched. Of course, Marcia Brock could be lying her head off, pretending an animus or disinterest that she didn't really feel, but somehow Hillary couldn't see it. And from what she was beginning to learn about the personality of the victim, she doubted if Malcolm Dale would have been stupid enough to start an affair with his secretary anyway. Especially such a physically unprepossessing one.

'Yeah, it seemed to work, from what I could see of it,' Marcia said after a thoughtful pause. 'I mean, I didn't really see a lot of Mrs Dale, but she seemed the type.'

'The type for what?'

'To be a Tory politician's wife, of course, what else?' Marcia said, with a twinkle in her eyes. 'She had the right look, the right voice, the right connections. Oh, I'm not saying that she was one of these dragons who push hubby on, but she was certainly behind him. Attended all the rallies, pressed the flesh, flattered the matrons, and so on. Part of the reason Malcolm Dale was put forward as a candidate was because he had the right wife to back him up, believe you me. Nowadays the Tories are very keen on family values.' Marcia couldn't resist the dig. 'And make sure their candidates toe the line. And I think Valerie knew it and knew her own worth. And, of course, with good old Daddy behind her, Malcolm knew he had to keep her happy, because there was nothing to stop her from walking if he didn't. And he'd be the real loser if she went.'

Hillary nodded. So it looked less and less likely that Valerie Dale might want to be rid of her husband due to financial reasons. But that didn't rule out other motives. More personal ones.

'And do you think he kept her happy?' she asked calmly.

Marcia Brock shifted uncomfortably on her chair. 'I expect so,' she said quickly. 'Look, like I said, I'm just his campaign secretary, not his bosom buddy. Or hers.'

There's something there, Hillary thought, but now was probably not the time to push it. It was getting on for the early hours of the morning, and her witness was getting cranky. And she herself was feeling the pull of her bed.

'OK, Ms Brock, we'll leave it there for now. But I'll be getting back to you within the next day or two for a follow-up interview. You will be available, I hope?'

Marcia Brock gave a wry smile. 'Don't leave town, huh? Don't worry, I won't be going anywhere. My lease on this place doesn't run out until the beginning of the next academic year for a start. If I'm not here, you'll probably find me down the job centre,' she added wryly, climbing wearily to her feet, but with relief evident in her eyes as she let them out.

Hillary had purposely not asked her anything about the actual finding of the body, knowing that Janine would already have covered it. Instead, she'd wanted to get her first real feel for their victim. And boy, did she have it.

'Didn't like him much, did she?' Janine said, once she'd joined her outside. She'd asked for and taken Marcia Brock's clothing, and would get it over to forensics first thing in the morning.

'No,' Hillary agreed thoughtfully. 'I don't think she even believed in his politics, either.'

Could you be a campaign secretary for someone whose politics didn't match your own? If you were a desperate student, eager for experience and to get a foot on the political ladder, she supposed you could. But could that dislike escalate and fester, leading you into banging someone over the head and killing him out of sheer frustration? She didn't think so.

No, if it was a woman who'd killed their vic, surely the motive was likely to be more personal than that.

'You noticed how she shied off when I asked her about the state of the Dales' marriage?' Hillary asked, following her sergeant up the path to their waiting cars. If Malcolm Dale was unfaithful, perhaps the mistress had got fed up with his promises to leave his wife, and had finally realised it was never going to happen. Or perhaps Malcolm Dale had chosen tonight to give her the elbow, and the woman had had other ideas.'

'Oh yeah. One or the other of them was definitely playing away, I'd say,' Janine snorted.

'Or maybe both,' Hillary said. Could it have been a lover of *Valerie's* who killed Malcolm Dale? It wouldn't be the first time the husband was killed by the other man. Could Valerie have put him up to it? Or aided and abetted. She really didn't like this flat tyre business.

Luckily, finding the body so soon had helped narrow down the time of death. Theoretically, Valerie *could* have killed her husband, changed her clothes, maybe even showered, and then left for her bridge club, arriving only a little late.

She sighed. 'I'm beat, and my head's spinning. Let's get some sleep, and tackle it head on in the morning.'

'Get no argument from me, boss,' Janine said. This was her third murder investigation now, and she'd learned, from the previous two, the need to pace herself. 'Night, boss,' she said, climbing into her Mini and roaring away.

Hillary got into Puff the Tragic Wagon and drove more sedately away into the night.

* * *

The tiny hamlet of Thrupp, where her narrowboat the *Mollern* was permanently moored, was hunkered down for the night, with not a single light showing. Parking in the deserted car park of The Boat pub, she locked her car and then walked up the muddy towpath towards her boat.

A sudden flap and splash from beside her told her she'd startled a sleeping duck or moorhen. With a fast-beating heart she cursed it softly under her breath, then climbed on to the back of her boat and reached in her purse for the key to the padlock.

Once inside the familiar, narrow space, she didn't bother turning on the light. She wasn't sure when she'd last charged the battery and besides, the moon was still shining brightly enough for her to see all she needed to.

She opened the door to her microscopic bedroom, shrugged off her clothes and let them fall on the floor, then climbed into the narrow single bed.

Within moments she was asleep.

# CHAPTER FOUR

Perhaps not surprisingly, Hillary awoke late. Outside she could hear the male thrush that was nesting in the willow tree overhanging her boat singing loudly, and a passing craft rocked the *Mollern* gently. Either one of her neighbours was taking to the open water or the very first tourist boats of the spring season were out and about.

She sighed and ran a hand through her hair. Ideally she could do with a shower and a hair wash but a quick glance at her watch showed her she just didn't have the time. She got out of bed, flung yesterday's clothes into the tiny hamper under the small round porthole and stood up. She didn't need to take even a single pace in order to open her wardrobe door, where she selected a smart chestnut-brown skirt and matching jacket with suede lapels. A cream-coloured blouse and low-heeled cream shoes completed the ensemble. She was out of fresh tights, so she grimaced and retrieved yesterday's pair out of the hamper. She splashed on some perfume and drew back the sliding door.

She walked quickly down the narrow corridor to the kitchen area and put the kettle on, wondering if her water tanks were low enough to make a visit to the communal taps worthwhile.

Another job she'd have to do tomorrow.

A cup of instant and a rather stale biscuit completed breakfast, and as she climbed the steps, careful to duck her head as she did so, she felt her stomach rumble a protest.

Outside, the March day was bright and sunny. Her neighbour's boat, *Willowsands,* boasted three tubs of daffodils, which were cheerfully swaying in a chilly breeze. A tiny Jenny Wren flew low across the water, and zipped right in front of her as she stepped off the boat on to land. She glanced down at the towpath, wondering if her cream shoes were ever going to survive the short muddy walk to her car.

Probably not.

Puff the Tragic Wagon started first time for a change, which was just as well, for the moment she walked into reception, the desk sergeant nailed her. 'DI Greene, the man from the Met wants you in his office pronto.'

Hillary groaned slightly at the summons, and waved a hand in acknowledgement as she headed for the stairs. The big electric clock on the wall told her it was nearly a quarter to ten. Well, sod 'em. She made her way to her own desk in the main office first and quickly checked there was nothing urgent, then walked the extra flight up to DS Raleigh's office. His secretary ushered her through at once. Inside were all the usual suspects — Mel, Regis and Tanner — and, seated to one side of Raleigh's desk, a tall, silver-haired man dressed in a dark grey suit. Hillary felt a slight sense of shock at the sight of him, but hid it quickly.

'Sir,' she said to the older man, wondering what had brought Detective Chief Superintendent Marcus Donleavy into the fray. And she quickly found out.

'DI Greene,' Raleigh greeted her pleasantly, without so much as a glance at his watch. Hillary nodded, not about to explain her late showing. If Mel hadn't done it, the super could just bloody well ask.

'As I was just telling the team, we've had something of a breakthrough. As you know, our source in Fletcher's gang had caught a whiff that the big man himself was going to be getting his hands dirty in the near future. He confirmed last night that a big shipment of "squaddie" was coming in, and this time he had a definite timetable — namely, nine tomorrow night.'

'Squaddie?' Hillary said, with some alarm, for she'd never heard of it.

Mike Regis shifted on his seat. 'It's brand new. Vice have only been able to get our hands on a few examples just recently, but the chemists tell us it's almost certainly a derivative of E, but with another kick, something from the amphetamine family. It's quick-acting and nasty. There's some talk among the medicos of possible brain damage in long-term users.'

Hillary sighed heavily. Great. This was just what she needed.

'So, as I was saying,' Raleigh said, again without even a hint of remonstrance towards the latecomer, 'the raid is definitely on for tomorrow night. We're almost certain it's going to be delivered to a farm owned by Fletcher, near the village of Bletchington. The location is perfect — the nearest house in the village is out of sight behind a small group of trees, and access to the farm is by a single track, leading to a narrow country lane that in itself lets out by a B road, so hardly any passing traffic. Fortunately for us, there's another farm on neighbouring land that can be accessed by another B road. The farmer is sympathetic and has allowed us to set up surveillance. Brian Doyle, the farmer, isn't a big fan of Fletcher, it seems. There was some dispute about land access. Course, we know why Fletcher doesn't want his neighbours too close. There was some talk last year, I believe, that Fletcher had set up a bootleg workshop there for DVDs and such?'

Mel nodded, but didn't go into details. He'd led the raid on the farm on that particular occasion, and although he'd found some wrappers for a recent DVD release of a big box-office hit, they hadn't found enough evidence to convict. Fletcher had evidently been tipped off.

'Yes,' Raleigh said heavily. 'For that reason, we're keeping this raid very close to our chests. Apart from the people in this room, and the officers on surveillance, of course, nobody, but *nobody* is to be told. Furthermore, I don't want a gathering of the clans here tomorrow either. I want you all to put in a normal working day, then we meet up at the neighbouring farm in Bletchington at 1800 hours. We use our own personal vehicles, and park them out of sight in a barn the farmer has let us use for the night. Is this clear?'

It was, and everybody nodded. It was a gloomy moment, as the super was all but stating openly that somebody at the nick had to be feeding Fletcher titbits, and nobody liked the thought of that.

But at least Raleigh sounded as if he meant business, which was heartening. Hillary watched him closely as he detailed the plans for the operation. Once more, she'd be working with the Tactical Firearms Unit, for it was almost certain that Fletcher and the rest of them would probably be armed, or have quick access to arms, but it was not her old friend Dobbin who'd be leading it this time, but a younger man she didn't know.

Raleigh's eyes were gleaming as he spoke, and as the sunshine outside picked up the more golden highlights in his light brown hair, Hillary could sense the tension in the man. Her mother had once had a Yorkshire terrier called Nero, who all but quivered with intense concentration whenever his ball was about to be thrown for him to fetch, and Raleigh suddenly reminded her of the animal. There was something almost inhuman about the energy he seemed to exude.

Once again she wondered what drove him. And how he'd got so close to Fletcher so soon. But perhaps she was just nitpicking. She knew that although the raid was an exciting development, and might well lead to nabbing Fletcher red-handed at last, she herself would be something of an also-ran at the event. It was obvious that Raleigh and Regis were to be the two main driving forces behind it. On the other hand, her own murder case was hers alone, where she was the big fish in the small pond, and was champing at the bit to get back to it. Could it really be that she was feeling nothing short of dog in-the-mangerish about the whole affair? Was that why she was so sceptical? She didn't like to think so.

Just then she glanced across and saw the heavy-lidded, pale-eyed gaze of Marcus Donleavy on her. Although he turned away the next instant, she had the definite feeling he'd picked up on her unease.

She glanced surreptitiously at her watch, wishing the briefing wouldn't take much longer. Although the whole force would celebrate if they actually nailed Fletcher, including herself, she had things to do and people to see.

\* \* \*

As it happened, it was nearly eleven o'clock before she went downstairs to her own desk, and Frank Ross, the poisonous little git, made a great show of looking at his watch. Janine, who probably knew from Mel that her boss had been upstairs in the big man's office, looked at her with far more interest, but Hillary merely sat down in her chair, and reached for the pile of reports in her in-tray. As expected, there was a full background report on both Malcolm and Valerie Dale, which she read quickly. Next came the preliminary forensics report — with nothing too startling. Most of the dabs taken at the scene had been eliminated as belonging to either the Dales, Marcia Brock, or a cleaning woman from the village who came in twice a week. But there were traces of another person, recently present, who hadn't yet been accounted for. These prints had been run through the computer, but matched nobody with a criminal record. Tommy was now running them through other databases that required fingerprinting — the armed forces, prison staff etc. — but Hillary had no great hopes of a match.

Still, the dabs would come in useful if they zeroed in on a suspect. Providing, of course, they didn't belong to a local plumber who'd been called in to unblock a sink, or any other stray person who might have had a legitimate reason to be in the Dales' kitchen recently. Nowadays, most killers wore gloves as a matter of course.

Unless the killing had been unpremeditated, Hillary mentally amended. And yet the lack of murder weapon at the scene made that decidedly unlikely. Unless the killer had snatched up a nearby object, then retained enough of a cool head afterwards to take it with him or her when they left?

'Janine, get Mrs Dale and the cleaner to check the kitchen and see if anything's missing,' she said, turning the last page over and closing the file shut with a slam.

'Already done it, boss,' Janine said, with quiet pride. 'I dropped in first thing this morning and found the cleaning lady in. It wasn't her usual day, but you know what it's like.'

Hillary did. People generally reacted to murder in one of two ways; either they went out of their way to avoid the scene and members of the family, or they homed in on it like pigeons returning to the coop.

'Get anything out of her?' she asked curiously.

'She was pretty sure there was nothing missing from the kitchen, other than what forensics had already taken away,' Janine replied. 'But she was a fount of gossip about the Dales — some of it interesting from our point of view. She thought, on the whole, that if either of them had been playing away it was more likely to be the hubby, but she didn't have any candidates for a possible mistress, and you could tell that that almost caused her pain.' Janine paused for breath, and to give a cynical smile. 'She said the kids were spoiled brats, although the little girl was still a quote "sweetheart" unquote.' Janine, who had no desire to have children of her own, couldn't understand some people's attraction to the little horrors. 'The bridge night was a regular occurrence, so there's nothing off there,' she carried on, reading out of her notebook. 'But she reckoned the missus might drink a bit more than was good for her. I'm inclined to take that with a pinch of salt, though,' she added, glancing up over her notebook at her boss. 'I noticed the Dales went in for really high-quality wine and spirits, rather than quantity. And I got the feeling the woman was just envious. She seemed to sort of resent being one of the have-nots.'

Hillary knew the type. 'She have keys to the house?'

'Nope, another thing that put her nose out of joint. The missus was always there to let her in and out.'

Hillary nodded, but could tell the cleaning woman hadn't roused anything on Janine's radar. She'd probably have to have a word or two with the woman herself, of course, but for the moment pushed her to the bottom of the list.

'OK. Tommy, I want you to get on with Mrs Dale's tyre-changing alibi. Until that's sorted one way or the other, we're just spinning our wheels.'

'Guv.'

'Frank, I want you to go house-to-house in the village. Pick up the gossip on the Dales.'

Frank sneered, but brightened up at the thought that the village was bound to have a pub. And since anyone interesting was bound to drop in, he might as well set up house there. Sod tramping from door to door.

'Janine, want to come with me to Woodstock? I want to have a word with our vic's main competition. What's his name again?'

Janine consulted her notebook. 'McNamara. George, J. A solicitor,' she added gloomily.

Hillary grunted. Along with Shakespeare, she knew what she wanted to do with most of those.

* * *

Woodstock, the town that skirted the famous Blenheim Palace, the Duke of Marlborough's little country pad, was a tourist hotspot in the summer, but on a sunny but cold March day, the ancient streets were mostly deserted. Antique shops, rather than anything useful, were the order of the day, but as she passed a small bakery, Hillary hastily averted her eyes from the chocolate eclairs and iced buns. That didn't prevent her nose from being assaulted by the delicious aromas of baking bread and melting chocolate though. She cursed at having to park so far away, but like all picturesque and ancient towns, parking was a sod.

McNamara's offices turned out to be in a higgledy-piggledy row of black and white cottages, with undulating roof, black ironwork, and window boxes full of scarlet geraniums. That must have set the cameras snapping whenever the Japanese tourists descended from the nearby city of Oxford, Hillary mused. Today, though, she barely gave the architecture a glance.

The brass plaque mounted to one whitewashed wall confirmed that Mulholand, Grath and McNamara did indeed keep their offices here, and she pushed through the glass-and-wood front door into a tiny anteroom. A secretary/receptionist, working like a troll in the mouth of a cave, peered out at them from a tiny recess under the stairs. She didn't stand, but then she probably didn't dare for fear of banging her head.

Hillary showed her credentials, smiling pleasantly as she did so. 'DI Greene, Thames Valley. I was wondering if I might have a word with Mr George McNamara?' She managed to make it sound like an order, not a request, but without throwing too much weight around. Janine wondered just how she did that.

The secretary nodded quickly and reached for the phone. She seemed like one of those women who'd come back to secretarial work after taking a break to have children, and her dyed blonde head drooped a little over the phone as she all but whispered the summons to her employer upstairs. When she put the receiver down, she turned a tight smile their way.

'Please, go right on up. Mr McNamara's office is second on the left.'

Hillary thanked her and climbed the deep, narrow stairs, holding on to the banister carefully as the boards creaked underfoot. At the top, thick and old glass window panes turned the sunlight a sort of milky colour, which reflected oddly against the hard-wearing dark grey carpeting underneath. The door in question opened before they reached it, and a man popped his head out. He wasn't tall, not much over Hillary's own five feet nine, and he had sandy blond hair turning silver. She saw his dark brown eyes run over her in quick summation. What he was seeing, she knew, was a woman with a Junoesque figure, a shoulder-length bell of nut-brown hair with chestnut tints, and, if he could see them in the odd light up here, wide brown eyes.

She was not surprised when his gaze moved on to Janine and widened slightly. Janine, with long blonde hair, ice-blue eyes, and a svelte figure with all the youth of a mere twenty-six-year-old, was used to hogging more than her fair share of male attention.

'DI Greene?' George McNamara said, his eyes going straight back to Hillary. 'Please, come in. I must say I was surprised when Clare told me you were here. We don't do criminal work, you see,' he added, as she hooked a dark brown eyebrow up in a silent question.

'Ah,' she said. Not the traditional enemy then. More of a neutral? 'I'm afraid we're here on a criminal inquiry, however, Mr McNamara,' Hillary said, as she took a quick glance around the office. A pair of uninspired but well-enough executed watercolours, one of Port Meadow in Oxford, the other of Worcester Cathedral, hung on opposite walls. Tomes and tomes of thick books in dark shades of leather lined both sides of a disused fireplace, and a couple of green and thriving pot plants sat on a broad windowsill. The floorboards underneath undulated as much as the roof, and she saw Janine totter slightly as she made her way to one of the comfortable-looking padded chairs facing a cherry-wood desk. Obviously, the firm did well for itself.

'Really? I'm intrigued. Tea, coffee?' the solicitor offered, waving her towards the other unoccupied chair.

Hillary never turned down the chance of caffeine.

In spite of the appearance of working in a lawyer's office that could have been lifted straight from Dickens, George McNamara reached out to press down the switch of a very modern intercom system and asked somebody called Daisy if they wouldn't mind popping in with the coffee pot.

'Well, I can't think which of my current clients could have fallen foul of the law, Inspector,' George McNamara said, leaning back in his chair. He was well-padded, with amiable button-like eyes, and wore a dark blue bow tie. Hillary hadn't seen a bow tie in years.

'It's about your political rival, Mr McNamara. Mr Malcolm Dale,' Hillary corrected him calmly.

McNamara's eyebrows shot up, and he suddenly straightened in the chair. 'Malcolm? But surely he can't have got into any trouble.' For all the words expressed doubt, Hillary saw definite hope and glee spring up in the other man's face.

'But if he had been caught out doing something he shouldn't, it wouldn't exactly break your heart, perhaps?' she asked, allowing just a touch of knowing amusement to creep into her voice.

As she'd expected, McNamara suddenly spread his hands in a helpless gesture, and a small, reluctant smile spread across his face. He had, she noticed for the first time, a moustache. It was so small and pale she'd almost missed it.

'Well, let's just say, all's fair in love and politics.'

'Mr Dale's campaign secretary seemed to think he had a good chance of getting the nomination,' Hillary said, throwing it into the pot just as the door opened and a plump elderly lady came in with a tray. On it was a genuine silver coffee pot, made somewhere around the 1840s, Hillary guessed, and what looked like genuine Spode cups and saucers. A matching silver creamer contained cream, not milk, and a sugar bowl was full to the brim with loose sugar, not lumps, with a small silver spoon nestling beside it.

'Ah, thanks, Daisy. Wonderful as ever,' McNamara complimented. Not one of the three women present knew whether he was referring to Daisy or the coffee, but Daisy smiled briefly and went out, without saying a word.

'Well, of course, his own campaign secretary would have to say that,' George McNamara said in response to Hillary's statement, reaching for the pot as he did so. 'But I'm hardly likely to agree. Yes, Malcolm has a lot of support, but most of it comes from the higher echelon of the party. My own strength is at grass roots level, which can sometimes be much more of an advantage. Cream? Sugar?'

Hillary murmured her choices and took a moment to think. So far, everything seemed on the up and up. McNamara was still talking about Malcolm Dale in the present tense, and seeing as the news of his death hadn't yet hit the papers, or been released to the local radio stations, there was no reason why the solicitor should know that his rival was dead. And right from the start, George McNamara had seemed to think that Malcolm Dale had been caught in some peccadillo that had for some reason caught the attention of the police.

But of course it could all be camouflage.

'So, tell me how I can help, Inspector,' McNamara said, raising the coffee cup to his lips.

'I'm afraid Mr Malcolm Dale was brutally murdered last night, Mr McNamara,' Hillary said calmly, lifting her own cup and taking a sip. Ah, wonderful. No mere instant spooned from a jar, this, but properly percolated Brazilian coffee.

'He what?' McNamara said blankly. 'Malcolm? Dead? But . . .' He slowly lowered his cup to the table, then looked at Hillary with a deliberate hardening of his face. 'I see,' he said, his voice taking on a much more solicitor-like tone. 'And you want to know where I was at the time?'

Hillary felt like smiling. He reminded her of nothing so much as a bird who'd had his feathers unexpectedly ruffled.

'Well, that would be a good start, sir,' she murmured blandly.

'And when *was* he murdered exactly?' McNamara asked, with a definite hint of you-don't-catch-me in his tone, which made Hillary feel like grinning. Or saying something equally fatuous, like 'touché.'

'If you can just tell me what you did from, say, five o'clock onwards last night, sir?' she said instead.

Somewhat appeased, McNamara nodded. 'Let's see. I left here at my usual time, that is, five thirty. The receptionist downstairs can confirm that. I live in Kidlington, so it took me, oh, say half an hour to get home. You know what traffic is like. My wife was home by then, and we made dinner together. Something simple — pasta of some sort, I think it was. We ate, and then I had some work to do in my study. Campaign work. I watched some television with my wife about ten — the news, that sort of thing. And we were in bed by eleven.'

'And did your wife disturb you in the study?'

'My wife, Inspector, I assure you, knows better,' McNamara said with a wry smile. 'Besides, she's a teacher, and had a lot of marking to do herself.'

'And when was it, would you say, that you retired to your study?'

'I don't know — seven thirty. Somewhere around then.'

'And did you take any phone calls in that time? Did you receive any callers?'

'No, and no,' the solicitor said, matching her matter-of-fact tone in unconscious mimicry.

So, Hillary thought, no real alibi. He could easily have slipped out, driven to Lower Heyford, clobbered his rival and come back. But would his wife not have heard the car? She'd have to send either Janine or Tommy over to have a word with Mrs McNamara before hubby could get home and give her some coaching.

'I see,' she said flatly.

'I rather doubt it,' George McNamara said wryly, having read with ease the way her mind was working. 'Let me enlighten you, Inspector. I've been a member of the Tory party all my life. I've now reached a point in my professional career where I have a solid client basis, and can afford a little time to devote to running for Parliament. But I'm not likely to be broken-hearted if I don't get nominated, nor am I likely to kill Malcolm Dale, for heaven's sake, in order to narrow down the competition. It's just not feasible, Inspector. I'm a law-abiding man. And not a violent one.'

Hillary nodded. She didn't think he was a particularly likely candidate either. In her experience, the power-hungry usually made their bid for the cherry long before they'd reached this man's — what — forty-odd years of age? Besides, she'd already summed up George McNamara to her satisfaction. A middle-of-the-road, unspectacularly successful man, having a mild mid-life crisis, he'd looked out for something to spice up his life. Not the type to have an affair, he'd seen the opportunity to try and run as his constituency's Tory MP as just the ticket. A respectable enough ambition not to frighten off his clients, or win the disapproval of the other partners in the office, but exciting enough to stir the blood.

It wouldn't surprise her, either, if McNamara wasn't really after a seat on the local county council, and saw being an honourable loser in a much higher stakes game as a clever way in.

'You know, I can't really believe anyone would actually murder Malcolm,' McNamara said now, distracting Hillary from her thoughts. It was as if the solicitor was only now taking on board the true enormity of what had happened. This reaction didn't particularly surprise her. Most people assessed news and dealt with it on a strictly personal level first — *how does this affect me, what will it do for or to me* —before taking on board its wider, more general effect.

'You surely don't suspect Valerie?' he added, his voice rising a touch in genuine indignation. 'I mean, I know that's the first thing people think of, but Valerie . . . I mean, I didn't know her all that well, but . . . well, she's just not the type.'

Hillary let that go without comment. How often had she heard that before?

'Do you know of anyone who might have a grudge against Mr Dale?' she asked instead. 'Your other running mate, perhaps?'

'Daniel Page? Good grief, no.' McNamara dismissed this suggestion with a wave of his hand. But then his whole face altered. 'Of course! Old man Matthews might have! I should have thought of him right away. He threatened to kill Malcolm often enough, heaven knows.'

Beside her, she sensed Janine nearly fall out of her seat. Hillary took another careful sip of her coffee. The man in front of her was now fairly bouncing around on his seat with excitement. 'Percy Matthews. Have you spoken to him yet?'

'This is the first time that name has come up in our enquiry, sir,' Hillary said flatly, trying to calm him down a little. 'You say this man actually threatened to kill Mr Dale? You actually heard this for yourself?'

'Oh yes. On more than one occasion too. He seemed to make no secret of it.' Some of the animation seemed to seep out of him, however, as he added reluctantly, 'Of course, Matthews is a bit barmy, and he *is* an old man. I mean, he's collecting his pension, and must be about seventy odd by now. But still, he's fit. Yes, he is fit.'

Hillary nodded. 'And do you know this Mr Matthews' address?'

'No, not offhand. But it's in the same village where Malcolm lived.'

'How do you come to know that?' Hillary asked curiously. 'Did Mr Dale ever confide in you that he was afraid of this man, especially as he was living so close?'

Surprisingly, George McNamara snorted with sudden laughter. 'Hell, no. Malcolm never gave the man a second thought. Mind you, he was being a bit of a nuisance. He brought the local press in, you know, and gained a lot of sympathy in some quarters. But since none of them were eligible to vote for or against Malcolm's name being put forward as a candidate, it didn't worry him as much as it could have.'

Hillary, out of the corner of her eye, saw Janine give her a 'what-the-hell' look, and noticed her pen was no longer scribbling shorthand notes. Hillary shared her confusion.

'The local press?' she repeated, bewildered. 'Mr McNamara, perhaps you can make yourself a little more clear?'

'Oh, yes, sorry. Not very professional of me. Let's see. Well, it all happened — oh, was years ago now. Malcolm was the master of Lower Heyford Hunt — a small gathering, and very new. It was only five years old or so. Anyway, during one Boxing Day hunt, the master of the hounds lost control of his dogs as they were passing through the village, and they got into one of the cottage gardens there and killed a family pet. A cat, I think it was.'

'Mr Percy Matthews' cat,' Hillary said flatly, picturing the scene. A cat, cornered by twenty or so hounds, wouldn't have stood a chance. By the time the pack had finished with it, it would be nothing more than a broken, almost fluid, hank of fur.

'Yes,' McNamara confirmed. 'Anyway, old man Matthews was furious. And I mean *furious.* I know one of the hunt members, and he told me the old man was literally beside himself with rage. Thought the old chap was going to have some sort of fit and pop his clogs then and there. Naturally, Percy Matthews swore up and down that he'd sue, that he'd kill every dog in the pack, that he'd kill Malcolm himself and so on.' George McNamara took a sip of now rapidly cooling coffee and shrugged. 'Of course, he didn't have enough money to take Malcolm to court, and although the local press and many of the villagers were on Matthews' side, nothing really came of it. Well, you know how these things go.'

Hillary smiled grimly. Oh yes, she knew how these things went all right. In spite of everything, and no matter what social historians said, the class system still ruled — especially in the villages. And she could well imagine the old man's sense of helplessness as he slowly came to realise that there was nothing he could do to get justice for his pet.

'Then hunting was banned, and the hunt sort of petered out,' McNamara went on, 'and things might have calmed down some but of course Malcolm wasn't going to take it lying down. Told everyone who would listen that Parliament had no right to dictate such matters. He even made it one of his pledges that, if elected, he would do everything in his power to get hunting reinstated. And that of course was popular with a lot of people. The Country Alliance was behind him one hundred per cent, as you might expect.'

Hillary sighed. Her only thought on the Country Alliance was that she was glad she was no longer in uniform, and therefore not obliged to turn out whenever they held a protest rally.

'I see. Well, thank you, Mr McNamara,' she said, climbing to her feet. 'I may need to speak to you again.'

The solicitor beamed. 'Any time, Inspector, any time.'

Out on the street, Hillary told Janine to go and talk to Mrs McNamara — who'd probably be at her place of work — and confirm the nuts and bolts of her husband's story. 'But hurry back, then we'll see what Percy Matthews has to say for himself,' she added grimly.

Janine didn't need telling twice.

# CHAPTER FIVE

Janine wasn't gone long, and reported back within the hour that Mrs McNamara's story supported that of her husband in all respects. And since she herself hardly knew either the victim or his wife, there had been little she could add to help move the case forward.

'So, McNamara's not officially out of it, but he's not high on the list,' Hillary responded gloomily. By now, she was hoping that she could at least have started ruling people out, but McNamara's alibi was still definitely iffy. She glanced at Tommy's desk, but it was still vacant, and she could only hope that he'd return with better news concerning Valerie Dale's movements last night.

'Right, let's see what the Matthews have to say for themselves,' she sighed.

Outside, they took Hillary's car, which was slightly bigger than Janine's, with Hillary opting to drive. According to Frank's somewhat cartoon-like map of Lower Heyford, the Matthews residence was at the top end of the village. She found it with ease — a tiny cottage, situated off the main road via a stone and mud farm track, overlooking a small set of allotments. Next to it stood an empty barn and some rusting farm machinery, with weeds growing through the metal.

As Hillary climbed out, she looked through the barely greening hawthorn bushes at the allotments, and could make out several ramshackle sheds, and, here and there, tepee-like beanpoles for runner beans, with some clumps of curly greens, and Brussels sprouts in frost-blackened rows. It instantly took her straight back to her childhood, for her father had kept an allotment, mostly for the cultivation of new potatoes and soft fruit. And sweet peas, for the local flower show.

Her father had been dead for several years now, and Hillary turned firmly away from the nostalgic sight and headed for the single dwelling, which had once, surely, been a farm labourer's cottage; a basic two-up, two-down. She knew from what she'd been able to glean during Janine's short absence that Percy Matthews was a retired shoe sales-man, who'd worked for nearly forty years in the same shop in Bicester, before it had closed to make way for a computer showroom. His wife, as far as Hillary could tell, had never worked beyond doing odd domestic jobs for the locals. The couple had five children, who'd all long since flown the nest.

Janine pushed open an old-fashioned picket gate, set in a matching but rather flimsy-looking picket fence. 'No won-der the hounds got in,' Janine muttered, eyeing the askew white-painted woodwork. 'This wouldn't have kept a hedge-hog out.'

'It was up to the master of hounds to control his dogs,' Hillary said sharply, making Janine shoot her a quick look.

'Anti-hunting, boss?' she asked, with genuine curiosity. She knew, from having lived in rural areas all her life, that the pro-hunters were talking rubbish when they insisted that the vast majority of country dwellers were all pro-hunting. In fact, nearly everybody that Janine knew, who were also coun-try-bred like herself, detested the practice. And that included not a few farmers! She suspected that her boss, like herself, was glad that the barbaric so-called sport had been banned.

Hillary merely nodded, then walked up the short flag-stone path and reached for the knocker. The garden was small but tidy, well-kept but uninspired. A small square of lawn played host to four flat flowerbeds on each side. A dwarf and weeping flowering cherry tree stood squarely in the middle.

'Sweet,' Janine said, following her gaze. 'At least there aren't any bloody gnomes.' Janine hated gnomes.

Hillary grinned, then quickly turned it off as the door opened, revealing a woman of about her own size and weight, but with iron-grey hair and eyes to match. She was wearing an old-fashioned flowered pinafore, the kind that looped over your neck and tied at the back in a bow. 'Yes?'

There were generations of country-bred Oxonian in that single word and Hillary smiled briefly. 'Mrs Rita Matthews?'

'Yes.'

Hillary held out her ID card, and nodded to Janine to do the same. 'I'm Detective Inspector Greene, this is Detective Sergeant Tyler. Is your husband in?'

'Yes.' For a moment, Hillary thought the woman was going to leave it at that, and simply stand there. Though she had considerable experience of country phlegm, that, she considered, would be really taking it too far. After another second, however, in which the old woman's dark eyes took stock of her visitors, she stood back. 'Come on inside. The kettle's on. I've just made some bread pudding.'

Hillary carefully wiped her feet on the rough mat out-side, before stepping straight into a kitchen. Of course, such a tiny cottage would have no call for anything so grand as a hall, or even a corridor, where muddy boots and coats could be dispensed with. Inside, instant heat hit them, along with the smell of cooking. 'He's in the living room,' Rita Matthews said, waving a hand at a large wooden door bearing a simple, hundred-year-old black iron latch.

Hillary nodded and went through, finding herself in a small room, with a real log fire blazing away in the hearth. A single settee, with a matching armchair, faced it. There was a utility cupboard, made just after the war by the looks of it, standing against the back wall, which was bedecked with photographs of the Matthews' offspring and assorted grandchildren, along with the usual selection of cherished but inexpensive ornaments. The pale cream walls were bare of any paintings or hangings. Bright emerald-green curtains hung at a single bay window. On the windowsill, in pride of place, was a big photograph of a grey cat.

The old man sitting in the armchair and reading a copy of the *Oxford Mail* slowly lowered the newspaper into his lap and looked at them in some surprise. Hillary heard the door close behind them and knew that Mrs Matthews had followed them inside. Janine cast a quick look at Hillary, wondering if she wanted her to usher the old woman out. Hillary gave a bare shake of her head as she headed around the sofa.

'That's a lovely fire, Mr Matthews,' she said, and again introduced herself.

'Police?' Percy Matthews echoed, surprised. 'Well, sit you down, sit you down. Want a cup of tea?'

'No, thank you,' Hillary declined. 'We're here to talk about Mr Malcolm Dale, Mr Matthews.'

At once, the old man's face darkened. He was a small, wiry man, with tufts of hair at his eyebrows that seemed to move like independent caterpillars. As had his wife, he had a lovely country accent. 'Oh, him,' Matthews sneered. 'What about him? Been complaining about me, has he? Ha, much good it'll do him. I'll get him yet.'

Behind her, Hillary heard Rita Matthews give a small sigh. Hillary settled a little more comfortably into the sofa, for she had the distinct feeling that she was going to be here some time. Percy Matthews, she noticed, was becoming flushed and animated as he charged on without waiting for any explanation of their presence.

'You see that, there,' he said, pointing imperiously to the photograph of the cat. 'That was Wordsworth, our cat. A beauty, weren't he?' Percy demanded, all but defying her to say otherwise. Not that Hillary was inclined to. Although not a thoroughbred, the photograph depicted a big, muscular tom, with a dense, short-haired, dappled grey coat. Big green eyes and slightly tattered ears showed signs of a battling nature. He wouldn't have surrendered to the hounds without a fight, she thought sadly. Not that his sharp claws, fierce hissing or brave heart would have helped him much in the end.

'He looks as if he were a real character,' Hillary said truthfully. She liked cats. She liked dogs. In fact, there weren't many animals she didn't like.

'He was,' Percy Matthews confirmed, his voice cracking. 'Ten years old he were, when that was taken, and he was top cat around here, I can tell you. He fathered some kittens.'

Hillary nodded sombrely. 'I know what happened to him, Mr Matthews,' she said, hoping to head off a graphic description. Without, of course, any luck.

'They came down this field, out back, see,' Percy said, glancing out the window to where a field of winter wheat stretched to a short horizon uphill. 'Following the hawthorn hedge down, in case the fox tried to cut across the main road into the gardens yonder.' He pointed to one side, where, across the road, was a small cul-de-sac of well-built council houses. Not that Hillary supposed many of them still belonged to the council now. 'But there was no fox, see, and those bloody dogs saw our Wordsworth. Even in the dead of winter, he liked to be out, watching the birds, or looking for queens in season. He were out by the bird bath,' Percy added, nodding at a rather small, bowl-shaped stone basin set almost into the ground. 'Had nowhere to go, did he? No way out. The bastards cornered him between the house here and the wall of the barn. I heard 'em, oh yes, and ran out, but I was way too late.'

Percy Matthews swallowed hard and took a much-needed breath, his small wrinkled face pursing in dismay as hatred and outrage gave way to a gulp. His eyes brightened suspiciously, and Hillary knew he wasn't far off tears. Beside her, she felt Janine stir nervously.

'It must have been an awful thing,' Hillary said, and meant it. 'You buried him in the garden?' she asked, knowing he'd have to get it all off his chest before she could even begin to talk about Malcolm Dale.

'Arr, what was left of him. Planted the little tree on top of him, as a remembrance, like. But you know what that bastard Dale said, that day? When he finally came prancing down here on that stupid black beast of a horse he rides to see what was holding up his precious hunt?'

Percy was sat on the edge of the armchair now, his face pinched and tight, his eyes blazing. His hands, she noticed with a touch of unease, were knobbly with arthritis, the fingers and one thumb curled in, as if he couldn't help but make a fist. Would those hands have been able to hold tightly on to a blunt instrument? And if so, would they have had enough force to crush a man's skull?

'Just imagine it — there I was, Boxing Day it were, the day after Christmas, with his bloody dogs boiling around in my garden making that hair-raising howling racket, and with my poor Wordsworth, like a hank of grey wool, all mangled and unrecognisable in my hands. And you know what he says, from up on that bloody horse of his, all dressed in scarlet, and looking like the biggest muckety-muck you ever saw? "Couldn't be helped, Mr Matthews," he said.' Percy shook his head, his thinning white hair flopping around his ears. 'Couldn't be helped?' His voice had risen almost to a hysterical pitch now, and Janine visibly winced.

'Percy,' Rita Matthews said, a weary warning in her voice. 'Take it easy, love.' It made Hillary wonder, with a sudden surge of sympathy for the woman, how many times she'd had to say that in the last few years.

'Well, it makes me sick,' Percy said defiantly. 'It couldn't be helped — what kind of rot was that? Course it could be helped — if they knew what they were doing. Bloody Heyford Hunt — just a few stupid idiots looking for an excuse to dress up and play real gentry, if you ask me. Only been formed for a year or two. Think they can make out they're someone a cut above the rest. That so-called master of hounds was about as much use as a fart in a colander.'

Rita Matthews walked a few steps to the window and stared out, her back firmly to the room, as if trying to disassociate herself from what was going on. Her gaze, however, strayed from time to time to the picture of the cat, Hillary noticed.

'Bastards never even said sorry,' Percy fumed. 'Well, that one woman did, the one on the white horse. She looked upset. But the others didn't give a toss. All they cared about was getting off again to see if they could track down Reynard. But I showed 'em,' Matthews snorted. 'Oh yes, I showed 'em. Went to a solicitor, got them to write a nasty letter, threatened to sue. That took the smile off their faces, I can tell you,' Matthews said, his angry face transforming suddenly into one of glee.

'Oh? Did you pursue it through the courts?' Hillary asked gently.

'No,' Matthews admitted grudgingly. 'Solicitor cost an arm and a leg just to write a letter. After that, though, I wrote to the local papers. I took a picture of Wordsworth, see, after they'd been at him. But the paper wouldn't publish it,' he added, aggrieved. 'Said it was too graphic. Might upset the kiddies if they saw it. But I wanted people to see it! If only people could have seen what those buggers did . . . But the paper did a nice write-up, I suppose,' he admitted grudgingly. 'Put that sod Dale's nose out of joint, any road,' he chortled. 'Then I heard that two members of the so-called hunt had retired. Yes, that put a dent in his pride, I can tell you. But it weren't enough.' He glanced at the photograph of the defiant Wordsworth, and again his eyes gleamed with ready tears. 'Not nearly enough.'

'I've been told you threatened to kill him, Mr Matthews,' Hillary said softly, and again she heard Rita Matthews heave a long-suffering sigh.

'Oh arr,' Percy said, with some of his old animation returning. 'Meant it too. Wanna see?'

Janine's pencil, which had been racing across the page of her notebook, came to a sudden halt, and Hillary herself blinked. Both women watched in surprise as Percy Matthews put aside the newspaper and got up, then went across to the utility cupboard. Inside, along with a tea service, some photo albums and other assorted bric-a-brac, he pulled out a big, untidy scrapbook.

Without more ado, Percy returned, not to his chair, but to the vacant third seat between the two women on the sofa.

His thin narrow frame fit in easily, but Hillary saw Janine hastily move her notebook to one side as his elbow threatened to dislodge it. The old man opened the cheap scrapbook and showed them the first page — which was a clipping of the newspaper article in question.

'You must be really pleased that hunting's finally been banned,' Hillary said, not sure where all this was heading. But to her surprise, Percy Matthews merely shrugged.

'Came too late for Wordsworth, didn't it?' he said belligerently.

Hillary supposed that it did.

'This is when I started to watch him,' Matthews said, suddenly turning the page. On the next one was a badly taken photograph of their victim, Malcolm Dale. He was astride a large black horse, but was not in hunting regalia. 'He keeps the beast stabled in Steeple Aston,' Matthews said with a sniff. 'Here's his shop.' Matthews pointed out another picture of the facade of what was probably Sporting Chance, Dale's shop in Banbury. 'Here's a list of his regular movements, see,' Matthew said, turning yet another page, and allowing a thin ruled notebook to drop out of the middle of the book. He opened it, revealing meticulous lists of times and dates. 'Course, his routine's changed some, since he began his campaign to get elected as Tory MP,' Matthews snorted. 'As if I'd ever allow that! He made our lives a misery when he killed our Wordsworth, and I vowed then and there that I'd make his life a misery too. And so I have. He'll get elected over my dead body. I've already sent out letters to everybody who's anybody, telling them all about Malcolm bloody Dale.'

Janine, who was gaping slack-jawed at this cheerfully offered evidence of stalking, shot her boss a quick, worried look. Was this a first-grade nutter or what?

Hillary was more interested in seeing the rest of the scrapbook than in speculating. 'What else have you got there, Mr Matthews?' she asked gently. 'That looks like an article on car maintenance to me,' she added softly.

She pointed out an article which Percy peered at short-sightedly. He snorted with impatience, and reached into the top pocket of his shirt for his spectacles. After putting them on, he tapped the page in fond remembrance. 'Arr, yes. That! That's when I thought I might get him by sabotaging his car. Thing was,' he added sadly, 'I'm not really mechanically minded. Never drove a car, see, always took the bus to work. And Rita can't drive either, so I've never had much to do with cars. Had to give up that idea,' Percy said regretfully, shaking his head.

'Get him?' Hillary repeated softly. 'What exactly do you mean by that, Mr Matthews.'

Percy Matthews craned his head around the better to look at her. His eyes, she noticed, were a sort of caramel-coloured butterscotch. 'Kill him, of course. What else?' he said, sounding surprised.

On his other side, she heard Janine draw in a sharp breath. Hillary noticed that her sergeant had gone rather pale and tense, as if ready to spring. Hillary could hardly blame her. She'd just heard what had amounted to a confession to commit murder. Hillary, however, being much more experienced than Janine, wasn't quite so excited. 'And what else did you think of, Mr Matthews?' she asked quietly, glancing quickly towards the window and Rita Matthews, to see how the wife was taking it.

Rita Matthews, however, was still staring outside at the uninspiring view of a plain green field. She showed no signs of surprise, or indeed even of interest in what her husband was saying.

So, it was like that, was it? Hillary mused grimly. Wonderful.

'Well, see, I thought of poisonous mushrooms next,' Percy said eagerly, turning a little in the middle of the sofa, the better to see Hillary. 'I read this novel where a man was killed by his wife picking poisonous mushrooms and giving them to him in an omelette.' Percy Matthews quickly trawled through the book, stopping at a page in triumph. 'See, got this article out of a magazine.' And there, indeed, was an illustrated guide to common, edible mushrooms, culled no doubt from one of his wife's magazines, and giving a clear warning at which ones were to be avoided. 'Thing was, I couldn't find any of the really deadly ones,' Percy said, sounding as petulant as a little boy who'd been denied a slice of cake. 'All that autumn — and a nice warm and wet one it was too, just right for mushrooms — I tramped about in the water meadows and the spinney, even on the side of the roads, and couldn't find a single damned poisonous mushroom. I blame the farmers — spraying this, spraying that.'

Hillary rubbed a hand across her eyebrow, feeling the beginnings of a headache. The police, of course, had a whole range of mental-health experts that she could call on for help, but once you went down that route things could get messy and — potentially — expensive. Mel, for one, wouldn't want his budget being cut into by having to pay for an independent assessment of a suspect's mental state.

'And did you think of anything else you could do to him?' she asked quietly. Over by the window, Rita Matthews finally made a noise, but it was more like a snort of quickly suppressed amusement rather than evidence of distress.

'Oh, now, let's see,' Percy Matthews said, lowering the book in his lap to stare into the fire thoughtfully. 'I thought of shooting him with a gun, but we don't own one, and even to get an air pistol or a shotgun nowadays you have to apply for licences and such. So that was out.'

'Boss,' Janine said impatiently, wondering what Hillary was waiting for. She had handcuffs looped to her belt, ready and waiting. Hillary held a hand out to silence her.

'Mr Matthews, you're telling me that you've been plotting to murder Mr Dale for some time now?' Hillary asked calmly.

'Arr. But it's not easy, see, not as easy as some people think,' Percy sighed. 'Thing is, you read all these whodunnits that they have in the library van, or watch them on telly — *Inspector Morse* and whatnot — and you get the idea that it's easy to kill somebody. I know I did. But really, when it comes right down to it, it ain't,' Percy explained in deadly earnest.

'You have to do no end of research, and planning, and more often than not, just when you get a really good plan up and working, something scuppers it.'

Hillary nodded, but her eyes were on Rita Matthews once more. Slowly, as if aware of her gaze, the old woman turned around, then moved across to the armchair and sank down. 'Don't listen to him, love,' she said tiredly. 'He's just a daft old fool. All talk and no trousers, that's him. Surely you can see that?'

Beside her, Percy stiffened in outrage, then scrambled to his feet, his face flushed. 'What do you know about it, eh? I'll get him yet, you just wait and see.'

'Mr Matthews, Malcolm Dale was murdered last night,' Hillary said quietly, and watched as all the colour drained from the old man's face.

'What? What?' he said. Then scowled ferociously. 'You mean someone else got to him first?' Again his voice rose to a squeak. 'That's not fair!' And he all but stamped his foot in frustration.

Janine, who'd leapt from the sofa at the same time as Percy had, now walked slowly towards him, keeping her eyes fixed on him all the time. Hillary simply sighed.

This was bad. Really bad. The trouble with mental cases like Percy Matthews was, there was no way a cop could win. In her own mind, she was almost sure that Percy was the kind who endlessly planned and talked and did nothing. But if she didn't take him in, and it later turned out that he really had killed Dale, then everyone from the media to the chief constable, from Mel down to her own mother, would ask her how the hell she could have been so stupid and not arrested him on the spot. On the other hand, if she *did* take him in, only for the police shrink to write him off as a fantasist, the press could get hold of it and ask how the unfeeling brutes at Thames Valley could victimize such an obviously confused and addled old boy.

So here it was — good old catch 22. And here she was, right in the bloody middle, as always.

'Mr Matthews, where were you last night?' she asked abruptly, surprising the old man in mid-flow. He stopped his swearing, complaining monologue on how the world was against him, and stared at her. He blinked. 'Last night? Well, I was here, wasn't I? All night, with the wife, watching telly.'

Janine didn't even bother to write that down, and when Hillary glanced at Rita Matthews, she just caught the tail end of the surprised look she gave him.

Now what?

The thing was, she really had no choice other than to take him in, at least for questioning. Once at HQ they could take his prints, and if they matched the as-yet-anonymous set taken from the Dales' kitchen, then at least they'd have good enough grounds to hold him. Nevertheless, she'd have bet her next month's salary that this man had never so much as set foot in the Dale house.

'Mr Matthews, I'm going to ask you to come with me to Kidlington. It's nothing to worry about,' she added firmly, as Rita Matthews suddenly sprang to her feet, for the first time a look of real alarm leaping to her face. 'I just need to take a formal statement from you both, and then take Mr Matthews' fingerprints, strictly for elimination purposes.' She quickly shook her head at Janine, who was reaching behind her for the cuffs. 'Do you have someone you'd like to call?' she asked Rita, who looked back at her blankly. 'One of your children, perhaps?'

'No,' she said shortly.

Hillary nodded. 'Right, then, let's go.'

* * *

Back at headquarters, she split them up. Outside the interview rooms, she nodded to Janine. 'You take Mr Matthews to room two. I'll take Mrs Matthews in here.' She wanted, if she could, to track down the source of that surprised look she'd given her husband when he'd claimed they'd been together all last night. 'Get Mr Matthews fingerprinted,' she added, 'and ask Mr Stevens to sit in with you.' Roger Stevens was a psychologist who consulted for them.

Janine grimaced but nodded and reached for her mobile to bring him in.

Hillary stepped into the interview room where Mrs Matthews was waiting and glanced at her watch. It was already nearly two. They'd have to feed them both. 'Please, have a seat, Mrs Matthews, I won't be a moment,' Hillary said. She left the old woman, still dressed in her pinafore, with a friendly-faced WPC to keep an eye on her, then nipped upstairs to find Mel.

Her old friend and immediate superior listened grave-faced as she outlined the latest developments. He didn't need the pitfalls outlining to him either, and when she'd finished, sighed heavily. 'Don't arrest him until you get Stevens' assess-ment of the old man's mental state, and the results of the fingerprints through,' he ordered curtly.

Hillary nodded, and was about to go when Mel called her back. 'What's your gut feeling about him?'

Hillary grimaced. 'I just don't see it, Mel. He's hoarded up his hatred like a miser hoards his gold, but I think he gets too much pleasure plotting and planning and gloating over the idea of killing Dale to ever actually go ahead and do it. And I'm not happy about the state of his hands.' Briefly she told him about what she suspected about his arthritis, and Mel agreed with her that they should get a medical opinion concerning the strength and flexibility of his hands as quickly as possible.

'He got any form?' Mel asked hopefully.

'Not a whisper.'

Mel grunted, and Hillary left.

* * *

'So, you're sticking to it that you and your husband were together all last night?' Hillary repeated, half an hour later, as Rita Matthews drained the last sip of tea from her mug and reached for the plastic triangle of sandwiches Hillary had ordered for her from the canteen.

'Like I said, we had our tea — it was Welsh rarebit and tinned peaches, then watched that *Eggheads* thing that Percy's so damned fond of. Then I did some knitting, while he watched the gogglebox. Some sort of soap, don't ask me, I don't watch 'em. I made some cocoa about nine, and we were in bed by ten, our usual time.'

She spoke with a doggedness that alone made Hillary suspicious. She wondered how much of this would match with what Janine was being told next door by Percy Matthews. Depressingly, she thought that probably a lot of it would. The Welsh rarebit, for instance. The cocoa. That all sounded genuine enough. But the bit in between?

The trouble was, the Matthews had one of those sorts of alibis that meant nothing, but, on the other hand, sounded so reasonable when outlined in a court of law. It was particularly frustrating because Hillary was sure that Rita Matthews was lying about something.

Of course, it might not even relate to her murder case. Hillary knew that people lied to the police all the time — it didn't make them killers. Rita was probably used to protecting her daffy husband from the consequences of his own actions. Perhaps she was worried that the social workers might put him in a home if it came to light how mentally ill he was. In which case, Rita's reticence might indicate nothing more than general caution on her part. Which, while understandable, was not something that a copper investigating a murder needed!

* * *

They were forced to call a halt at three. Roger Stevens, having sat in on the Percy Matthews interview, was not at all happy about his continued questioning, and asked to speak to Hillary.

'The thing is, Inspector Greene,' Stevens told her outside in the corridor, 'I suspect Mrs Matthews has probably been her husband's keeper for some time. He's not senile, exactly, but he's not far off either. I'd be inclined to take any confession he might make with a large grain of salt. Not that he's confessed to anything yet, but I can see he might well be working his way up to it.'

It was all very much as Hillary had feared.

'I need to have a quick word with Mrs Matthews, just to see how long her husband's been going downhill,' the psychologist added, 'and get some sort of idea about the dynamics of their relationship. I should be able to give you a better idea of what's what after that.'

The moment the psychologist went in to see Rita Matthews, and had shut the door firmly behind him, Janine went on the attack.

'Come on, boss, the man's as nutty as a fruitcake. By his own admission, he's been stalking Dale for years. He has motive, and no way you're going to tell me the wife isn't covering up for him. If he was in all night watching telly, then I'm a Dutchman's uncle.'

Hillary sighed heavily. 'Do his fingerprints match the ones we found in Dale's kitchen?'

Janine's glare faltered. 'Well, no. But that doesn't mean anything. Even a fruitcake knows enough to wear gloves these days. Come on, boss, you can't just let him walk!'

'Janine, the press will crucify us if we get it wrong. Look, I'll tell you what. See if you can get a search warrant for the Matthews' place. If we can come up with a murder weapon, forensics, anything solid that'll link him to the killing, I'll feel a lot happier. Until we do, we're not arresting him and that's that.'

Janine nodded and went off, glad to have something positive to do, but Hillary had the nasty feeling that she was going to complain to Mel behind her back, maybe even try and persuade him around to her way of thinking. Hillary wished her the best of British luck. It was one thing for gung-ho sergeants to go rushing in where angels feared to tread, but those who had to take the backlash if things went wrong were a different breed altogether.

For now, though, the extraordinary Matthews pair would have to be left to simmer.

# CHAPTER SIX

Tommy got in a few minutes later and headed for his desk. He listened with a worried frown as Hillary filled him in on the latest development with Percy and Rita Matthews, and its possible repercussions, then wondered aloud if Janine would have any luck with the search warrant. During his time, he'd had to apply for many warrants, and the grounds for this one sounded perilously slim to him.

'I'm not exactly holding my breath with anticipation,' Hillary agreed glumly, then added firmly, 'But you've brought me better news, right?'

Tommy nodded, opening his notebook and arranging his thoughts.

He was a big man, standing well over six feet, and had done a fair bit of running during his college days. He knew his dark skin and level gaze made many people uncomfortable — most of them his fellow cops. With villains, the appearance of Tommy Lynch on their patch was hardly a cause for celebration either, but rather for colourful and mostly racial comments — usually said from a great distance, for his speed was well known. But for all that, there was no noticeable chip on his shoulder, which Hillary, for one, greatly appreciated.

'Valerie Dale did have a flat, guv,' he said at once. 'I talked to her this morning, and she pinpointed the place easily — it was just on the hill, as you come into Adderbury. Another couple of hundred yards or so and she'd have made it to Mrs Babcock's front door. I found evidence of where a car had pulled in, and flattened grass where a tyre might have laid. Better than that, the spot was overlooked by two houses. In one, nobody was in, but in the other, I found a bloke who does the nightshift. He was going out the night in question, heading for work, and remembered seeing a car pulled up and a woman changing the wheel. His description was fairly spot on for Valerie Dale.'

Hillary sighed. 'He give a time?'

'Fits in with Valerie Dale's statement, guv,' Tommy said.

'OK. So, it's looking less and less likely it was the wife. Course, she could still have bopped hubby over the head before she went out — but that puts time of death right at the early outer limit. I want you to chase up Frank — see if he can find anyone who can confirm what time Valerie Dale left that night.'

Tommy grimaced. 'Trouble is, it would have been dark, guv,' he said, somewhat unnecessarily. 'Hardly anybody out walking their dog, and most people would have got home and been putting their feet up in front of the telly round about the time in question.'

Hillary nodded. 'I know. But try it anyway.' She didn't add that that should already have been covered by Frank — that went without saying. She glanced at Frank Ross's empty seat and desk, and wondered when he'd surface. She was pretty sure he would have set up almost permanent residence in The Bell by now — Lower Heyford's only pub. Still, while he was in there rotting his liver he wasn't getting in her hair, so she could hardly complain.

'Forensics in yet, guv?' Tommy asked.

Hillary nodded, and tossed over a thick document. 'Nothing much we didn't already know. The shower showed signs of recent use, but not, they reckon, within a few hours of our vic dying, so if Valerie did kill her husband before leaving, she didn't shower afterwards. And there's nothing suspicious in the washbasin or U-bend. So the killer must have cleaned up somewhere else.'

'Not looking like the wife, is it?' Tommy muttered.

'No, it's not,' Hillary agreed. 'Forensics found evidence of car tracks on the roadway, but only the Dales' own. So the killer either parked up on one of the village roads, or they walked.'

Percy Matthews could have walked it easily, and although his cottage was at the top end of the village, and the Dales lived in the valley, it would have been dark, as Tommy had pointed out. And he could have kept to the shadows between the street lighting, if anyone had been about.

She reread the pathologist's report, but it was all very much as Doc Partridge had said at the scene — Malcolm Dale had died as the result of several blows to the head with a heavy, rounded implement. Apart from that, he'd been relatively healthy, although the pathologist had marked him down as a heavy drinker from the state of his liver, and noted that he was headed towards clinical obesity. So no surprises there.

Fed up with reading reports and getting no further forward, Hillary reached for her jacket. 'Come on, Tommy, I want to re-interview Marcia Brock. I'm sure she's got more to tell us.'

* * *

Tommy drove to Witney, a small smile on his face. He was out alone with the guv, and the sun was shining, even if a cold wind was blowing. They were on the hunt for a killer, and he was sure he'd done well on his sergeant's Boards. He was also sure Hillary Greene would give him glowing reports. Who knows, by the time his wedding came around, he might be pulling in a sergeant's pay. The only thing was, with two sergeants already on her team (even if Frank Ross hardly counted), he couldn't see Mel keeping him on with Hillary. Far more likely he'd move him somewhere else, and assign another fledgling DC for Hillary to train up. She was known to be good at it — having both patience and the gift of imparting knowledge.

The logical part of him told him that this state of affairs would probably be a good thing. Jean, his fiancée, was the only woman he'd slept with in years, and he had no doubts that marrying her would be good for them both. And he wanted kids. Pining after his boss was just plain stupid.

'This is it — the semi, here,' Hillary said, jerking him out of his morose thoughts and bringing his foot to the brake.

Marcia Brock opened the door after the first ring, and took a surprised step back when she saw Tommy standing on her doorstep. Then she spotted Hillary behind him, and her shoulders slumped. 'Oh, you said you'd be back,' the campaign secretary acknowledged, standing to one side and trying to summon up a smile. 'I just didn't expect you back so soon.'

'The first few days in any inquiry are vital, Ms Brock,' Hillary said, and introduced Tommy. Marcia nodded without interest, and Hillary thought that Janine's snap judgement about this witness's sexual preferences were probably spot on. Not that it mattered to Hillary — unless it somehow impinged on the case. And since, somehow, she couldn't see Marcia Brock and Valerie Dale as illicit lovers plotting to get rid of the unwanted male in their lives, namely Malcolm Dale, Hillary simply gave a mental shrug.

'Tea? Coffee?' Once more Marcia showed them into the kitchen, rather than the living area, and Hillary took her seat once more at the small table.

'Coffee would be fine. Any luck at the job centre?' she asked.

Marcia shrugged. 'Sure, if I want to spend five months stocking shelves at Tesco's or driving the home-delivery van for Iceland. Oh yeah, or working in a bakery.'

Hillary smiled. 'I'd take the bakery job in a heartbeat.' The thought of free chocolate eclairs was enough to corrupt any copper off the straight and narrow.

Marcia Brock managed a wry laugh, and returned with three steaming mugs which she set down, with some spillage, on to the table. She pushed the sugar bowl towards Tommy, who smiled but ignored it.

'Well, we have a much better picture of our victim now,' Hillary began, 'but we're still searching for things in his private life that might have led to his murder.'

Marcia gave a tight smile. 'He hasn't been fiddling the books at the shop then?'

Hillary, who had yet to read the reports from the constables who'd been assigned to check out Sporting Chance, shook her head. 'Can't go into details, I'm afraid. But I got the distinct feeling, the last time we spoke, that you were, shall we say, being somewhat less than fully candid with me?' She let her voice drift up at the end, making it a question, and watched as Marcia's hands tightened around her mug. The younger woman kept her head firmly bowed over it, then blew on her coffee, and finally shrugged. 'I told you everything I know.'

'But not everything you suspect,' Hillary prompted at once, making it a statement this time, and not a question. 'What is it? Financial irregularities in his campaign?'

As expected, that made her head shoot up, and Hillary noticed a dull flush of anger stain her cheekbones. 'Hell, no. I run an honest ship,' she said hotly.

Hillary nodded. When questioning a reluctant witness, it was always best to lead with something they could indignantly deny. That way, it made admitting to the truth somehow easier. She'd have to ask a psychologist why that was sometime. 'So it was something in his personal life,' she pressed on. 'What was it? An affair?'

'Why do you coppers always assume the worst?' Marcia demanded belligerently. 'The poor sod's dead, isn't he? I didn't like him much, but he deserves some privacy, some respect.'

Hillary nodded. 'Yes, he's dead,' she said flatly. 'And it's up to me to find out who killed him.' She paused a moment, to let that sink in. 'He's got nobody else who can help him now. Only me. And I can only help him in that one, single way. To find out who did it, why, and make sure they're brought to account for it.' Hillary waited until the other woman was looking her in the eye, before adding quietly, 'So anything you can tell me will really be appreciated. And useful. Really.'

Marcia's high colour slowly ebbed, and she looked away, but this time, Hillary thought, with a sense of shame. It was always easier to reach the ones who still had consciences.

'I thought he was having an affair, yeah,' she said at last. 'But I've got no proof, mind. I never saw nothing, no notes or anything. He didn't ask me to send flowers or anything icky like that.'

'Do you know the woman involved? It was a woman, I take it?' Hillary said softly.

Marcia sighed softly. 'Yeah, it was a woman. A GP. Name of Gemma Knowles. She works at the Oxlip Health Centre. I saw them having lunch, once, in this little out-of-the-way pub in Oxford. Course, I could have got it wrong.'

Hillary nodded. She talked to Marcia for a while longer, but was finally satisfied that she'd got everything out of her that she was going to. She thanked her, then left.

By the time they made their way out of Witney it was fully dark. 'I'll be glad when the clocks go on. This Saturday, isn't it?' she mused to Tommy, who nodded.

'OK. Finish the paperwork and then you can get off,' Hillary said, as he pulled into the parking lot back at HQ. 'You can drop me off here. I'm having an early night for once,' Hillary said, making Tommy look at her in some surprise. He couldn't remember the last time his governor had gone home much before six, and never when she was working on a case. And, of course, Hillary couldn't tell him about the raid tomorrow night until much closer to the time, mindful as she was about the super's desire to keep this totally hush-hush. 'Get some sleep yourself,' was all she said, as she shuffled across into the driver's seat.

Tommy watched, fascinated, as her skirt rode up her thighs, and mumbled something indistinctly.

* * *

Hillary drove home, making the three quarters of a mile or so out of town and to the tiny hamlet of Thrupp in less than five minutes. Now that was what she called a commute.

Walking along the dark towpath, she shivered as the cold wind rippled around her. The dried sedges on the opposite side of the canal whispered to her as she opened the padlock and duck-walked down the stairs. When she'd first moved on to the boat, supposedly as a temporary measure nearly three years ago now, she'd hit her head constantly on the hatchway. Now she didn't give it a second thought.

She'd recharged the battery yesterday, so she turned on the lights as she went, and threw her coat and bag on to one of the two chairs in the *Mollern*'s forward cabin. She rifled through the cupboards, and came up with a can of chicken in white wine sauce, a tin of garden peas, and one of new potatoes. These three items took up every saucepan the tiny galley owned.

As she reached for the tin opener, she gave a brief thought to the fine cuisine that the modern working woman was supposed to enjoy, as a matter of course, and snorted. As the assorted gloops started to simmer on the small gas stove, she promised herself a meal at The Boat that weekend. Something with French words in it. And a pudding that would make calorie counters sit up and weep. For a week.

She ate quickly, and had to admit that the tinned fare really wasn't all that bad. Either that, or her taste buds had finally packed up on her. She washed up carefully after her, having long since learned the need for neatness and method when you lived in such a confined space.

Still, less space meant less housework, and she didn't regret her decision to put the house she and Ronnie had once shared on the market. Not that it was moving yet. Trust her to hit a slump in the property market, just when her main financial asset suddenly became free. She wiped the small table down, then folded it away, and walked two paces forward to peruse her small library. It consisted of three shelves, tucked down in the bottom right-hand corner, and was already overflowing. She'd studied English literature at college, and her eye ran restlessly over all her old favourites — every Bronte ever written, the same for Austen, with some modern poetry and the odd biography thrown in.

Her eyes stalled over the tattered paperback of a single Dick Francis book, and her heart did its usual slump into her boots. She was going to have to do something about that. Something soon. If she was caught with it, and somebody worked out what it contained, it could send her to prison for up to five years.

And for a cop, prison was not a good place to be.

Pushing the thought aside, she selected *Jude the Obscure*. For some reason, she was in the mood for Hardy. Perhaps she saw herself as one of his flawed, inevitably doomed heroines?

Now there was a thought to take to a cold and lonely bed with you on a windy March night.

* * *

She got in the next morning, to find Janine already ahead of her, and fuming. The moment she used her key-card to gain access to the big open-plan office, she could feel waves of frustration emanating from her pretty blonde sergeant.

She hadn't even put her bag down on the desk before Janine swivelled her chair around to face her, a dark glower ruining the effects of her perfectly applied make-up. 'Bloody judge wouldn't roll over on the Matthews search warrant, boss.'

Hillary sighed, but she'd expected as much. 'Who did you try?'

'Phelps.'

Hillary nodded. The most pro-police of the lot.

'Should I try going round him?' Janine asked, but without much heat, and wasn't surprised when Hillary firmly shook her head. No, the last thing they needed was to piss Phelps off. He came in very handy at times.

'We'll just have to wait and watch them,' Hillary said. And hope the press didn't get a hold of it. So far, she'd been dodging reporters with ease, with most of them content to go through the press liaison officer, with the odd harassment of Lower Heyfordians thrown in. So far, most of the press speculation had, almost inevitably, centred around Valerie Dale, but that would quickly change when they got whiff that she wasn't a serious suspect any more. Nobody but a tiny and rather ridiculously radical tabloid took the political angle seriously. Who'd want to knock off a man who hadn't even been elected MP yet? But if the vultures got hold of Percy Matthews, and his story, she shuddered to think what the headlines would be.

And how long would it take the batty old coot to realise that he now had the perfect opportunity to immortalize his Wordsworth once and for all? All he had to do was show them his scrapbook and that would be it. Feeding frenzy.

*Please, please, please, don't let him 'confess' to a reporter live on air*, Hillary pleaded silently to whoever might be listening.

'OK. Well, it's not all doom and gloom. Tommy and I winkled a nice tit-bit from Marcia Brock yesterday afternoon,' Hillary said, by way of cheering her up, and filled her in as Janine drove them towards the small village of Oxlip, not far from the Oxford suburb of Headington.

\* \* \*

'Brings back old memories, this,' Janine muttered, as they parked up in the health centre's large car park.

Hillary nodded. They'd had cause to come here before, on a previous case, to question one of the doctors. He'd since been struck off, or so she'd read. She wasn't sure that that had been altogether fair, but then, she didn't sit on the Medical Council.

Inside, the waiting room was half full, and Hillary felt all eyes on her as she showed her warrant card to the receptionist. She felt guilty about pushing in ahead of the queue and lengthening their wait to see Dr Gemma Knowles, but that was life.

'Dr Knowles is out on a home visit,' the receptionist said worriedly when she heard what the policewoman wanted, and Hillary had to grin. Oh yes, that was life all right. It wasn't fussy about who it shafted.

'Will she be returning here when she's finished?' she asked hopefully.

'Oh yes. And she shouldn't be too long. She's usually in before ten. She has patients starting at a quarter past,' the receptionist added firmly.

Hillary smiled grimly. Not any more she didn't.

'We'll wait,' she said. 'Please inform us the moment Dr Knowles comes in.'

Janine heaved a sigh as she selected a month-old *Homes & Gardens* magazine from the pile on the table, and took the seat farthest away from the children's play area, where a loud three-year-old was playing with a wooden engine.

* * *

Hillary spotted Gemma Knowles the moment she stepped out of her car. She'd been gazing out of the window at a pretty, early-flowering almond tree for the last ten minutes, when a smart and zippy new Mazda pulled in. The doctor wasn't tall, but was dressed in a well-tailored, navy blue pair of slacks, with a matching, quilted Barbour coat. She had a short cap of dark hair that had been professionally high-lighted with auburn streaks, and, even from a distance, big pansy-brown eyes. As Hillary suspected, she didn't use the front door, but trotted off to a private entrance round the back.

Hillary tapped Janine on the top of her arm and got up, making her way to reception. The same receptionist noticed her approach and spoke quickly into the phone, then put it down. She nodded, and directed them to the first office down the corridor. Gemma Knowles opened the door before they reached it and pulled it open. She looked rather relieved to find two female police officers, and Hillary suddenly knew that she wasn't going to have much trouble with this witness.

'Oh, hello. Yes, I've been expecting this,' Gemma Knowles said, pointing to the single chair standing beside her desk. 'Er, I'm afraid one of you will either have to stand, or if you prefer . . .' She waved vaguely to the padded narrow couch where patients could stretch out for more intimate examinations. Janine shuddered and leaned against the door, getting her notebook out. Hillary sat.

Gemma crossed a pair of legs, clad in expensive hosiery, and fiddled with a pen. Hillary guessed there was money somewhere about — either she'd married well, or she had private means.

'It's about Malcolm, I take it,' Gemma Knowles said at once. Obviously the kind who liked to take the bull by the horns, which was fine by Hillary. Her face, though perfectly made up, was pale, and she had hollows under her eyes that looked dark, in spite of the powder. The GP was genuinely upset about her lover's death, Hillary realised, and gave a mental nod.

'Yes. We understand you and he were intimate?' She asked the question bluntly, but her voice was kind. Gemma Knowles blinked, and Hillary could almost see her shoulders straighten. She'd been right to choose this no-nonsense but non-brutal approach. As a doctor who must have grown used to being firm but compassionate, it struck just the right chord.

'Yes. Yes, we were. For about four months now.'

'Was it serious?'

'Oh no. I mean, neither of us was going to break up our marriages or anything,' Gemma said. 'Apart from the odd lapses, created by boredom mostly, I'm quite content with Larry,' Gemma said frankly. 'And Malcolm, of course, had so much more to lose than I did. So, no, we were very discreet, and we both knew exactly where we stood.'

Hillary nodded. Well, if that was true, then Gemma Knowles had no reason to kill Malcolm Dale. If it was true. If it wasn't, well, it opened up a whole lot of potential. Had she really loved the man, and been angered by his refusal to leave his wife, so killed him in a fit of jealousy and rage? Or had *he* been the one pushing *her* to leave her husband, and had she then killed him to keep her marriage safe?

Of course, a lot of people were appalled by the thought of doctors, people who dedicated their lives to tending the sick and curing the ill, actually killing someone. But they were human, just like everyone else. And Harold Shipman had probably changed the British public's conception of GPs for ever.

'You'll understand that I need to know where you were, two nights ago, from, say, five o'clock onwards, Dr Knowles.'

The GP nodded. An intelligent woman, she'd of course have expected that. 'I can tell you all right, but I'm afraid it's not ideal. We see the last of our patients here at four thirty. After that, we usually stay in the office for up to an hour or so finishing off our paperwork. That night, I'm afraid I had to stay even later. I'd had a few emergency call-outs the day before, and had more than two days' worth of notes to put into the computer. I worked until nearly eight, then left.'

Hillary gave a mental head-shake. Yet another one with no solid alibi. 'What time do the secretaries leave?'

'About five.'

'And that night, did you see anyone? Did one of the partners pop his head around the door to say hello, anything like that?' Hillary asked, although the other woman was already shaking her head.

'I'm afraid not,' Gemma Knowles said ruefully. 'I wish they had.'

So did Hillary. Just for once, it would be nice to categorically rule someone in or out.

'So, you got home about what time?' Hillary ploughed on.

'About twenty past. I only live in Bletchington, not far away.'

'And your husband, Larry, was in?'

'Yes, he'd cooked dinner, bless him.'

'And you stayed at home all that night?'

'Yes.'

Hillary nodded. Not that *that* helped. According to Marcia Brock and the pathologist, Malcolm Dale had been dead by then. So Gemma could have left earlier, motored to Lower Heyford, parked up somewhere dark, then walked to her lover's door, been invited in, and killed him. And she could so easily have come back here to clean up. Even if she got forensics to go over the place, it was a doctor's surgery, for Pete's sake. They'd come up with scores of blood traces and who the hell knew what else.

Hillary sighed. 'And your husband? Had he been in all night?'

'Larry?' Gemma said sharply. 'No. I'm pretty sure he said he'd been out to the pub.'

'I thought you said he'd cooked you dinner?' Hillary pointed out softly.

'So he had, but only chicken Kievs from the freezer,' Gemma said. 'Look, I promise you, Larry didn't know about me and Malcolm. I'd have known if he had.'

Her voice, for the first time since the interview began, showed signs of strain. Hillary reached into the bag for her notebook and scribbled a quick message: 'Go and speak to the hubby. I don't want them to have time to confer. Grill him hard.'

This she handed over to Janine, who read it, poker-faced, and got up and left without a word. Gemma watched her go, a real look of alarm on her face now.

Yes. Gemma Knowles seemed very worried about her husband all right. But then again, perhaps she was simply afraid that he'd find out about her affair — if he really did know nothing about it, as she insisted. It didn't necessarily mean that she was secretly worried that he had killed her lover.

'So, Doctor Knowles, tell me how you met,' Hillary said, settling down to a nice long chat.

# CHAPTER SEVEN

Janine got the home address of Gemma Knowles from the receptionist, who didn't like handing it over, and quickly headed towards Bletchington. It was a small village, with a surviving village shop overlooking a triangular village green. The GP and her spouse lived in a small cul-de sac in one of six large, similar-looking mock-Tudor detached houses that would be forever out of Janine's price range.

But as she parked her sporty little Mini by the double set of wrought-iron gates, she checked the house out with a small smile of satisfaction on her lips. Mel's house in The Moors was older, bigger and better-looking than any of these.

When they'd first started dating over two years ago now, she'd gradually begun to spend more and more time at his place, since the house she rented out with three other girls was hardly the place for romance. She had most of her stuff moved in now, including her CD set and her favourite chair. She loved living in the big house, with the pond and weeping willow in the front garden, and nodding hello to neighbours in the morning who were judges and architects, computer designers and art collectors. She was even thinking about approaching her three friends and asking them to find somebody else to help out with the rent. It seemed such an unnecessary expense.

But just lately, Janine had become less sure. She might be wrong, but she thought she'd begun to detect a distinct sense of 'cooling off' in Mel. Nothing concrete, nothing she could put her finger on. Just stupid little things that rang warning bells. Like him insisting on watching a football programme on Sky, when she wanted to watch something else. In the early days, she'd always been able to wangle control of the remote. And he hadn't come home with a bottle of wine or box of Belgian chocs for a while. And sometimes, when she'd be talking to him, chatting in the kitchen or wherever, she'd suddenly realise he hadn't been listening to her.

As she walked up the path and rang the doorbell of the Knowles's family home, she wondered seriously, and for the first time, if Mel was getting ready to dump her.

She didn't like that thought. Usually, she was the one that did the dumping — only two boyfriends of hers had ever been the first to break it off, and both times it had left her smarting and fuming. She didn't take rejection well.

And this was far more serious than either of those losers dumping her. Mel was her first boyfriend to be on the job as well, in a position to do her career prospects good; the first to be so much older than her, to actually be marriage material. But perhaps she was reading it wrong. Mel had a lot on his plate, what with working under the boy wonder from the Met, Jerome Raleigh. Maybe he was just feeling generally stressed out.

Maybe.

But if Mel thought he could just dump her, he'd soon learn differently.

She leaned on the doorbell again, but nobody was going to answer. At this time of day, hubby was almost certainly at work. She went back to the car, made a quick phone call to records, and learned that Lawrence Peter Knowles worked, surprisingly, for a construction company, as a bricklayer.

They were currently throwing up a series of warehouses out near Kidlington airport.

Mindful of her boss having to keep Gemma talking until she gave her the all-clear, Janine put her foot down.

* * *

Larry Knowles was a tall, lanky man with a mass of sandy hair, a smattering of freckles, and watery blue eyes. He was working steadily on an outer wall, laying bright red bricks at a surprising rate. His motions were fluid and unthinking, and when Janine walked up to him he didn't notice her at first. A wolf-whistle from across the construction site eventually made him look around.

He smiled and straightened up. 'Take no notice,' he said dismissively, as another wolf-whistle followed the first. Janine, who was used to attracting male attention, had already filtered it out. She showed him her ID and saw the usual wariness enter his eyes. She cast a quick look around. A cement mixer was grinding noisily away a few yards to their left, giving them as much privacy as anybody could hope for on a building site.

'Mr Knowles, can you tell me where you were two nights ago, between five and ten?' she jumped right in.

Larry Knowles slowly lowered the brick in his hand back on to a pile and lodged his trowel into some still-wet cement. 'What's this all about?'

'Just routine, sir,' Janine lied.

Larry sniffed, then wiped the back of his hand across his nose, making the sergeant wonder what had prompted such a chic and sophisticated woman like Gemma Knowles to marry a man such as this one. Perhaps opposites really did attract.

'I worked until six, as usual. Went home. Gemma, my wife, was still at work. There was a message on the answer phone to say she'd be working late. I got something out of the freezer and cooked it. We ate when she got in, watched some telly, and went to bed.'

Janine jotted it all down, her face giving nothing away. 'Did you go out at all? To the pub maybe?'

Larry Knowles shook his head. 'Nope.'

Janine nodded, a sharp tug of excitement making her short hand fly faster. It didn't tally — well, not exactly — with Gemma Knowles's statement. 'Did you tell your wife that you'd been to the pub?'

Larry Knowles slipped his hands into his trouser pockets. It was a defensive gesture that didn't go unnoticed. He stared at his feet for a while, then looked up at Janine. She realised he wasn't going to answer and tried a more aggressive approach.

'Does the name Malcolm Dale mean anything to you, Mr Knowles?'

The bricklayer sighed heavily. There was something really weary in that sound. 'What is this? What's up?' he demanded bluntly.

'Just routine, sir,' Janine repeated the lie. 'Do you and your wife have a good marriage, would you say, sir?' she asked, knowing she was hardly being subtle. If her boss was here, Hillary Greene would no doubt be handling this very differently. But what the hell. This was *her* way of doing things.

Something interesting happened to Larry Knowles's face as Janine asked the question. Not anger, but a knowing, almost shamed expression darkened his face.

'In other words, what was someone as smart and classy as Gemma doing marrying a working-class know-nothing brickie like me?' Larry said, repeating almost word for word Janine's earlier thoughts.

So he had a chip on his shoulder. Not surprising. A lot of people must have wondered the same thing. And boy, did this man know it. Janine, having learned the trick from Hillary, said nothing. Most people didn't like silence, and would say anything just to banish it.

'My marriage is none of your business,' Larry Knowles finally said and bent down to pick up his trowel. 'Now, if that's all . . .'

'You never said whether or not you knew a Mr Malcolm Dale, sir,' Janine said quickly.

'No, I don't,' Larry said, laying the next brick in three short movements, and reaching for the next.

'And you don't want to change your statement about what you did two nights ago?'

'No, I don't.'

Janine nodded, and walked away.

* * *

Hillary, now back at HQ, listened without interruption as her sergeant reported her conversation with Larry Knowles almost verbatim. When she'd finished, Hillary sighed heavily. Another one with no alibi. Great.

'Sounds to me as if he turns a blind eye,' she mused out loud. She'd managed to snatch a rather wilted salad from the canteen and was still feeling hungry, and thus grumpy. Tommy, who'd been updating the Murder Book, glanced across.

'Blind eye, guv?'

Hillary nodded. 'He married up, and he knows it. Wife's better looking, got more brains, more class. And I reckon there's money in her background too. So if she occasionally strays — well, he thinks, that's only to be expected, isn't it? Can't expect to keep her, can he? She's bound to realise what a mistake she made. Best just to pretend it isn't happening. Perhaps she won't leave him. I've seen that sort of mindset before.'

'What the shrinks call low self-esteem,' Janine put in with a twist of her lips. Men could be such wimps.

'Or sound common sense.' Hillary was never loath to play devil's advocate. 'Thing is, the poor mutt doesn't realise that his wife, by and large, is probably perfectly happy with her marriage. She's got a husband who doesn't compete with her on a professional level, who's got a steady well-paid manual job that keeps him fit and healthy. The last thing a GP would want is hassle at home. If she gets bored and strays now and then, so what?' Hillary shrugged. Ronnie had cheated on her with every blonde bimbo that wandered across his path. Fidelity was something he thought only applied to sound systems. She knew all about maladjusted marriages.

'Even so, he could have got jealous,' Janine said. 'One affair too many? The straw that broke the camel's back.'

Hillary nodded, going along with the hypothesis. 'He could have thought the "working late" message really meant she was with her lover. Could have gone over to confront them, expecting to find his wife there.'

'But she wasn't.' Janine carried the scenario further. 'So he thinks this is the perfect opportunity, goes in, bops our vic, and takes off.'

But even as she said it, it didn't quite gel. If he'd gone hot-foot to Lower Heyford expecting to find Gemma and Malcolm together, wouldn't he have been relieved to find Malcolm alone after all? Or at least, wouldn't some of the heat have gone out of him? And why would Malcolm Dale have invited him in? Did he even know what Gemma's husband looked like?

'And did he take the murder weapon with him?' Hillary asked quietly. 'So far, there seems to be nothing missing from the family home. So the murder had to be premeditated.' She too didn't quite like the ring of it. But with no alibi, both the Knowles pair were still firmly in the frame.

'Check it out, Tommy,' Hillary said. 'See if he really did go out to the pub — what's the local called?' she asked Janine, who checked her notebook.

'The Black's Head.'

'Oh, very funny,' Tommy said, and they all laughed.

'No, that's really what it's called,' Janine insisted.

'Well, see if he was in that night. He might have forgotten about calling in,' Hillary said wearily. 'If not, see if any of his neighbours can put him at home, cooking dinner, when our vic got clobbered.'

'Guv.'

Janine looked up as Frank came in. He tossed some reports on to Hillary's desk, then jerked his head up to indicate the ceiling. 'Have to go upstairs in a bit.'

Hillary's face tightened. She hadn't forgotten. The raid was on tonight. But exactly why Jerome Raleigh was keeping Frank Ross, of all people, so tightly in the loop, still worried her. When Frank had gone, leaving the scent of old beer, cigarettes and stale sweat behind him, Janine reached into her bag and brought out some air freshener.

Hillary glanced at her watch, saw it was getting on for three, and decided it was time to fill her team in. There was no one within earshot, but she pulled her chair a little closer to her desk anyway, indicating she wanted a private huddle. 'Tommy, Janine, something's on for tonight.'

Janine instantly caught her tone, and scooted closer. Tommy, looking more surprised, simply sat and waited. Slowly, carefully, and leaving nothing out, Hillary told them about the raid, and the super's instructions to keep it quiet. When she was finished, Janine looked ready to chew the table legs. To think that Mel, the bastard, knew all about it, and hadn't told her.

'I wondered why you lot seemed to be upstairs so often just lately,' she snapped. Then, remembering Frank Ross's unsubtle head-nod a while ago, flushed with genuine rage. 'Don't tell me that toe-rag Ross has been in on this all the while?'

At this insult, Tommy jerked a little in his seat.

Hillary shrugged helplessly. 'Don't look at me,' she told her outraged team. 'It wasn't my idea. The super has his own way of doing things.'

Janine subsided a little. 'He was right to keep it quiet,' she agreed grudgingly. 'Everyone knows Fletcher's got ears in this place.' It galled her to say it, as much as it galled Hillary to hear it.

'So, it's back to Bletchington,' Janine said. 'Funny, the Knowleses living there. But it's got to be a coincidence, right?' she asked sharply.

Hillary, who didn't usually like coincidences either, had a quick think about it, then reluctantly nodded. Fletcher was blamed for nearly anything and everything dirty that went on in their patch, but even she couldn't see why he'd want to murder a wannabe Tory politician. Or have anything to do with a local GP and her husband who might or might not have anything to do with it.

That was taking paranoia a little too far.

'The Fletcher farm's a mile or so out of the village proper,' Hillary said. 'And, besides, everyone's got to live *somewhere*.'

* * *

As per the super's instructions, everyone worked their full shift, then left as if nothing out of the ordinary was going on. Because she lived so close to work, Hillary went home and changed into black trousers and black sweater, and wore her oldest, dullest brown coat, before heading out to the rendez-vous point at Brian Doyle's farm, half a mile from Fletcher's place. She suspected that all the others had gone straight from work to the farm, and only hoped they'd had the sense to stagger their arrival. The last thing they wanted was for a Fletcher lookout to spot a load of cars in convoy, turning into Doyle's place.

She headed for an open barn, where a man stood in the darkness, beckoning her. She could only just make him out in the moonlight. She nudged Puff the Tragic Wagon under cover, noting Mel's car, but not Janine's Mini. They'd prob-ably arrived together, cutting down on the volume of traffic. Likewise, she saw Tommy's car, but not Frank's, and a luxury saloon that could only belong to the super.

The Tactical Firearms Unit, she supposed, would have come in the usual heavy-duty vehicles, and would have been parked well away, and probably hidden by ex-army camou-flage gear.

So, she was the last to arrive. More demerits with the new super? It was hard to tell with Raleigh. He never seemed to show either approval or disapproval of her. It was discon-certing, to say the least.

'They're all in the kitchen.' The man who'd beckoned her into the barn appeared at her car door the moment she opened it, and hissed into the darkness. She wondered what the farmer was making of it all. Was he excited, or scared? No member of the criminal fraternity would ever have even given a passing thought to helping the police nail Luke Fletcher. But an honest farmer was a different proposition altogether. It made Hillary uneasy as she walked to the farmhouse and tapped quietly on the door. She only hoped nothing bad would touch this family, or this home, tonight.

Sometimes, the weight of being a copper seemed to land on her from a great height. Sometimes, she thought about a million pounds sitting in a Caribbean bank account, and thought about retiring to the sun. About never having to worry about someone else's safety again.

The door was opened, and Mel gestured her inside. The farmhouse kitchen was warm, smelt of stew, and was full of people. Mike Regis was there, although she hadn't seen his car in the barn, and he looked across at her the moment she walked in. Like her, he was dressed in his darkest, oldest clothing. His green eyes watched her move across the room, then he turned back and resumed his conversation with Colin Tanner, the man who'd been his sergeant for years.

Superintendent Raleigh nodded at her, but remained in one corner, a radio clamped firmly to his ear. Obviously, the TFI were already at stage A, and were closing in quietly on the target.

'Make sure you're loaded up with flat-nosed ammo,' she heard Raleigh say into the mike, and felt a chill go down her spine.

Flat-nosed bullets were often used by the police because there was less chance of a flat-nosed bullet going straight through a body and killing someone else behind the target. It brought home to her, more than anything else, the seriousness of the situation.

She saw Tommy frown, and wondered if he'd caught her shivering like a terrified whippet. She turned away from the quiet, tense atmosphere and glanced outside. Brian Doyle was nowhere to be seen. Come to think of it, none of the

Doyle family was present. Perhaps the wife and kids were holed up in the living room watching *Emmerdale* and pretending that none of this was happening.

She hoped so.

Although none of the 'regular' coppers in this room would be going in until the Tactical Firearms Unit gave the all-clear, you could cut the atmosphere with a knife.

Tommy appeared at her elbow, a big, quiet, calm presence. 'Guv, you really think we're going to nail Fletcher tonight?' he whispered.

Hillary shrugged. Nailing Fletcher was everybody's fantasy. The untouchable, murderous, drug-dealing scumbag who lived high on the hog right under their noses. They'd tried to get him before, and always failed. But this time?

'Who knows,' Hillary whispered back. 'If Fletcher is there. If the drug shipment arrives. If Fletcher's caught red-handed. If the paperwork's in order. If someone doesn't bribe the judge, if the stool pigeon testifies and doesn't end up dead in the canal . . . Hell, Tommy, your guess is as good as mine.'

The drugs might never arrive, and then everyone would stand down and go home, sick with a sense of anti-climax.

After nearly twenty years in this game, Hillary wouldn't have bet a penny on the outcome either way.

\* \* \*

It was nearly two hours before it was confirmed that the drugs shipment had arrived. Or at least, that the three-man team their source *said* would be carrying the new drug squaddie, had arrived.

According to Raleigh's supergrass, the three-man team was from up Liverpool way, anxious to sell their wares down south. They were doing an 'introductory' deal with Fletcher, who should, right now, be holding 100,000 quid in ready cash in his hot and greedy little hand.

She glanced at the clock, as Raleigh, over in the corner, listened intently, the radio seemingly glued to his ear. Every now and then he'd speak, giving a running commentary to the deathly silent room, as relayed by one of their lookouts.

'The car's pulled into the outside rear barn.' Raleigh sounded tense but controlled. 'Two have entered the premises — the third has stayed with the car.'

Hillary, like the rest of them, was following the action intently, and thinking it through as and when the information came in. Someone staying with the car was a complication. It meant the TFI would have to send a two-man unit in to neutralize the car driver.

They'd also have to start 'mopping up' the outer perimeter too, in one smoothly co-ordinated effort, before anybody moved in on the farmhouse proper. Nobody wanted to get caught in crossfire, and Fletcher was bound to have lookouts scattered throughout the farmyard and surrounding area.

'Direction microphones are picking up voices. Being recorded.' Again Raleigh spoke, again everyone listened. Janine began to pace, then stopped.

Still, everyone waited, everyone imagining what was going on at the site. Fletcher's chemist would be testing the drugs for sure. Would they have a guinea pig, a volunteer, who would take a sample and see how high it got them? Fletcher would have no shortage of volunteers. He liked to keep some of his dealers hooked. Not all. Just some.

'The team leader has given the go-ahead for stage B.'

Hillary tensed. That was the point of no return. Stage B called for the TFI to simultaneously move in on the targets patrolling the outer perimeter. They'd have been in position for hours, pinpointing the lookouts and guards. 'They have a go,' Raleigh added simply, for the first time lowering the radio and looking at the others. 'Let's get to Checkpoint Charlie.'

The order acted as a safety valve, with everyone moving, letting out pent-up breaths, and glad to have positive action at last.

As Raleigh walked outside ahead of everyone else, Hillary saw him reach into his pocket for his mobile phone.

He must have pressed speed dial, for he only pressed one button. As he disappeared into the dark of the farmyard, she saw him put the phone to his ear, but he spoke so quietly she couldn't hear what he said. Then she forgot about it in the co-ordinated rush to get moving.

Checkpoint Charlie was the first position near Fletcher's farm where the unarmed team were to congregate. Far enough away from any possible gunfire to be deemed safe, it was also close enough to satisfy Raleigh and the rest of the brass that they were in a prime position to move when the TFI gave the all-clear.

It had all been mapped out before who would go with whom. Hillary and Tommy followed Regis and Tanner, who'd parked their car behind the barn, not in it, and piled into the back seat. Mel, Raleigh, Ross and Janine went in Raleigh's saloon. The two cars left, Raleigh's leading, and headed into the darkness of the cold March night.

They drove down a narrow lane, with bare-branched trees crowding in on them on either side. For a moment, the eyes of a deer, two blank yellow disks, showed up between the tree trunks, then was gone. Hillary tried to breathe normally, but it wasn't easy. She could feel adrenaline bubbling through her veins, making her want to fidget in her seat, and knew it would be the same for the others.

Even with the car windows shut, Hillary distinctly heard the first burst of gunfire. The sounds were flat, hard, and alien, and beside her she felt Tommy flinch.

'Didn't think they'd surrender without a fight,' Mike Regis said flatly from the front passenger seat.

As if to confirm it, a second barrage of gunfire ricocheted through the night.

* * *

At Checkpoint Charlie, they pulled in off the road and doused the lights. The entrance to Fletcher's so-called farm lay just a few yards off up to the right. All was now quiet.

'What's going on?' Regis said, the moment Raleigh got out of his car. 'Is anybody down?'

The superintendent held up a hand, as ever, the radio glued to his ear. 'They went in a few moments ago,' Raleigh said.

'We know, we heard,' Regis responded grimly, making Hillary wonder if he had wanted to go in with them. Frank Ross lit up a cigarette, and she saw Colin Tanner peel off to intercept him. A moment later, she saw the cigarette end glow and arch in the darkness as Ross threw it away.

'We're moving up to Checkpoint Romeo,' Raleigh said without warning, and suddenly they were all headed into the cars again.

'Isn't it a bit early to be going in?' Hillary said to Regis sharply. Checkpoint Romeo was just off the entrance to the farmyard proper. She hadn't expected them to get so close for a good half an hour yet. Didn't the Tactical Firearms Unit prefer to do several sweeps before calling in their unarmed colleagues? Had the plan been changed at the last minute? Had the super heard something on the radio that altered everything?

'I dunno,' Regis muttered, but his eyes met hers in the mirror. He looked calm enough, but Hillary got the feeling he was as surprised as she was to get the go-ahead so soon. And, like her, didn't like it.

They were driving fairly fast up a rough tarmac road, and now, just up ahead, the lights from Fletcher's farm spilled out on to the ground. They pulled up just outside a traditional five-bar iron gate. The farmhouse had light coming out of almost every window. It was a large, square, rundown building, with paintwork peeling off the doors and window frames. Off to one side was a series of disused barns.

As she climbed out, in one of the barns she could see two men in Kevlar standing either side of a man dressed in jeans and leather jacket. He was clearly not happy. Her breath feathered white and ghostly in the frosty air as she glanced further along. In another barn, several more handcuffed suspects were being guarded by three more men in Kevlar. All were carrying the regulation-issue .38 handguns that the TFI preferred. So all the scouts and lookouts had been accounted for. The gunfire must have come from the farmhouse itself, when the main strike force went in.

She knew ambulances were standing by just off the main road, ready to be called in if needed. She only hoped no copper had got shot tonight.

The light spilling from the open doorway suddenly dimmed, and Hillary instinctively crouched down behind the car. But the figure that emerged was wearing Kevlar and she slowly straightened up again. She felt no shame at her reaction. Janine, however, gave her a rather sneering look.

Hillary felt too tired to give her a lesson in real life. Perhaps if someone had been shot inside, then Janine might learn something. Being called to a murder and looking at a corpse was not the same thing as having to look at blood and guts that had just been spilt, or smell the cordite, or listen to pitiful moaning as some poor sod who wondered whether or not he'd live to see morning called pitifully for his mother.

The man in the doorway paused, as if surprised to see the two cars parked outside the gate. He spoke rapidly into the radio strapped to his chest as Raleigh began to walk forward with Frank Ross, of all people, by his side. Hillary was so surprised you could have knocked her down with a feather.

She could understand why Raleigh would be mad keen to get in on the act — this was, after all, his show — but she'd have bet her last pair of tights that Frank was too careful of his own skin to be one of the first inside.

The others, taking their cue from Raleigh, began to follow, Regis trotting to catch up. At the door, the member of the firearms unit was already holding up a hand to halt them. Behind him, the team leader suddenly appeared. At least, Hillary assumed it was the team leader, for he spoke hard and fast, and with obvious authority. He didn't seem to like it they were here.

Had Raleigh called them in without waiting for the go-ahead? Hillary gave a mental head-shake. How arrogant, not to mention bloody stupid, could you get?

She knew how hot Raleigh was to nail Fletcher but this was sheer stupidity. And if true, she thought it highly likely that, before long, Raleigh would find himself up before a disciplinary board.

She slowed down her pace, not wanting to get caught up in it, and glanced across at Mel, who was also frowning. Tommy, sensing something in the air, also slowed to a stop and looked back at them, as if looking for orders. Only Janine kept going.

Raleigh and the armed cops in the doorway talked for a while, or rather argued, and then Raleigh and Frank Ross stepped inside. Mel stepped forward, as did Regis. Hillary heard another muttered and hot argument, and walked slowly back towards the gate. Whatever was going down here, she'd rather let them all get on with it. They didn't need her sticking her oar in.

Instead, she glanced around, getting a feel for the lay of the land.

The car the three drug dealers had arrived in was a large Japanese model, and was parked neatly and tightly into one corner. Three other cars, supposedly belonging to Fletcher's gang, were parked in the last of the ramshackle sheds. Light continued to spill out on to the dirty cobbles and the weed-strewn courtyard. Inside, everything was quiet.

After a few minutes, Mel finally walked over to join her. Regis and Tanner remained by the doorway talking animatedly to the TFI member guarding the door. Janine stood off to one side, impatiently shifting from foot to foot, anger coming off her in waves. She was desperate to get in there and see what they'd scored. Had *she* ever been that keen? Hillary wondered. And concluded, with a small sad smile that, yes, she probably had. In fact, if she were Janine, she'd probably be harbouring fantasies of putting the cuffs on Fletcher herself.

After a while, men in Kevlar started coming out. In the quiet night, she heard one of them call for the ambulance to come to the gate at the bottom of the property and her heart fell. She knew what that meant. There was no hurry. Someone (or more than one) was dead, and simply needed a ride to the mortuary. By the way the TFI man spoke, it wasn't one of their own.

For the first time, Hillary wondered if Fletcher himself could be dead. She was just wondering how she felt about that, when gunfire suddenly exploded inside. There was a frozen moment of disbelief, and then suddenly everyone was running back inside — the men in Kevlar, Regis, Tanner and Janine.

Hillary shouted helplessly 'No!' and took a step forward, then stopped herself and grabbed Mel's arm as he moved to sweep past her.

'Mel, have some sense!' she screamed, almost getting her arm torn out of her socket before her friend caught her words and saw the sense behind them. He came to a halt and glanced back at her, his face conflicted, then looked back to the farmhouse. Hillary followed his gaze and yelled, 'Tommy, stop!' as the detective constable ran on ahead. He turned his head to look back at her, and with her free hand she frantically waved at him to get to one side. He was stood in a direct line with the open door, right in the highest concentration of light. 'Take cover!' she yelled frantically.

To her enormous relief, Tommy quickly nodded and moved forward, but angled off to one side, flattening himself against the outer wall of the farmhouse.

Mel began to angrily shrug her hand off his arm. 'I don't need—' he began, then abruptly stopped, for the horrified look on Hillary's face had him turning around to glance once more at the farmhouse.

Coming through the door was a man with a gun. He was a tall man, over six feet, with dark brown hair and what looked like a thick moustache. But he was not dressed in Kevlar. Hillary's breath caught in her lungs and stayed there.

Her thoughts seemed to move into hyper-speed. He was not dressed in Kevlar, so he was not a cop — he had to be either one of Fletcher's gang, or one of the Liverpool drug dealers. Somehow, he'd survived the initial TFI sweep and had just gunned his way out of the house.

He was now looking around, like a cornered rat seeking a drainpipe. And Hillary instantly thought about the cars. The cars in the barn were too far away for him to get to quickly. The jeep was parked in the corner and hemmed in. And then, even as the gunman's eyes turned their way, Hillary thought about the only other two cars around that could give him any hope of an easy getaway. The two cars they'd come in. Parked right behind them outside the gate.

Even as the gunman ran forward, even as he raised his hand, even as she saw the darkness of the gun, glinting like the carapace of a beetle in the artificial light spilling into the courtyard, she knew what was going to happen.

Tommy was safe, being out of sight with his back to the wall, but she and Mel were in plain sight. *And standing right in front of his only means of a getaway.*

'Mel, down!' Hillary screamed, but even as she spoke she was launching herself sideways, using all of her solid frame to deliberately cannon into her old friend.

Beyond the man running towards them, appearing in the doorway, she saw the blonde head of Janine. Saw her mouth open into a silly 'O' of shocked horror. A millisecond later, she thought she saw someone looming up behind Janine, pushing her out of the way.

Then she was crashing into Mel, her hands dragging at the tops of his arms, desperate to get him out of the line of fire. She knew from statistics that men with guns tended to shoot at other men first. Women afterwards. It made sense in a way — they perceived men as the far greater threat.

She felt her feet slither out from under her, and her knees folded as she finally succeeded in pulling him down. The gunman, who was now running right at them with his arm fully extended, didn't pause. He simply pulled the trigger.

Hillary heard it as a loud, huge noise, detonating the night and turning, as if by magic, into pain.

Pain in her side, low down. Pain that burned and made her scream in fright. Pain that turned liquid, hot liquid, pouring down her side, down her leg, as she hit the ground, Mel underneath her.

She felt herself roll, and knew she had no strength to do anything about it. It was as if she'd been zapped by a Taser. Her limbs felt weak and useless, her brain giving them messages they simply couldn't obey. Something was dreadfully wrong.

She opened her eyes, but saw the world at an odd angle. Dirty cobbles and weeds, right in front of her. Then she could see pounding feet — a pair of incongruously well-cleaned boots. Suddenly, she understood.

They belonged to the gunman, still running towards her. Towards *them*. She was helpless — nothing about her body seemed to work anymore. Mel was moving, swearing, trying to get to his feet, so he was OK, but he had no gun. There was nothing to stop the perp from shooting them both, unless all he could think about was getting away, of leaping over them and getting to the car.

But no. They weren't that lucky. She heard that sound again — the ear-piercing, head-bursting sound of another bullet being fired from a gun. She wanted to yell in fury, to shout at the universe that it wasn't fair.

But she hadn't enough breath left to even whimper.

So this was it. This was what it all came down to, just before you died.

# CHAPTER EIGHT

Hillary heard Tommy Lynch shout, but the sound seemed to come from very far away. Had he moved from his position by the wall, legged it for the outer fields? No, that didn't make sense, because his face was right in front of her.

'Guv, stay still,' he said, his voice wavering slightly. 'I've called the ambulance up; they'll be here in a flash. I'm going to put some pressure on your wound. It'll hurt.'

Hillary nodded — or thought she did. It was hard to tell when she had one side of her face pressed into hard and dirty cobbles. As if he was a mind reader, she felt Mel lift her face to put his jacket under it. 'Bloody hell, Hill,' he muttered, his voice as shaky as Tommy's had been. His hands, as he placed his jacket under her head, were visibly shaking. It was hard to imagine the supercool and immaculate 'Mellow' Mallow coming this unglued. Even his trademark nifty suit looked crumpled and stained.

Her throat felt dry, as did the inside of her mouth. She wanted to lick her lips, but couldn't seem to unglue her tongue from the top of her mouth.

When Tommy moved to one side, she saw a man lying on the ground a few yards away, with one of the Tactical Firearms Unit personnel stood over him, holding a gun to him. Hillary gave a mental nod. OK, the gunman was down. She wasn't dead. OK, that was all good. She was hurt, because Tommy was talking about a wound, but she was still conscious, and apart from a fire in her hip and side, she wasn't in too much pain. That had to be good, too, right?

She'd been wounded in the line of duty before, of course; the worst time, when she'd been sliced with a knife when a drunk who'd been brought in as quiet as a mouse had suddenly gone berserk. It had taken her, the desk sergeant and the two arresting constables to restrain him. She'd remembered a sharp, flickering pain in her arm, and realised she'd been cut only when the dark blue of her uniform sleeve had turned darker and wet. Twenty stitches that had earned her, and a lifelong scar, faded now to nothing more than a thin pale line that refused to suntan in the summer.

So, she could get through this as well. Piece of cake, really. She closed her eyes a moment, and heard Mike Regis shouting her name. He sounded desperate, but she couldn't be bothered to open her eyes again. They felt glued shut. What was it with this gluing thing? Hillary frowned. First her tongue, now her eyes. Perhaps she should just go to sleep.

The pain in her hip suddenly worsened as she felt Tommy pressing down on it, and she heard herself moan. She bit her lip, but couldn't stop another yelp of pain from getting past her clenched teeth. Yes, sleep was probably a good idea right about now.

Mike Regis called her name again, but this time, Hillary didn't hear him.

* * *

Janine Tyler didn't know what to do. It was a new feeling for her, and one she didn't appreciate. When the firing had started, she'd headed inside the farmhouse along with everyone else, but two TFI men prevented her from going further into the house than the first empty room — a sort of makeshift living room. There had been shouts from somewhere deeper in the house, and Janine could clearly make out one of them as being the super's voice. A moment or two later, she'd noticed movement in the corner of her eye, as if someone was slipping into the hall out of the room opposite. She'd shouted a warning instinctively and headed towards it, only to bump into one of the TFI in Kevlar just as she got to the front door, where she was just in time to see a man shoot her boss.

It wasn't something Janine had been prepared for. Oh, she knew the risks, and could quote the statistics along with the rest of them. Coppers sometimes got shot. But the ones who were most in the firing line were people like the TFI or the uniforms out on the street. DIs in plain clothes should, in theory, be the safest of the lot.

She'd felt herself being catapulted out of the door by the TFI guy behind her, and had fallen on to her hands and knees on the cobbles, feeling sharp pains lance through them. When she looked up, one of the TFI team was levelling a gun and firing it and another body hit the ground. She heard Mel swearing, and felt her body go suddenly cold. Hillary had been standing right in front of Mel. What if the bullet had gone right through?

She got up and staggered forward, her hands and knees bleeding and wondering where Tommy had suddenly come from, because there he was, running towards Hillary Greene, shouting her name, sounding as if he was on the verge of losing it.

Then Mike Regis was suddenly beside her.

'What's going on?' he said. 'Who fired the other shots?' He could see a gaggle of people crouched on the ground further out in the courtyard, and felt a coldness invade his gut.

'The boss has been shot,' Janine heard herself say.

'DCI Mallow?' Regis said sharply.

Janine felt her head shake. 'No, my boss. DI Greene.'

Now, they were all grouped around the figure lying so still on the ground, and Janine didn't know what to do. Tommy seemed to be coping with the first aid — he'd been the last to do a refresher course, so she left him to it. Mel was knelt down at Hillary's head, talking to her, but she didn't seem to be responding. Her eyes were closed. Was she dead? Janine tried to see where the wound was, but Tommy was blocking her view. His hands seemed to be pressing down on her lower stomach. A gut wound? Janine began to shiver. Those were bad. Really bad. She didn't want to think how bad those could be.

She looked around and saw DI Regis, standing stiff and white, staring at the woman on the floor. His eerily silent sergeant, Tanner, stood beside him. Members of the TFI were standing around, guns ready, waiting and watching everything and everyone. Suddenly, the flashing blue lights of the ambulance came around the corner, and Regis raced off towards it, no doubt to direct them to Hillary as quickly as possible.

Janine sat down. She didn't care that the cobbles were hard and cold and dirty. She just needed to sit down.

* * *

Hillary became aware of movement, of different voices, of being lifted. She suddenly felt warmer. Her whole world began to shift — faster, smoother, and it took her a while to realise she was in the back of an ambulance.

OK. That was probably good too.

She went back to sleep.

* * *

When she woke up, her mother's face appeared above her, and she jumped. 'Mum?' she mumbled, wondering what she was doing waking up in her bed back in her old childhood home. It wasn't Mother's Day, was it? She often spent the weekend at her mum's then.

'How's the wounded hero then?' a gruff masculine voice said, and suddenly her favourite uncle was there too.

'Uncle Max?' she said, frowning. What was going on? 'Nothing's happened to the boat, has it?' It was the first thing she could think of. Technically, the *Mollern* still belonged to Max, although she'd come to think of it as her own.

'The *Mollern*'s fine. I've kept an eye on it, made sure it was all battened down,' he said. He was a small man, neat and tidy, who looked as if he should have been a retired military man. In fact, he'd worked for the Post Office for most of his adult life.

'How are you feeling, love?' her mother asked, reaching out and taking her hand. It was then that Hillary noticed all the white — white walls, white ceiling, white sheets. Other beds — three of them. Nurses in white. Oh God. She was in hospital.

Then it came back — the gunfire. The man rushing out in the night, lifting the gun. She and Mel in direct line of fire. The sudden pain.

'Bugger, I got shot,' she said flatly.

Max Granger gave a sudden grin, and hugged his younger sister. 'See, told you, June,' he said, giving her grey curls a quick kiss. 'Nothing wrong with your girl a few days' rest won't cure.'

Hillary reached for her mother's hand. She looked older than she remembered, greyer, smaller. 'Oh, Mum,' Hillary said helplessly. 'Please, don't worry.' But her daughter had been shot. Of course she was worried. Hillary felt a great wave of guilt wash over her for all that her mother must have gone through. In her mind's eye, she could see it all, how it must have been.

Mel would have been the one to tell her, of course. He'd have driven, not phoned. The moment she'd seen her daughter's superior officer on the doorstep, June Thorpe would have known that it was bad. Had she had nightmares about this very scenario? Mel would have told her quickly and calmly what had happened. Had he driven her back to the hospital? Had she stayed all night?

Again, guilt nibbled at her. She shouldn't be putting her mother through this. She was in her mid-seventies now, too old to take such traumas in her stride. And somewhere at the back of her head a little voice piped up, telling her that if she took early retirement, June Thorpe would never have to worry again. Hastily, she thrust it back, and glanced at the pale grey blinds lining the window. It was broad daylight. She was assuming it was the next day — but what if it was the day after that? Suddenly she felt utterly disorientated.

'Did I have to have surgery?' she asked, and her mother sighed and slowly sank back on to the chair. It was wonderful to hear her girl speak again. To sound so like her old self — calm and in charge. That was her Hillary. Always the sensible one. Always the one who knew what she wanted and how to get it.

'Yes, they had to remove the bullet.' Her words quavered a bit on the last word. 'But there was no real damage. It came close to a major artery though,' June carried on quickly, as if needing to gloss over that bit, 'but there was no real muscle or bone damage. Apparently the bullet lodged in the fatty tissue.'

Hillary began to shift to her side, the better to see her mother's face and tell her that she didn't have to worry, the shooting had been a one-in-one-thousand glitch, then bit the words off as a sudden pain shot through her backside.

Her backside! Lodged in the fatty tissue? 'Oh no,' she wailed. 'Don't tell me I was shot in the bum!'

'Ssshh,' June Thorpe said, casting an anxious glance at the other three women in the beds around her. 'No, you were shot just above the hip — through the waist, more or less.'

Hillary closed her eyes and grinned in sheer relief. She would never have lived it down if she'd been shot in the backside. She could already imagine the jokes the desk sergeant would have had lined up. Not to mention what that sneering git Frank Ross would have said. To have Ross, of all people, laughing at her, would have been simply too much.

\* \* \*

Hillary wasn't quite awake later on that evening, when Mel arrived. They'd served tea — or what had passed for it — and she'd taken so many pills she was almost sure she could hear herself rattle. The drone of the television sets that her fellow patients were watching acted as a soporific, but a stealthy screech had her eyes popping open. Mel was positioning a chair beside the bed, and had caught the chair leg against the tiled floor.

He looked up and winced as he saw Hillary's big brown eyes looking at him. 'Sorry, didn't mean to wake you.'

Hillary smiled. 'No problems. So what the hell happened?'

Mel sat down and grimaced. 'Hell, Hill, you've been shot. The least you can do is moan and gripe a bit before giving me the third degree.'

He was once more the immaculate 'Mellow' Mallow, well-dressed, and looking like something out of a Brooks Brothers catalogue. His first marriage had quickly faded because they'd both been too young, and his second marriage to a very wealthy woman had also ended amicably enough. It wasn't hard to see how Mel would never have any trouble attracting the ladies. He'd also earned his 'Mellow' tag with a soft voice and apparently easy-going personality that hid a will of steel.

'Fine,' Hillary sighed. 'The dinner was so bad, it made me feel as if I was a cordon bleu chef in comparison. My hip hurts, they keep making me take drugs that bring on the DTs and the bed is as hard as iron. Happy now?'

Mel grinned. 'Much better.'

'OK, now what the hell happened? Did Raleigh jump the gun?'

Mel shook his head. His face looked more gaunt than she remembered it, and for the first time ever she thought he could do with a shave. Hell, he must be having a rough day. 'I'll say,' he confirmed wryly. 'We should never have been in that courtyard. Shit, Hill, when I saw you go down, when I realised you were hit . . . hell, I've never felt so sick in all my life.'

Hillary went hot, then cold. She hadn't really thought about that yet. She grunted, and said, 'Give us a hand sitting upright, would you? There's a lever thingy under the bed — push it in. Or out. It makes the back of the bed come forward.'

Mel, successfully distracted, fiddled with it, the bed first going down, then up. Wincing with pain, Hillary finally got herself sitting more or less upright and comfortable. Her hip throbbed. 'Bring us another pillow behind my head. Thanks. Right, now tell me. What's the state of play? Were there drugs? Was Fletcher there? Did we nail the bastard at last?'

'Fletcher's dead,' Mel said flatly, and Hillary blinked. So that was it. Just like that, the big bad bogeyman had been dispensed with. Somehow, it didn't seem real.

'Was the shooting righteous?' she asked automatically, although why she asked, she couldn't say. Any shooting by the TFI was almost always righteous.

To her astonishment, however, Mel shrugged and spread his hands. 'We don't know. As far as we can tell, he was shot by one of his own men.'

Hillary blinked again. She felt her chest tighten — not, she was sure, due to anything medical, but with a tension she'd felt before. A tension she always felt when anything was somehow off. 'Come again?' she said slowly, and listened as Mel told her what they had worked out from the evidence gathered and the witness statements taken during the day.

'It started off great. The outer perimeter sweep went without a hitch,' Mel began. 'Then they raided the house. So far, so good. The TFI went through, room by room, in a classic sweep, but in the first bedroom encountered resistance.'

'The first bout of gunfire we heard, when we were driving to Checkpoint Charlie?'

'Right,' Mel confirmed. 'They mopped that up — one of Fletcher's gang was hit, and killed. They surrendered pretty quickly after that. Then another member of the TFI came under fire, this time from one of the Liverpool gang. They returned fire, and quickly persuaded the Scouser to

113

surrender. The drugs were there all right, but at that point there was still no sign of Fletcher.'

Hillary frowned. How had Fletcher managed to hide himself when none of the others had? Then she shrugged. The farm was Fletcher's home ground — he'd obviously have had a few good bolt-holes mapped out beforehand, in case he needed them. He'd always been a careful bastard — that's why they'd never managed to catch the slippery sod.

'The TFI were doing a more detailed sweep through the house when we rolled up,' Mel went on, and Hillary frowned, holding a hand up to stop him.

'The team leader hadn't given Raleigh the all-clear?' she asked, eyebrows raised.

'No,' Mel sighed. 'That's why one of his men stopped us at the door, and called the team leader down. Raleigh insisted on going inside. He checked out the upper rooms, according to one of the TFI sergeants, but when they came up empty, went back downstairs. He and Frank Ross went into one of the rooms off the kitchen that had already been cleared. The team leader took point again, and went back upstairs, where the rest of the team was still doing its second, more thorough search. After about a minute, there was another burst of gunfire, and this is where things start to get cloudy.'

Hillary tried to put the memory of that moment out of her mind. What came immediately afterwards wasn't something she wanted to deal with just yet.

'Go on, what happened?' She was still struggling to make sense of all this. Why had Raleigh wanted to go in so early? What difference did twenty minutes make?

Mel laughed. 'You might well ask! Just what did happen next? We're not really sure. Any of us. Even now, and we've been going over and over it all day. Apparently, Fletcher had a hidey hole in a cupboard out in the back wall of the kitchen. Raleigh and Ross had gone back downstairs by then, but they were in one of the living rooms — the right parlour, we've called it, just to save confusion. They heard gunfire in the kitchen next to them, but saw nobody. When the team leader and his immediate team came downstairs, they found Fletcher dead on the kitchen floor. Then they heard gunfire outside. The first one out the door nailed the bastard who shot you. Oh yeah, Janine was in the left lounge, and Regis and that sergeant of his were upstairs. Nobody saw Fletcher get it, so nobody knows what really went down. At the moment, we're working on the theory that Fletcher and one of his thugs had holed up in the kitchen, but argued about whether to stay put and trust that their hiding place would remain undetected, or try to make a break for it.'

Hillary frowned. 'Staying put wouldn't be a good idea. Fletcher would know that the cops would be at the farmhouse for days, logging evidence.'

'Yeah, maybe. Perhaps he wanted to leg it, but his sidekick got scared and wanted to stay. So he shot Fletcher when Fletcher insisted on making a run for it.'

Hillary gave Mel a quick look. 'That make sense to you?'

'Nope. Janine said, when she was in the left lounge, that she thought she saw someone slip out of the door opposite. If that's true, it could have been the one who shot you. But Raleigh and Ross were in there, and they're both saying that nobody came through the kitchen via the right lounge.'

'So whoever it was must have come from the kitchen and straight up the corridor and Janine saw him pass as he went across the open doorway?'

'She must have.' Mel shrugged helplessly.

'Could Janine have seen the super slipping out of the room opposite, trying to see where the shooting was coming from? Did he go into the kitchen?'

'Yeah, he did. The team leader found both Raleigh and Ross there. So, perhaps that's it. Janine doesn't really know who she saw — she only sensed movement. Hell, Hill, it's all a bit of a mess. Regis, Tanner and Janine shouldn't have been in there at all. The TFI are up in arms about it, and who can blame them? The team leader is telling all and sundry that he's not going to take the rap for this. But when they heard gunfire they all piled in. Regis and Tanner headed straight for the stairs and only got to the top just in time to get out of the way as the rest of the TFI came racing down! It must have been like an episode out of the Keystone Cops in there.'

Hillary opened her mouth to defend Regis, then shut it again. She understood why he'd gone racing inside, of course. But Mel was right. It had been stupid. Brave, but stupid. 'So how are the brass playing this?' she asked curiously, and Mel laughed cynically.

'The drugs haul was big, and seeing as it's a new concoction, it has the appeal of being novel. Fletcher is dead — so a "force for evil" has been removed from our streets, according to the assistant CC. As you can imagine, the PR boys are having a field day. They've even got a hero cop to put a cherry on the icing.'

'Aye? Who?' Hillary asked blankly, then felt herself flush as Mel gave her a long, level look.

'Oh,' Hillary said.

'I put your name forward for the gallantry medal,' Mel said quietly. 'Marcus Donleavy backed it. You're bound to get it. You saved my life, Hill,' he muttered, looking down at his hands. 'I just stood there like a lemon.'

Hillary looked quickly away, and found the woman in the bed opposite watching her. She was the young one, who'd come in yesterday with appendicitis. She quickly dipped her head to her magazine, pretending she hadn't been straining her ears to listen in.

'A man came at me with a gun and I hit the dirt,' Hillary said dismissively. 'What the hell's so gallant about that?'

Mel leaned back in the chair and ran a tired hand over his face. Hillary supposed he hadn't slept at all last night. 'Come on, Hill, we all know that you were thinking on your feet, as always. You stopped me and Tommy from going in and making the farce even worse. And you knew exactly what Brian Conroy wanted when he came out that door, waving that bloody revolver around. He was making for one of the cars, wasn't he?'

'It seemed obvious,' Hillary agreed. So that was the name of the man who'd shot her. Brian Conroy.

'Sure, it was obvious,' Mel echoed wryly. 'All the other vehicles were too inaccessible. I thought of it about five minutes later, when we were following you in the ambulance. Let's not kid ourselves, Hill, I'd be dead if it wasn't for you.'

Hillary saw Mary, the woman in the bed next to her own, glance across. She was about her own age, and had come in to have her cancerous ovaries removed. They'd chatted that afternoon, when Mary had told her that, since she already had three kids, it was no big deal.

Mary had clearly heard Mel say that she'd saved his life, but for some reason, Hillary found herself unable to meet the other woman's look. No doubt it was admiring, maybe even respectful. And in this day and age, with tales of heroism being too precious and far between to be ignored, Hillary supposed she should just accept the compliment and then forget about it.

The trouble was, she felt such a complete fraud. OK, so maybe she'd thought a bit faster than everybody else, and had managed to keep a clear head when everybody around her had been losing theirs, to paraphrase Kipling. And she'd been unlucky enough to get shot in the arse. Well, nearly. But did that make her a hero?

Her mind skipped forward to a possible awards ceremony. The press would be out in force, with her mother and brother and sisters and Uncle Max all there to cheer her on and slap her on the back. She'd have to step up on to some sort of stage and shake hands with the chief constable as he handed her a bit of metal. Then she'd have to have her picture taken over and over again, followed by interviews with the press, where she'd give modest disclaimers and refuse to comment about the ongoing Fletcher investigation.

She'd have to wear her best dress uniform, of course. Hell, did it even still fit her? She'd have to have it let out. At this, Hillary suddenly laughed out loud. 'Hey, Mel, did I tell you, the bullet didn't do any serious damage because my fat stopped it? If ever there was a good excuse not to diet, that's gotta be it.'

Out of the corner of her eye, she saw her third roommate smile. She was a plump, middle-aged librarian, who was having her gall bladder removed tomorrow.

'Trust you to find a silver lining,' Mel laughed.

Hillary glanced over at the movable tray beside her bed. It was filled with bags of fruit, a couple of vases of flowers, a book of crossword puzzles and now, a bottle of lemon barley squash.

'You brought lemon barley?' Hillary said. 'Most people bring grapes.'

'I know you like lemon barley,' Mel said, surprised.

'Yeah, and how do you know?' Hillary asked. 'Because we've been friends for ever, that's why,' she answered her own question. 'So let's not indulge in any more breast-beating, yeah? Someone was going to shoot us, and I made sure we both hit the deck. I only got winged because there was more of me to get shot at, that's all. I always said you were a skinny little git.'

\* \* \*

After Mel left, the nurses came round to take blood, check pills had been taken, and monitor blood pressure. Hillary's particular favourite, a little brown sparrow of a girl called Tracy Wall, wasn't there, but another nurse brought with her a copy of the *Oxford Mail*. And sure enough, there on the front page was a picture of a younger Hillary, and the confirmation of Fletcher's death and a large drugs haul. To please everyone, Hillary read it. It did indeed mention that she was in line for a police medal for gallantry.

She was saved from having to accept everyone's congratulations and sly hints for her to give them some inside gen by the arrival of Superintendent Marcus Donleavy.

He looked like a banker — grey/silver suit, grey/silver hair, grey/silver eyes. He fairly radiated power and prestige, and the nurses and curious patients melted away at his approach. Hillary was not surprised when Donleavy pulled the curtains around, giving them some privacy. He sat close to her and put a small tape recorder on the tray beside her bed, letting her see it was running. So, this was to be an official debriefing.

Hillary nodded.

'So, DI Greene. What can you tell me about the events last night?'

* * *

The next morning, Mel came back. He brought a box of chocolates with him. 'Since you don't have to diet anymore, I thought you might like these,' he said, sitting down.

'You rotten sod,' Hillary said, and added heavily, 'Donleavy came by last night.'

'I know. He's heading up the internal inquiry.' There was a certain air of satisfaction about the way Mel said that that had her radar instantly sending out a 'bleep' of interest.

'You think the man from the Met might be out on his ear?' she asked. She could understand why that would please Mel. Superintendent Raleigh was always going to be a thorn in her old friend's side. He'd been given the job that Mel had thought was his, for a start. Now it looked as if he'd come a cropper, and who could blame Mel for having a good old gloat?

Mel shrugged. 'Well, let's just say Raleigh jumped the gun. He didn't follow procedure, hell, didn't even stick to the plan. And as a result, a senior female police officer was shot. So he's hardly going to get any brownie points, is he?'

Hillary sighed, not liking the sound of that. 'So I'm going to be the stick they use to beat him up with? Wonderful.'

'Come on, it won't matter to you. Anyway, he's bound to be transferred out of Thames Valley.'

Hillary nodded, then shot him a quick look. 'Ah. Which means they'll need to appoint an acting super for a while. Has he been suspended yet?'

'No. Not yet.'

'How's he taking it all?' Hillary asked, genuinely curious.

'I'm not sure,' Mel said, after a thoughtful pause. 'You'd think he'd be miffed. Not showing it, of course, but definitely antsy. But I don't know. He looks tired, but not . . . I don't know. He almost seems to be . . . up, somehow. You know, like a man who's been vindicated, instead of possibly in the shit.'

Hillary frowned. This was still making no sense to her. Then Mel cleared his throat, and Hillary shot him a quick glance. She knew that throat-clearing gesture of old. It didn't bode well.

'Since you're going to be off work for some time to come, I've decided to put Janine in working charge of the Malcolm Dale case,' Mel said quickly. 'Well, I can't let Frank Ross run the show, and Tommy's too junior,' he rushed on, giving her no chance to object. 'I'll keep an overall eye on things, naturally.'

Hillary stared at him for a moment, thought about it, opened her mouth, then closed it again. She waited until he was looking at her before she let him have it with both barrels.

'You're going to dump her, aren't you?' she accused flatly. 'You can practically taste that promotion to acting super, and know that if you want it, you're going to have to jettison the baggage. And you think that giving her her own case will help get her off your back.'

Mel flushed but didn't deny it. 'It's time to get back on track, Hill. Come on, be fair. Who else can take over the case while you're away?'

Hillary shook her head.

*First you get shot nearly in the backside, then you have to accept a medal, then your blonde bombshell of a sergeant gets to run your case while you sit in a narrowboat and twiddle your thumbs, going slowly mad with boredom.*

Whatever it was that she'd done in a previous life to deserve this, she hoped it had been worth it.

# CHAPTER NINE

Superintendent Jerome Raleigh slowly steepled his fingers together and met the eyes of the man sitting across from him. His desk, stretching between them like a no-man's land, was unusually clear. Perhaps because his workload had suddenly lessened. A clue perhaps of things to come?

He said as much to his superior officer.

Chief Superintendent Marcus Donleavy shrugged. 'Until we can clear up the events of that night to everyone's satisfaction, you're still, technically, in the saddle. But nobody's anxious to load you up with new cases or committee appointments, at least not until they're sure how things will pan out.'

Jerome smiled thinly. 'Can't say as I blame them. And how long do you think it's likely to be before that happens?'

Again, Marcus shrugged. 'Depends how quickly the evidence can be sifted, and how fast the review board can process it. But it might get bogged down because the TFI are going to fight their corner every inch of the way, and are adamant that they're not going to take any flak over this.'

Jerome Raleigh nodded. 'Nor should they,' he agreed quietly.

Marcus watched the man from the Met as he leaned back slightly in his swivel chair, making it creak slightly. His steepled hands fell to the arm rests and lay limply. 'Is that an admission that the faults all lie with you?' he asked curiously.

Jerome shrugged. 'If blame has to be apportioned, then yes. Do you think it will?' he asked, the question either very candid, or unbelievably naive. And Marcus Donleavy didn't think the man was naive. Which meant he was asking for honesty.

Suddenly he sighed, and they were just two men who'd managed to climb the ladder high. Up until now, Donleavy had had no complaints about the man who'd taken over his old job. He'd seemed to settle in and he'd heard no management complaints or grumbling from the lower orders. And certainly nobody had doubted his dedication to putting away the scum. So was this Fletcher fiasco just a glitch? Or was it indicative of a more ingrained problem? But then, surely a man couldn't reach the position of super without somebody noticing if he were either reckless or stupid. And what had happened during the Fletcher raid had to be either one or the other.

Marcus frowned, then realised the man was still waiting for his answer. He thought carefully before speaking. 'Unless something drastic happens, I think we're OK,' he finally said, a shade reluctantly. 'The killing by the TFI man of Marcus Shandy has already been ruled justified, as has that of the killing of Conroy. The fact that Hillary's injuries weren't serious also helped your cause. The TFI are making it clear you came in too early and without clearance, but nobody's looking to cut you off at the knees for that. And with the killer of Fletcher also dead, it's not looking nearly as bad as it could.'

In other words, Raleigh thought, the brass considered it best to keep it in-house and sweep it under the carpet, and content itself with giving him a rap over the knuckles.

So, with a bit of luck, he could simply take his medicine, keep his head down, and get on with things. The only two flies in the ointment were Ross and Greene.

Raleigh was confident that Ross was too shit-scared to grass. But Greene might be a problem. She was too smart by half — and, incidentally, the last person in the world he'd wanted to get shot. Good coppers were too few and far between to lose any of them. Yes, in spite of the fact that she worried him, Jerome Raleigh still felt guilty about what had happened to Hillary Greene.

But that didn't stop him from looking out for number one; he still needed to know if he was safe. He shifted in his chair and glanced past Donleavy, to stare at the wall. 'I'm really sorry about DI Greene,' he said flatly. 'That was never meant to happen,' he added, sincerely. For one thing, he knew that a wounded and pissed off Hillary Greene was probably far more dangerous than a merely curious DI Greene. 'You're sure she's all right?'

'She's fine,' Marcus said curtly, then added grimly, 'She was lucky. If the bullet had been over to the right a few inches, she'd have been gut shot.' He could still remember the phone call that night that told him one of his officers had been shot during the Fletcher raid. And when he'd discovered it was Hillary Greene, his anger and concern had escalated. So he wasn't in any mood to soft-soap the officer who'd been in charge. Even before knowing all the circumstances, it had never seriously crossed his mind that Hillary might have been the one to make a mistake. She was too savvy for that.

Raleigh winced. 'Is she . . . is she going to file a complaint? She'd have every right to.'

'Against you, you mean?' Marcus clarified in a hard voice, still not willing to let the younger man get away with anything. He let the question hang for a moment, then shook his head. 'I doubt the thought even crossed her mind,' he said flatly. 'I've known Hillary Greene for years. That husband of hers put her through misery — both personally and professionally. She'll probably never recover from the stigma of being investigated for corruption. Which is a great pity — she's one of the best detectives we've got. She's also straight up and down, one of us, through and through. The last thing she'd ever do is put the screws on a fellow officer. So you can relax.' He made no effort to hide his distaste, or belief that Raleigh was getting off lightly.

Raleigh nodded and took it. He deserved it. But it had been worth it. Everything had been worth it. Now, if he could just sit tight and weather the investigation, everything would be fine.

He'd just have to make sure that worm Frank Ross knew enough to keep his mouth shut. But he was fairly confident of that. Self-interest alone would ensure his silence.

\* \* \*

Mel glanced up as Janine knocked on the door to his office, then stepped in. 'I've updated the Dale case, sir,' she said, waving a folder at him, then glanced behind her and closed the door. 'Thought you might want to see it,' she added, coming to stand in front of his desk. 'I daresay you'll have to take it over now.'

Mel smiled, seeing right through her. She wanted to be SIO so bad she could taste it. Which was good. Very good.

'Yeah, bit of a bugger when I've got so much on my plate already,' he played along.

Janine nodded. 'You think Raleigh's gonna get the elbow?' she asked, with genuine curiosity. When things got shaken up, interesting things tended to fall out of the tree.

Mel shrugged. The truth was, he wasn't so sure anymore. The murmuring on the grapevine didn't sound too promising. And, naturally, the last thing the brass wanted was a scandal. Still, maybe a quiet sidelining would be on the cards for him some months down the line.

Which would leave him with plenty of time to get his house in order, and make the brass look seriously at him for the superintendency. Thinking of that . . . He sighed, and nodded to the chair. 'Janine, sit down. We have to talk.'

He'd thought about doing this tonight, when they were both at home, but quickly realised that Janine would be uncontrollable then. At least here she'd have to curb her temper. It was, he knew, the coward's way out, but he'd always favoured the line of least resistance.

Janine felt her heart give a little kick, and something cold dropped into the pit of her belly. Her eyes glittered and her chin came up defiantly as she sat down. Mel saw the look and felt his stomach clench. She'd already guessed what was coming. Had he been so obvious?

He took a long deep breath and began.

\* \* \*

Hillary gritted her teeth as she put her left foot down. 'Ouch. Ouch. Ouch,' she muttered, every time she took a tottering step forward. This morning she'd done the same journey with a Zimmer frame, of all things, but now she had a walking stick. Tracy Wall was walking close beside her, one hand on her arm in case she fell.

'You're doing great,' she encouraged as Hillary slowly began to take longer and more confident steps towards the opening into the corridor, where the nurses' station was situated.

'That's easy for you to say,' Hillary huffed, feeling the sweat running down the side of her nose. She was in one of her mother's long flowered flannel nightgowns (since she only slept in old T-shirts back on the boat) and she felt about a hundred years old in it. On the other hand, it had matched the Zimmer frame to perfection.

She winced but managed to refrain with the 'ouch' as she took another step. This morning, her hip and the crease in her waist felt on fire as she moved, but it had still been good to be out of bed. Now, on this second outing, she didn't feel half so stiff or uncomfortable. She'd always been one of those people who heal quickly, and never had she been more glad of it.

'I hear your boss came by last night,' Tracy said chattily. 'Tessa told me he was a dreamboat. All silver hair. Very Paul Hollywood.'

Hillary laughed, wondering how Marcus Donleavy would react at being compared to the sexy baker.

Her thoughts strayed back to the murder victim, Malcolm Dale. Dammit, she should be trying to figure out who'd killed him, not shuffling around hospital corridors. To make matters worse, Donleavy had told her she'd been scheduled to take three weeks' sick leave, which might stretch to a month, depending on doctors' reports. A month! What was she going to do for a month?

As she began to march down the corridor with growing confidence, she tried to think positively. She could put all her energy into selling the house, and then finally buy the boat off Max, all nice and legal. For a long time now she'd been putting that off, but perhaps it was time to admit that she was perfectly content to live on the boat. All of that could fill in some time. Then she could do all the odd jobs around the boat she'd always put off. That might take all of two days.

She shuddered. The thought of so much inaction scared her. But she could still work the Dale case, if she was sneaky. She was pretty sure Tommy could be persuaded to come by with the latest news and copies of reports. If Janine didn't cotton on to what he was doing.

Janine, she thought glumly. By now, Mel must have told her that she'd be the senior investigating officer on the Dale killing — her first time in charge of such an important case. A chance to shine. Just what she'd always wanted. Right about now, she must be over the moon.

\* \* \*

'You bastard,' Janine hissed. 'Why the change of heart? You were all over me last night.'

'Keep your voice down,' Mel said calmly. 'Do you really want to give Frank Ross a show?'

Janine took a deep breath, feeling her fingernails cut painfully into her palms as she clenched her hands into tight fists. There was a throbbing in her temples and she wanted to scream in frustration, but a colder, harder voice of reason stopped her.

If she went ballistic now, she'd never live it down. She could almost hear the sneering. The cracks from all the misogynists that bred in this place like malaria mosquitoes. And Mel was right — Ross for one would just love to see her make a scene. She'd be hearing 'hysterical female jokes' and reference to PMT for months to come. And it was bound to get back to the brass. As well Mel knew, the bastard. That's why he'd broken up with her here and now.

'Don't think you're going to get away with this,' Janine warned him. 'I can still make your life a misery. I could file a sexual harassment suit for a start. What would that do to your chances for promotion then, hey?'

Mel felt himself go cold, but managed a smile and small shrug. 'What would that do to yours?' he countered softly, and then sighed heavily as Janine went pale.

'Look, let's not be like this,' he cajoled. 'We're both grown-ups. We both know how it goes. We tried it out for a while, but it just wasn't working—'

'It was working for me!'

'And now we have to carry on working together. Look, Janine, this won't affect your career, I promise. I'm not the sort of man who can't stand to have his ex-lovers around, or go all postal on them. In fact—' he leaned back in his chair and tossed the folder she'd just brought in back to her, '—I want you to head up the Dale case. I'll be in overall charge, of course, but I want you to lead the investigation. You've worked with Hillary for three years now — you've picked up a lot of good stuff from her. This is your chance. Don't screw it up just because you're mad at me.'

Janine stared at him for a long while, then slowly reached forward and picked up the folder.

'I'll be round tonight with a mate's transit van for my stuff,' she said coldly. She got up and added a sneering, 'Sir.'

When she left, the air in the office hovered somewhere just below freezing point.

Mel let out his breath in a long slow release, and felt suddenly anxious. And bereft. Janine, in spite of everything, had been fun. His last sip of the summer wine? Fifty was looming, and for a moment he wondered if he'd made a mistake in letting her go.

Then the moment passed.

* * *

Mike Regis stared at her nightgown and tried not to smile. Hillary twirled one of the pink ribbons that rested coyly just below her chin and grinned. 'My mum's.'

'That's a bloody relief,' Regis said with a laugh, and indicated a big plastic bag. 'Brought you some of this muesli mix stuff. Nuts and raisins and whatnot. Don't know if you like it.'

Hillary didn't either. It wasn't something she'd normally try. 'Considering the food in this place, I'll take it,' she said, and opened the bag for a rummage. 'So, what's the latest?'

Mike drew up a chair and shrugged. He was wearing a pair of dark grey slacks, white shirt, and black leather jacket. With his thinning black hair and penetrating green eyes, she'd noticed all her other ward-mates giving him the sly once-over. Now they pretended to be reading or watching daytime TV.

'I reckon your boss, Donleavy, is going to do a gloss-over on Raleigh,' he said flatly. 'Can't blame him. Why give the press ammo? Apart from your mishap, it was a bloody good night.'

Hillary grinned. She couldn't help it. 'Next time you get shot, I'll come over and sit by your bedside and say the same.'

Regis watched her nibble a hazelnut and smiled. 'Seriously, I'm glad you're all right.'

'Seriously, so am I. So, how does it feel to have Fletcher out of the way?' she asked curiously. As a Vice officer, Fletcher must have always been more of a thorn in his side than in most. She herself was glad the villain was off the streets, but she couldn't help but wonder who'd be taking his place in the pecking order, and when. Still, during the vacuum, Vice should be able to make a good sweep of a lot of low-lives who'd be scuttling for cover and panicking now that the big kingpin was dead.

'Don't really know, to be honest,' Mike said. 'I think I'd have preferred to see him banged up. See how he liked to swap his swimming pool and his holiday villa in Marbella for a fourteen-foot cell and a toilet that doesn't flush.'

'But you'll go to his funeral?' she asked, biting down on a surprisingly chewy, but nice and sweet, sultana.

'Oh yeah, I wouldn't miss dancing on his grave for all the tea in China.'

'Nice,' Hillary said. 'I think I've just cracked a tooth on a piece of barley. Do people really eat this stuff for pleasure?'

Regis shrugged. 'Beats me. I'm a pizza man myself.'

'So, you any closer to figuring out exactly what went down that night? There seems to be some confusion,' Hillary said, and Regis laughed bluntly.

'You can say that again. Neither Col nor me can quite figure it out.' Hillary had wondered where his sidekick, the ever-present, ever-quiet Colin Tanner was, but didn't ask. It was just one less male to see her in her mother's tent-like nightie.

'We were upstairs when we heard the shots, the ones that must have killed Fletcher,' Regis said. 'We both headed for the stairs at a rate of knots, along with nearly every other TFI guy up there. Col was nearest the stairs first, and didn't see anybody come out of the kitchen, where Fletcher got it. Not a TFI guy, not your guv'nor, and not the bloke who shot you.'

'Brian Conroy?'

'Right. They're doing his PM now, by the way.'

'That's late.'

'They're backlogged. Fletcher's was done yesterday.'

Hillary shrugged. 'Then Conroy must have got out the kitchen the moment he shot Fletcher, and you weren't in time to see him.'

'That blonde sergeant of yours was in the left front room. She says she saw movement, but thought it came from the room opposite.'

Hillary frowned. 'Is there access from the right-hand living room into the kitchen?'

'Nope.'

Hillary frowned. 'Wait a minute. According to what Mel said, Raleigh and Ross were in the other living room, and went to the kitchen after they heard shots. That must have been what Janine saw.'

'I didn't see them, neither did Col. They must have moved bloody quick. Mind you, that boss of yours does have a tendency to jump the gun. But if you were in the house and heard gunshots, and you were unarmed, would you go rushing to see what was happening?'

Hillary gave him the eagle eye. 'You know damned bloody well I wouldn't. And didn't. Which is probably what got me shot! Now what does that say about life?'

Regis grinned. 'That sod's law is alive and well?'

* * *

It was dark when Hillary looked up from the copy of *The Mill on the Floss* that she was reading, and saw Tommy Lynch. He was hesitating in the wide opening, a big bunch of lemon-coloured chrysanthemums in his hand.

She was out of bed, having had yet another walk about and this time moving much easier and almost without pain, and she was now sitting in the chair beside her bed. She held up a hand so that he could spot her, and when he did, he smiled and came towards her.

'Hello, guv. Mel told me you were seeing visitors.'

He glanced down somewhat helplessly at the flowers in his hand, and a nurse spotted him and came to take them away. She smiled at him as she took the flowers, but Tommy didn't seem to notice. Hillary would have to let it drop that the DS was due to get married in June. And that reminded her — she still hadn't got them a wedding present yet.

'Sit down.' Hillary put the book away on the wheeled tray beside her bed, and watched him as he took a seat. He looked tired and drawn. When he sat down on the moulded plastic chair, he let his big hands drop between his splayed legs and leaned forward, an obvious sign of fatigue.

'How's the Dale case going?' Hillary asked at once. 'Any new developments?'

Tommy nodded. 'The guv made Janine acting SIO. First thing she did was pull Percy Matthews back in.'

Hillary winced. Great going, Janine. No doubt Mel would have something to say about that.

'You got anything else on him? Forensics?'

'Nah, but the wife gave us permission to search the house. We spent all afternoon tossing the place, but there was nothing obvious. Janine kept at Percy and Mrs Matthews all afternoon, but they're both sticking to it that they were in together all that night.'

Hillary nodded. 'And that's all they'll have to keep saying,' she mused glumly. 'It's up to us to disprove it.' If, indeed, there was anything to disprove. Rita Matthews letting them search the house was a fairly sure sign that she thought they had nothing to hide. Or that she was sure there'd be nothing for them to find — which was not quite the same thing. But somehow, Hillary just couldn't see Percy Matthews as the culprit. He was not a doer, in her opinion, but a planner. An endless prevaricator. Still, she could be wrong.

'Janine's been out all afternoon questioning the neighbours, trying to break his alibi. Trouble is, with him living on that top road, he hasn't really got neighbours to speak of,' Tommy carried on. 'The sarge is determined to interview everyone in the village. All the uniforms are complaining about having to do third and even fourth interviews again.'

Hillary shrugged, but wasn't about to criticize. She knew how Janine felt. This was her first time leading a case, and she wanted results, fast. Especially if Mel, the prat, had already given her the push. Her ego would be smarting, and her pride would demand even more that she close the case fast, just to show him and the brass that she had the smarts and could be trusted with more responsibility.

The trouble was, Hillary was not at all sure that she was barking up the right tree.

'Well, they're letting me out of here tomorrow,' she said, and nodded as Tommy looked surprised. 'Need the bed, I reckon. Nowadays they get you out as quick as possible. I've got to have the district nurse in once every two days to change the dressing, but apart from that, and a really bad limp, I'm free and clear. They're giving me enough painkillers to fell an elephant, so I'll be OK.'

'Won't getting around on the boat be a bit of a hassle, though? The narrow steps down and all?' Tommy asked

Hillary shrugged. 'Less room to fall over in,' she said philosophically.

* * *

The next day, Hillary left hospital in a taxi. Getting down the narrow set of steps was a bit of a grind, but once settled inside, Hillary felt much better. To be surrounded by the familiar was wonderful. She made herself a cup of coffee just how she liked it (a real luxury after hospital java) and sat in the single armchair in the tiny living area and listened to the sounds of the canal.

A blackbird was singing in the hawthorn right beside the boat, and across the canal on the other side, where a field of winter barley was growing, a skylark was competing. Even the sun was shining, and tomorrow the clocks went on, giving her another hour of light at night.

All those hours, and nothing to fill them. She could take up watercolours, except she couldn't paint for toffee. Pity, because the stand of bulrushes she could see out of her window across the way would make an ideal subject. She could catch up on her reading, of course — an English Lit major could never get enough books. Trouble was, you could only read for so many hours a day.

The painkillers were doing a good job, and for someone who'd been shot only two nights ago, she was feeling fairly fit and relaxed. It was not as if she felt ill. She'd only been in the boat an hour, and already she could feel it closing in on her. And it had nothing to do with claustrophobia. No. It had to do with incipient boredom. By the time she'd fixed herself some beans on toast for tea, she knew she was going to go mad unless she could come up with some sort of plan of action for the next week or so.

The trouble was — what could she do? If she went in to work, Janine would throw a fit and Mel would only chase her out again. Her eyes fell speculatively on the Dick Francis book in the shelves of classics. She could do something about that, she supposed. But that would mean notifying the brass. Raking up the scandal that was Ronnie Greene all over again. On the other hand, it wouldn't be hanging over her any more. And since her credit as a 'hero cop' was running high, now might be a good time to tell the brass she'd miraculously discovered where her corrupt, late and totally unlamented hubby had stashed his million-plus in ill-gotten gains. Then she shook her head. Why rock the boat? Best just to ignore it.

As darkness fell, she heard moaning coming from the next boat. Her neighbour on *Willowsands* was entertaining her latest. Nancy Walker, a very merry widow of uncertain age, liked her students young.

It was all right for some, Hillary thought grumpily. She tried the TV, but it was all rubbish. Restlessly, she turned it off and finally thought about the night she was shot. Faced up to it, relived it, cried a bit, felt sick, had a slug of whisky, and got past it. She felt shaky, but better. She was now confident that she wouldn't wake up with the sweats in the middle of the night. Better yet, she was fairly sure she hadn't lost her nerve either, but couldn't know for certain. And she'd never *be* certain until she faced physical danger again.

Always something to look forward to.

In the meantime, she'd forget about that particular sword of Damocles hanging over her head, and think about Luke Fletcher instead, and the way he died.

And the more she thought about it, the more she didn't like it. Things just didn't add up.

By the time she finally went to bed, she knew just how she was going to survive the boredom of her recuperation.

# CHAPTER TEN

Hillary took the bus into Oxford rather than drive herself, just to be safe. Although her side was still painful, she found she was able to manoeuvre on and off the boat with growing ease, and the bus presented her with no difficulties. Walking for any length of time tended to ratchet up the pain a bit, and she made a mental note to herself not to hoof it too much.

Luckily for her, the internet café in St Giles wasn't far from a bus stop, and she treated herself to their best blend of Brazilian as she surfed the net. She took a fresh notebook with her, and was glad, since she found that Jerome Raleigh had quite a few hits to his credit. Most of it consisted of newspaper reports of his busts back in London, but once or twice she found some good titbits about his social life. Surprisingly, she could find no trace of a previous marriage. A bachelor boy then, obviously, but only of the wolf variety, for she'd found several pictures of Raleigh taken at fairly high-profile social events, with a different and attractive woman on his arm each time. She made careful note of the women's names, and details of the busts that had made the headlines.

After a couple more hours of solid digging, she could see why the man was a superintendent at forty. He'd played the game well, and had obviously cultivated the right people carefully. With some perseverance (and a lot more coffee), she managed to trace his rise from humble police constable beginnings to his current position. And as she did so, making a scrupulous timeline as she went, a single fact began to stand out more and more.

Raleigh had been born and bred in London. His father had been a solicitor at a large firm, his mother a dentist. He'd enjoyed all the privileges of a good, solid, middle-class upbringing, and had attended a local grammar school, following it with a degree from his local university in political science. Perhaps joining the police had been a surprising choice, but it was obvious right from the start that Jerome Raleigh had intended to go places. And go places he had. His rise to sergeant had been swift, following a brilliant showing at his Boards. A bare three years later and he made inspector. A long stint followed, with Raleigh logging up a good record of solved cases, but he'd also volunteered for several committees and high-profile initiatives that had been bound to get him noticed. His position as chief inspector had been all but a foregone conclusion. He never put a foot wrong as far as Hillary could tell, and none of his immediate superiors had anything but praise for him.

So why, last year, had he made the sudden move to Thames Valley? Why would a Met man, born and bred, suddenly move out to Oxfordshire? He hadn't pissed anybody off that she could tell; in fact, quite the opposite. Reading between the lines, an ACC seemed to have been grooming him to take on a superintendency in his own department.

So why had he left? It wasn't for more immediate promotion prospects, that was for sure. He had no family commitments. It wasn't for more money. Burnout might be a possibility, but in that case, why go for a superintendency on one of the largest and most active forces in the country?

The net was great, but it couldn't tell her everything. After another two hours, Hillary walked slowly and carefully to the nearby South Park, opposite the red and white brick monstrosity that was Keble College, and found a quiet bench on which to think. Her only neighbour was a squirrel looking for a handout. Occasionally, mothers pushing well-wrapped toddlers in pushchairs went by.

The more Hillary had learned about Raleigh, the more uneasy she had become. Now, taking out her mobile and her personal telephone diary, Hillary started making calls.

Over the years she'd made friends and contacts in all sorts of places, both high and low, some of whom were living and working in London. One, a sergeant she'd trained up many years ago now, and was now a chief inspector in the Met, owed her more than a few favours, as did some snouts who would have crossed Jerome Raleigh's patch.

But after an hour of careful digging, Hillary was still none the wiser. Which could mean only one of two things — either all her sources were lying to her, or nobody really knew why Jerome Raleigh had left London. And she wasn't paranoid enough yet to think that everyone knew something that she didn't.

As she sat on the park bench, shivering a little in the cold March afternoon sunshine, Hillary thought about the Fletcher raid. And the more she thought about it, the more something about it kept sending back to her the distinct whiff of something rotten.

Well, at least she wasn't bored.

* * *

Janine Tyler tried not to sound excited as she watched the man opposite her pull out a cigarette and light up. She was in a small cottage in the village of Lower Heyford's main thoroughfare, Freehold Street, and had all but given up hope of finding anyone who could put Percy Matthews out and about on the night of the Dale killing.

She'd done nothing all day but re-interview people who were all eager to please but unable to help. The murder of Malcolm Dale was still a matter of high interest, of course, and would be for years to come, if Janine knew villages, and everyone she met had a theory and wanted to try it out on her. Opinion seemed to favour Valerie Dale as the culprit, but only, it seemed, because most killings were done by spouses. Some favoured a political angle, although none could offer any real basis for this when challenged. Two old dears were convinced that animal rights fundamentalists had done him in because of his very public promise to get fox hunting re-established if he'd been selected to run as their MP, and Janine had given Frank the task of seeing if any of their local animal nutters could indeed have been responsible. He'd griped about it continuously since, so that was a definite bonus.

But house after house, interview after interview, nobody believed Matthews could have done it. Loony but harmless was the general consensus when it came to the retired shoe salesman. And certainly nobody had seen him that night.

Until now. Sitting opposite her, looking rather bleary-eyed because she'd woken him up, Oliver Rogerson puffed long and hard on his fag. 'Been trying to give them up, but can't. Wife keeps nagging me. Good job I work the night shift, otherwise I'd never get a drag.'

Janine nodded. Rogerson worked as a night watchman on 'The Camp,' what Lower Heyfordians referred to as the now abandoned RAF/USAF air force base at Upper Heyford. Now it housed a giant car lot, and Rogerson patrolled it at night to prevent car thieves. Janine wondered how many hours he spent smoking around the back of his little cubby hole and how much patrolling he actually did. But she wasn't about to carp. Not after what he'd just said.

'So, just to make sure,' she said, glancing at her notes. 'You leave for work at six thirty p.m.?'

'Right. Have my main meal at five — I cook it, 'cos the wife comes home from her job then.'

'And you bike it to Upper Heyford?'

'Only got the one car and it seems daft for me to take it to work when the camp's only a mile away, and the missus works in Bicester.'

Janine nodded impatiently. 'Right. So every night you get out the bike and push it up the hill?'

'Can't ride it up. Legs ain't as good as they used to be.'

'And on that night, the night Malcolm Dale died, you saw Percy Matthews walking towards you. That is, coming from his house at the top of the village, and heading downhill?'

'Right.'

'And you're sure it was the same night that Malcolm Dale died?' she pressed.

'Course I'm sure. The wife was full of it when I got back the next morning.'

'And you saw him clearly?' Janine insisted.

'Yeah. He was just coming out from under one of the streetlights.' Oliver Rogerson grunted. 'Don't know why the council bothered putting them up in the first place.'

Janine's fingers tightened on the pencil. 'You say he was just coming out from under the light? But you could see his face? He wasn't in darkness, or half in darkness?' She knew only too well what defence barristers could do to witness statements of this sort.

'He was still under the light when I saw him,' Oliver said, narrow brown eyes watching her through the smoke haze. 'Don't know why you're getting so excited. I sometimes see Percy, now and then. He does live in the village, you know.'

'But you'd be willing to swear in a court of law that you saw him that night, at about six thirty-five or thereabouts?'

Oliver Rogerson suddenly looked nervous. Janine knew this reaction too. The old I-don't-want-to-get-involved syndrome. 'Mr Rogerson, this is important,' she said severely, and the older man shrugged reluctantly.

'Suppose so,' he grunted.

Janine grinned and stood up. That was good enough for her.

\* \* \*

Tommy's call came just as she'd taken her seat on the bus back. The bus was nearly empty, since it was still only three o'clock in the afternoon, but one old lady gave her the gimlet eye as the cell phone's ringtone disturbed her.

Hillary quickly snapped it open and put it to her ear. 'DI Greene,' she said. And the old lady quickly stopped giving her the eye and faced front again. Hillary smiled wryly. That was her all right — the scourge of little old ladies everywhere.

'Guv,' Tommy said. 'You wanted to be kept informed about the Dale case. Janine just arrested and charged Percy Matthews.'

Hillary blinked. 'That was quick. What's up?'

Tommy told her the latest, and on impulse, Hillary told him she was going to drop in. Ostensibly to show everyone she was all right and touch base, but they both knew she was hot to see how this latest development panned out.

She got off at the stop opposite the station, but found the walk up the short drive and across the big parking lot more arduous than she'd expected. She stopped at the main entrance to dry-swallow two more painkillers, then pushed inside. The desk sergeant hailed her, and she spent several minutes accepting congratulations and commiserations, and swapping war stories about injuries of the past. They agreed that his split skull beat her bullet, and then she took the lift upstairs. Normally she'd have had no trouble trotting up the stairs, but by now she was beginning to feel distinctly iffy. A hot-cold thing was going on, making her alternately sweat and then shiver, and she knew that she should really be back at the boat, taking it easy. The nurse was due to change her wadding soon, too.

She made her way to her desk without stopping, accepting the calls and queries of all the others in the big open-plan office without detouring. Once sat down, she felt a whole lot better.

Tommy was the first to come to her desk, since he was expecting her. Taking one look at her pale face, he went to Mel's office, where the CI kept his own personal coffee machine, and pinched some of his finest roast and brought her back a mug.

Hillary accepted it with a smile. 'So, what's happening?'

'Mel's down there interviewing Percy now. Janine's hopping about it.'

'I'll bet,' Hillary said. 'What do you think?'

Tommy shrugged. 'Percy Matthews was definitely lying about staying in all night. The wit Janine found seems sound. It puts Matthews out and about without an alibi at the time of the murder.'

'So Mel's happy with it?'

Tommy frowned. 'Dunno, guv. I think he thinks Janine jumped the gun in charging him. And I think he's annoyed that she didn't consult him first. But he hasn't given her a rollicking.'

No, he wouldn't, Hillary thought, hiding a grin. He'd be stepping on eggshells around Janine Tyler for some time yet. Serve him right.

'Well, let's go down and observe, shall we?' she said, the mug of coffee giving her a new lease of life. Even so, she took the lift back down.

There was no one else in the observation room. She took the only chair and sat down, but even through the glass, she could feel anger and excitement shimmering off her blonde sergeant. Mel, doing the questioning, was as smooth as ever.

'But, Mr Matthews, we have a witness, a very reliable witness, who says he saw you on Freehold Street, at six thirty or thereabouts, on the night that Mr Dale died.'

'Must have been wrong then,' Percy Matthews said belligerently, folding his thin arms over his scrawny chest. He was dressed in a white shirt and a dark green V-neck, hand-knitted sweater over black trousers. He didn't look the least worried. In fact, he looked positively chipper.

'He's the sort who likes to scrap,' Hillary said thoughtfully. She'd met a lot of people like that — but very few of them had, funnily enough, been prone to real violence.

'Come now, Percy,' Mel said, slipping in the Christian name craftily. It always helped if you could do that — it gave the inquisitor a distinct psychological advantage. 'Don't you see that you're not helping yourself by continuing to lie?'

Percy Matthews shrugged. 'Can't help it if you've got it wrong, can I?'

Mel abruptly changed tack. 'You do realise, don't you, Percy, that you've been charged with first degree murder?' He paused to let it sink in. 'That's very serious. You could be looking at life inside — twenty to thirty years. And with a man your age . . .' Mel shrugged eloquently. 'Well, let's face it, Percy, you'd die in prison. Don't you think it would be better if you just told us what happened? Who knows, if there was adequate provocation, perhaps the Crown Prosecution Service might consider reducing the charge to manslaughter?'

Hillary sighed. *Careful, Mel.* She turned to Tommy. 'Did Mr Matthews waive his right to a solicitor?'

Tommy nodded. 'Yeah, he did. Right away. Said he didn't need him.'

Hillary didn't like the sound of that. How fast would a good defence barrister claim that Percy had been unfit to make that decision, thus rendering anything he said here and now inadmissible in court? If it had been her in there, she'd have insisted he have legal representation.

She had to remind herself that this wasn't her case anymore. Not that it did any good. It still *felt* like her case.

Someone knocked on the door to the observation room, and Tommy opened it. Hillary heard him murmuring quietly for a moment, then he came back. 'Guv, Mrs Matthews is here. She's mad as a hornet, apparently, and demanding to see someone in charge.'

'Wasn't she there when Janine brought Percy in?'

'No. She was doing the grocery shopping, it seems.'

'Oh hell! Is there an interview room free?'

'Five is, guv.'

'Have her in there then,' Hillary said, getting up with a wince.

Tommy frowned. 'Guv, you're still on sick leave.'

'I know. But it won't hurt to see what she has to say.'

Tommy went reluctantly, and Hillary had only just sat herself down in room five when he came back in with Rita Matthews. She was dressed in a shin-length brown dress, and a long raincoat in more or less the same colour. Her face was flushed red, and her eyes glittered as she sat down. 'What's all this nonsense about our Percy being arrested?' she asked, without preamble. 'I hadn't stepped off the bus when Julie told me about it.'

Hillary didn't ask who Julie was. She didn't need to. In any small village, information was relayed faster than the speed of sound.

Hillary quickly set the tape running, introduced herself, Rita Matthews and Tommy Lynch, and stated the time and place. Only then did she answer the question. 'I'm afraid we've found a witness who saw your husband in Freehold Street at around six thirty, on the night Mr Dale was murdered, Mrs Matthews,' she said. 'Won't you tell me why you lied about your husband's whereabouts that night?' she asked gently.

Rita Matthews sighed heavily. 'Because the daft sod had already said we were at home together, hadn't he?'

Hillary nodded. 'But you knew that wasn't true?'

'Course I did. He was where he always is every Monday night. Playing cards with his mates in Fred Turnkey's garden shed.'

Hillary opened her mouth, then closed it again. 'Tommy, I think you'd better get Sergeant Tyler in here,' she said quietly, and then for the tape, added quietly, 'Detective Constable Lynch has just left the room.'

* * *

Janine Tyler could feel her face flame as Rita Matthews snapped, 'Listen, you daft bugger, stop playing the fool and tell them what's what.'

Rita and Percy Matthews, Mel and herself, were now all in interview room three. She'd taken Rita Matthews' testimony in interview room five with a stony face, suspecting that Hillary Greene was watching her from the observation room and crowing with glee.

In that, she was wrong. Hillary, after Janine had returned with Tommy, had left to go home. She knew Tommy would explain everything, and she had no desire to watch her young sergeant's humiliation. Besides, she had to get back to meet the district nurse.

In the parking lot she'd snagged a patrol car going out, getting a lift to Thrupp. The two youngsters had been only too pleased to do it, and Hillary knew that her status would remain high for some time to come. She was now the cop who'd got shot bringing Fletcher down. Whatever the actual facts of the matter, she knew that's how she'd now always be known. But she didn't buck it. Better that than to be known as corrupt Ronnie Greene's missus.

Now, with her wound cleaned and the bandaging changed, she lay out on her bed, trying to doze, but unable to do so. Although the painkillers had made her drowsy, she couldn't help but wonder what was happening back at the station.

Although she was fairly sure she knew.

* * *

Janine listened, feeling herself shrinking further and further into a small ball, as Rita Matthews continued to harangue her husband. 'You've got no more sense than to fly a kite in a thunderstorm. What were you going to do? Just sit here and let them bang you up? You tell them where you really were, or I'll . . . I'll . . . box your ears, you twit!'

'Mrs Matthews, please calm down,' Mel said sternly, but he was trying not to laugh. 'Mr Matthews, is what your wife said true?'

Percy Matthews looked sulky. 'Well, I was playing cards with Fred and the others, yes. We always play on Mondays.

For bottles of beer, and cheese and stuff. We all bring something and bet with it. Winner takes the pot. I took a farmhouse cake that night.'

'I baked it,' Rita put in, looking less ferocious now that her husband had capitulated.

'I see,' Mel said. 'I need the names of all the others who were there.' Rita provided them quickly, and once more Percy Matthews sulked. Janine wanted the floor to open and swallow her up, but nothing happened.

'Right. Now, what time exactly did you arrive at Fred Turnkey's house?'

'His garden shed,' Percy corrected. 'I went straight to the shed — we all did. His son-in-law's an electrician. Fitted it out nice. Electric fire and everything.'

Mel nodded. 'What time, Mr Matthews?' he persisted.

'Twenty to seven, I 'spect it was.'

'Were you first to arrive?'

'Course not. Fred was there first. It was his shed. Vern was there as well. Cyril and Harry came last.'

Mel nodded. 'Sergeant Tyler, perhaps you'd like to take DC Lynch and confirm Mr Matthews' alibi?' Mel said, careful not to catch her eye. 'They all live in the village?'

'Cyril and Harry live in Rousham,' Percy said. 'Cyril's got a car, and gives Harry a lift.' He provided the addresses and without a word, her face averted, Janine got up and left.

Mel watched her go, not sure whether to laugh or cry.

* * *

That night, Tommy dropped by. A big man, he found the boat a bit of a novelty. It reminded him of a child's Wendy house. He insisted that Hillary stay seated, and as he made drinks for them both, filled her in.

When he was finished, he was sitting on the floor, his back to the bookshelves. There was only one armchair in the tiny room, but he seemed comfortable enough.

'So it all checked out?' Hillary said. 'I hope Janine's OK?'

Tommy grimaced. 'She's embarrassed, but trying not to show it. Frank isn't helping.'

Hillary grunted. So what else was new? 'Is she still in charge?'

'Mel hasn't said anything. Janine's got Ross checking out the loony animal rights movement, see if any of them were active that night. He's carping on about needing help with it. I'm just hoping she doesn't send me.'

Hillary nodded. After a radical animal rights group had tried to sue her for possession of her house, she wasn't exactly keen on the breed. Ronnie Greene had made his dirty money from an illegal animal parts smuggling racket, as investigation into his corrupt activities had proved. But they hadn't found where he'd stashed the money, and an animal so-called charity had tried to scare her by threatening to sue her. Their argument had been that Ronnie had bought their house with illegal money obtained through animal suffering — and so the house should be sold and the money donated to their 'charity.' Hillary had asked a friend, who was also a first-rate solicitor, to defend the case, but it had never come to court, with the animal rights people eventually backing off.

Thinking of it made her eyes move to the Dick Francis novel, now sitting on the shelf not six inches from Tommy's head.

It had been her stepson Gary who'd given it to her. Ronnie's son by his first marriage, Gary had cleared out an old locker of his father's at Bicester nick, and had thought she might like to have the book back, because of the personal inscription inside.

Hillary had been puzzled to read the rather sick-making message inscribed by her to Ronnie on the inside page. Very puzzled, actually, since she'd never written it. It was only then, leafing through the pages, that she'd noticed several words underlined. 'Too, heaven, ate,' etc. And realised they were all numbers. Two, seven, eight, and so on. From there it had been a quick jump to realise that they probably belonged to a numbered account in a bank in his favourite spot in the Caribbean. She'd surfed the net and found the bank some months ago, and also found the missing money. All million-plus of it. Since then, she'd dithered about what to do with it.

'Anyway, it looks as if we're back to square one on the Dale case,' Tommy said, wrenching her thoughts back to the here and now.

Hillary sighed heavily. 'It sure looks like it,' she agreed glumly.

# CHAPTER ELEVEN

The train service to London from Oxford was good, and within an hour, Hillary found herself in Paddington. The first woman she wanted to see lived not far from the station, and the office where she worked was even closer.

Marilyn Forbes was a woman on the way up, if the size of her office in the well-established PR firm was anything to go by. A window with a view of endless traffic was double-glazed, letting only a mild whisper permeate the beige-and-cream space. Black leather and chrome chairs grouped around a smoked glass table, while colourful and successful advertising campaigns adorned the walls.

Marilyn still looked very much like her photograph, taken at a large charity ball a few years ago, which Hillary had found on the internet. She still wore the same short cap of ash-blonde hair, and her big grey eyes were highlighted with careful make-up. There were a few more wrinkles around the nose and mouth perhaps, but her figure was still reed-slim. Hillary disliked her on sight.

'Please, take a seat,' Marilyn said, indicating a chair. 'Ms Welles, I think you said?'

Hillary smiled and held out her hand. 'Yes. Thank you for agreeing to see me. I know a lot of people don't have time for journalists.'

Marilyn laughed. 'Except for people in my profession.'

Hillary smiled again. Marilyn's professional instinct to be kind to the press was exactly the reason why she'd chosen to take on the persona of a reporter.

'You're freelance, I think my secretary said?' Marilyn prompted, taking a seat opposite the table, and reaching unrepentantly for a cigarette. 'Hope you don't mind,' she said, waving the offending article in the air. 'I don't care what the current thinking is, I need a fag every four hours to get me through the day. And since this is my office . . .'

Hillary shook her head with a smile, and opened her notebook. 'Of course I don't mind. And yes, I'm freelance for my sins, but hope to sell the story to several quality magazines. Superintendent Raleigh is very much man of the moment back in Oxford.'

Marilyn made a small approving sound around her cigarette, and lit it. 'Yes, I heard. Good for him, I say.'

Hillary nodded, trying to look earnest. Obviously, their split had not been acrimonious if she still wished him well. 'You and he were an item once, I understand?' she asked delicately.

Marilyn Forbes grinned. 'A while ago now, but yes, we were close for about six months or so.'

'And what do you feel comfortable telling me about him?' Hillary left the question deliberately open-ended and unthreatening and, as hoped, Marilyn quickly launched into a careful but seemingly candid description of the man, both as a policeman, and as a partner.

'I see from my research that the superintendent never married,' Hillary mused, again keeping her voice bland.

Marilyn grinned. 'A bachelor through and through. Well, who can blame him?' Marilyn shrugged. 'He's good-looking and not too badly off, so he has no problem getting the ladies, but his job simply eats him alive. No time for a wife, that's the impression I got. And after a brief matrimonial disaster in my early twenties, I never wanted to tie the knot again either.' The PR executive shrugged again. 'So, we both knew it wasn't going to lead to orange blossom and vows.'

Hillary nodded. 'Did he ever talk about his work with you? I mean, obviously not specific details. Or was he the kind of man who kept it all bottled up?'

Marilyn was obviously flattered at being the recipient of an interview herself, rather than simply arranging them on behalf of clients, and again Hillary took copious notes as she talked. She remembered best the cases he'd been working on while still with her, naturally, and that had included the case of a man who'd battered his stepdaughter to death. From what Marilyn described, Hillary could tell that, even back then, Jerome Raleigh had been a dedicated investigator, the kind who never let go once he'd got his teeth into something. So, this thing he had about nailing Fletcher wasn't particularly uncharacteristic. Perhaps he was just the type who took chances when he thought the pay-off was big enough to warrant it? Maybe she was just wasting her time.

'He seemed to take it really personally,' Marilyn carried on, as if in confirmation of her hypothesis, taking a last puff on her second cigarette and putting it out. 'It was as if he really despised criminals. You know, it wasn't just his job. He told me once, as a young copper on the beat, he was called to a house where an old lady had been beaten up for her pension money. He said it made him so angry he could feel himself burning up. I suppose something like that sticks with you.'

Hillary nodded emphatically. Oh yes, things like that stuck with you all right. She herself could vividly remember her first battered wife case, and the overpowering sense of revulsion it had awoken in her. However, all she said mildly was, 'His bosses must have liked that attitude.'

'I'll say,' Marilyn said with a grin. 'He was still a DI when I knew him. He was trying for promotion to DCI when we split up. I wasn't surprised to hear a few years later that he'd got it.'

'He did well at the Met,' Hillary agreed, not making it a question. 'I can't seem to find the reason why he left to join Thames Valley. It puzzles me a bit.'

Marilyn nodded seriously. 'Sorry, can't help you there,' she said with a frown. 'You know, it surprises me too, now that I think about it. Jerome was such a big city animal. He loved London — knew it inside and out.'

Hillary sighed. Damn! 'So you've no idea why he might have left? Nothing in your previous relationship with him gives you any insights?' She knew an appeal to a woman's intuition when it came to discussing men would never go unchallenged.

'It can only be to do with his ambition,' Marilyn said at last, after a long, thoughtful pause. 'He was determined to be chief constable one day. Literally, I mean. We used to talk about it. I sometimes laughed, but he never did. If he left the Met, he must have got something really serious in return for it. He was the sort who could make sacrifices too, if he had to. You know, personal sacrifices. He had a lot of self-discipline.' A certain amount of bitterness crept into her words just then, and as if sensing it, she shook her head and smiled. But her self-defences were being raised.

Hillary, detecting the change in mood, swiftly changed tack and kept it innocuous. When she'd finished, about ten minutes later, she thought she probably knew a bit more about what made her boss tick than she had before, but still, she had nothing solid to go on. Nothing specific to the cock-up that surrounded the Fletcher bust.

It wasn't until Hillary was putting on her coat in preparation for leaving that she was given a final small nugget. 'I'd be glad if you could let me know if you sell the piece,' Marilyn said, reaching out to shake her hand goodbye. 'Not for myself, naturally, but I'm sure Jerome's mother would like a copy for her scrapbook. I still see her occasionally. Not that we were close or anything.'

Hillary blinked. Mother. She hadn't realised Mrs Raleigh was still alive. She must be in her late seventies, early eighties, at least. 'Oh. She lives locally then?' she asked casually, and without a thought, Marilyn waved a hand vaguely at the window.

'The other side of Chepstow Gardens. Linacre Road, I think it is.'

Hillary thanked her and left.

\* \* \*

Linacre Road was depressingly long and lined with smart-looking but small terraced properties on either side. Paintwork gleamed, and black railings were the flavour of the moment, and someone had started a trend for planting terracotta pots with miniature daffodils. Early-flowering cherry trees, planted at intervals, were already displaying their first pink buds. It looked very prosperous and demure, and had one of those streets-that-time-forgot feelings about it that you sometimes stumbled upon in the capital.

Hillary stood at one end of the road with a vague sense of frustration. There was no way she could talk to Jerome Raleigh's mother, of course, not even in her current disguise as freelance journalist. What proud mother could resist the urge to phone her son and tell him all about the fame and interest he had garnered with his latest exploits? True, Raleigh might not think anything of it. No doubt, back at HQ he was having to fend off reporters all the time. Still, he might find someone digging around and asking questions back in London and pestering his mother a bit much. And if Mrs Raleigh should describe the so-called journo . . .

No, Hillary thought with a shiver. She didn't want her super knowing she was investigating him. He could make her life a misery. Just as she was about to turn around and try to seek out another of Raleigh's past loves, she noticed an old woman get off a bus, which had stopped at the head of the road just behind her. She started to come towards Hillary, her shoulders stooped forward from the weight of the heavy shopping bags in each hand, white head bowed.

Hillary quickly walked forward to meet her and smiled. 'Hello, can I give you a hand with one of those?' The old woman's head shot up, instantly alert, and Hillary gave a big inner sigh. Sign of the times, she thought cynically, but she always felt defeated whenever something like this happened. She smiled again, and took a step back. 'Sorry, didn't mean to scare you.'

The old woman, relieved to see not a bag lady, or a member of a teenage gang, but a well-dressed woman in her forties, gave a tremulous smile. 'Sorry, dear, but you hear of such awful things nowadays,' she apologized.

'I know,' Hillary said flatly, and nodded to the bigger bag. 'I promise not to run off with your shopping. At least let me take it as far as the end of the road for you.'

The old woman nodded, and handed it over, still a shade reluctantly, Hillary thought. It weighed a fair bit, and Hillary felt her hip twinge as she took it in her left hand — the same side she'd been shot — and quickly transferred it to the right.

Together they started to walk down the pavement. 'I think I'm lost,' Hillary said, as an opening gambit. 'I was trying to find a Mrs Raleigh. Her son's a policeman. Quite famous just now,' she said. 'I was hoping to do a piece on him.'

'You mean Sylvia? I know Sylvia Raleigh,' the old woman said at once. 'She's always going on about that son of hers too. Well, he's an only child. Me, I had four. But I still think the world revolves around each and every one of them too, so I'm no better! I'm Geraldine Brewer, by the way.'

Hillary quickly gave her false name in return and then looked worried. 'I'm not really sure if I should bother her at the moment,' she confessed. I'm trying to do a piece on Superintendent Raleigh's latest arrest in Oxford. Maybe you've heard about it?'

'Not seen Sylvia for a few days, dear,' Geraldine Brewer said, and gave a short laugh. 'And I don't read the papers nowadays. Too depressing. But I dare say I'll hear about it from her soon enough, when I meet up with her in the super-market or on the bus.'

'Well, I didn't want to bother her unnecessarily. There's been just a little bit of trouble about it,' Hillary said, deliberately lowering her voice. Taking somebody into your confidence was the surest way, she'd found, of learning their own secrets. 'And I'm only a freelancer. I don't believe in bullying people for interviews and such,' she added. 'Some of my colleagues in the press can be very unfair, I think,' she added, just to reassure the old woman as to her own, more gentle bona fides.

She felt her hopes rise as the old woman's eyes lit up.

'Bit of trouble, huh?' Mrs Brewer repeated avidly.

'Oh, nothing really bad,' Hillary hastened to add. Although it was human nature to be interested in other people's woes, she didn't want to alarm Mrs Brewer. Just get her talking. 'I wonder — did you know Jerome Raleigh at all?'

'Oh yes! Well, sort of. I met him a couple of times, when he visited his mother. Look, this is me here,' Geraldine Brewer said, indicating a house with a dark blue door and the ubiquitous terracotta tub full of daffodils. 'Why don't you come in and have a cup of tea?'

The policewoman in Hillary immediately wanted to lecture her about the dangers of inviting strangers into her house. Good grief, this garrulous and friendly old lady would have been a conman's dream. Instead, she smiled brightly. 'I'd love to. And if you can give me some good background stuff, then perhaps I won't have to bother Mrs Raleigh at all.'

\* \* \*

'So, I suppose you can see why Sylvia is so proud of him,' Mrs Brewer said, ten minutes later. They were sitting in her tidy, sunshine-yellow living room, sipping tea and nibbling homemade fruit cake. Geraldine had just got through telling Hillary all about Sylvia, who had long since retired from dentistry, and now lived a quiet life of widowhood on an adequate pension, punctuated by visits to the local church. Which, according to Geraldine Brewer, she kept going almost single-handed. 'But you can only do so many flower arrangements, and organize so many jumble sales, can't you?

That's why she always makes a fuss when her boy comes to stay,' she explained.

Hillary nodded. 'And what do you think of him, Geraldine?' Hillary asked. 'When you're trying to write a piece about someone it's so hard if you can't get a clear idea of what they're like. Talking to someone who knows them, and can give an unbiased opinion, is such a help.'

'Oh, I can imagine. I couldn't do it. Well, let's see. He's good-looking, of course — never has trouble with the ladies, I can tell you. Sylvia's been quite driven to despair. She so wanted to be the mother of the groom, you see.'

Hillary nodded. 'She must be disappointed not to have grandchildren,' she said vaguely. 'You don't think, then, that all those women might be . . . well, camouflage, so to speak?'

'Oh no!' Geraldine said at once. 'Nothing like that. And of course, there was Elizabeth, so Sylvia didn't miss out on grandchildren. No, he was just too fly to settle down, I reckon,' Geraldine said with a sniff. 'Mind you, he wasn't the sort to shirk his responsibilities, I don't think that was it. I know for a fact that he paid out regular for the little tot.'

Hillary felt a jolt go through her. 'Sorry, what was that about grandchildren? Who's Elizabeth?'

'Elizabeth. Oh, sorry, am I not making myself clear? Elizabeth is Sylvia's granddaughter — Jerome's daughter by one of his women. She was always over here as a little girl, but I haven't seen her for ages now. Well, the mother moved away when she was only twelve or so, so I suppose that's only to be expected. She must be quite grown up by now, but I don't think she's married or had kids of her own yet. If she'd become a great-grandmother, Sylvia would have said.'

Hillary took a deep breath. 'I see. I'm surprised they didn't marry. Jerome and . . . what was her name? The mother's, I mean?'

'Ah, now you've asked me,' Geraldine said, putting down her teacup and frowning. 'Something beginning with A, I think. My word, it must be over ten years ago now since I saw her.' Her old fingers tapped the edge of her chair arm, and Hillary felt herself tense, but even before the old woman started to shake her head, she sensed she'd just run out of luck. 'No, it's no good, I can't think what it was,' Geraldine sighed. 'Audrey, maybe? No. Too old-fashioned. It was more modern than that, I think. Allison . . . No, I don't think so.'

'Alice?' Hillary proffered, trying not to sound impatient.

'No, that was my mother's name.' Geraldine smiled. 'I would have remembered if that had been it. Oh bother, it's such a nuisance to get old. Your memory's one of the first things to go, you know. I expect it'll come to me in the middle of the night or something.' Geraldine sighed. 'That's usually the way. I'll be sleeping soundly, then I'll wake up, and think, hah, *that's* her name. Subconscious working and all that.'

Hillary nodded, biting her lip. She wanted to leave her number with the old woman and ask her to call if she ever remembered it, but of course she couldn't. She sometimes had to leave her mobile turned off for hours at a time, and even someone as trusting as Geraldine Brewer would wonder why 'Ms Welles,' freelance journalist, would have voicemail for someone called DI Greene.

'You know, I have to come back to town in a few days,' Hillary lied. 'Perhaps I can call on you again?'

'Love it, my dear — I don't get many visitors nowadays. I'm in most days.'

Hillary nodded and quickly turned the talk back to Jerome Raleigh. It turned out Jerome had been only a young man on the beat when he'd fathered his illegitimate daughter. Why they hadn't married, Geraldine wasn't sure, but she thought it was the mother who'd vetoed the idea. 'Young girls nowadays,' Geraldine said, sighing. 'Like as not, they're the ones that don't want to be tied down. It was different in my day, of course.'

Apparently, though, there had been no hard feelings, for the baby and her mother had been regular visitors at Sylvia Raleigh's home for many years, with Jerome Raleigh paying maintenance without a fuss.

'I remember, Elizabeth used to have these long fair pig-tails,' Geraldine mused. 'She must have been — oh, ten, eleven then. Very smart at school she was too, I seem to recall. Sylvia showed me some of her reports once. Pleased as punch she was. Sure she was going to go on to university. Well, with Sylvia being a professional herself and all, she'd want her only granddaughter to do well, wouldn't she?'

'But you say they haven't been around lately?'

'No. I think Sylvia told me that they were moving up north. The mother had got a promotion in her job or some-thing, but it meant they had to leave London. Oh, I wish I could remember her name.'

'Presumably the little girl took her mother's maiden name?' Hillary prompted.

'Quite right,' Geraldine said. 'Sylvia was a little put out by it — wanted the Raleigh name to be perpetuated, I expect. But it's no good. I can't remember the surname either. Not Smith or Jones exactly, but nothing really uncommon either. Nothing about it that stood out.'

Hillary spent nearly an hour in the little house, and by the time she'd left, she had a notebook full of interesting data. And maybe the first inkling of why Jerome Raleigh had left the Met? Could he have moved to be closer to his family — albeit his unofficial one?

Hillary was pretty sure that keeping his daughter under very tight wraps had been a deliberate ploy on Raleigh's part, and that was understandable, for many reasons. It wouldn't have done his promotion chances any great boost for his bosses to know that he'd fathered an illegitimate daughter while still on the beat for one thing, and privacy could become a habit. Then, too, he must have felt safer knowing that villains in particular had no idea that he had a child. Sometimes having dependants could be used against a high-ranking cop, and why take the risk if you didn't have to? No, she could understand why Raleigh would want to keep his daughter a secret.

But according to Geraldine, his ex-girlfriend and daughter had left the capital some years ago. So why would that make him leave London now? Could one of them be sick, perhaps?

Hillary took the train back to Oxford, wondering if she was really any further forward, or if she was just kidding herself. Besides, what any of this had to do with Fletcher or why Raleigh had mucked up the raid so badly, she couldn't begin to say.

She might have been a lot more worried if she knew what Superintendent Jerome Raleigh was doing right at that moment.

\* \* \*

Raleigh slowly lowered the telephone and leaned back in his chair. He jumped as a knock sounded on his door, and quickly wiped the scowl off his face.

'Come in.'

His secretary entered with a folder in her hand. 'You wanted a copy of this the moment it came in, sir.'

Jerome nodded and took it from her, feeling his heart pick up a beat as he saw what it was. The final pathologist findings on the Luke Fletcher autopsy.

'Thank you, Sandra.'

His secretary nodded and left, and Jerome quickly scanned it. It was all as he had known it would be. The bullet that had killed Luke Fletcher did not match the bullet that had been taken out of Hillary Greene. So by now the brass would know that their current working hypothesis — namely, that the dead man, Brian Conroy, had shot Fletcher then tried to escape, shooting Hillary Greene in the process — was wrong. Had to be. Unless he had two guns. And Jerome didn't think that he could make that fly. So now they'd have to come up with another working theory. And when forensics finally put in their own report, and the brass learned that the gun that shot Fletcher hadn't been recovered at the farm at all . . . what would they think then? Jerome sighed heavily and his eyes fell to the phone. First that phone call from Marilyn, now this. Things were definitely coming unravelled.

Of course, he'd always known that the inquiry into the Fletcher incident would be riddled with holes, holes that would never get filled, and would irritate the hell out of the brass. That he could live with, and survive. He might not get promoted again, but that had been something he'd been willing to chance.

What Marilyn had told him, however, was another matter altogether. He'd been surprised to hear from his former girlfriend after so many years. Less surprised to hear that a reporter had interviewed her for some background to a piece they wanted to do on him. The press were like vultures, after all, and right now, he was hot news. Perhaps they were already scenting blood? Perhaps it was the fear that they might have that had prompted him to ask Marilyn to describe the journo. Perhaps just coppers' instinct.

But was he glad he had! Now he took a long deep breath and slowly closed his eyes. Although the description of a forty-something woman with a long bell-shaped cut of nut-brown hair and a curvy figure could describe many women, Jerome knew it simply had to be Hillary Greene.

What had put her on to him so fast? She couldn't have seen or heard anything that night to rouse her suspicions. He opened his eyes and sat up, shaking his head. Since when did a cop as good as Hillary Greene need reasons to know when something was off? Her sense of smell had probably been telling her for some time that her new boss needed watching.

It made him sad. Under other circumstances, having someone like her on his team would have been a dream come true.

As it was . . . He got up and slipped on his jacket. Time to do some snooping of his own. If he was to survive the next few months, he needed something on her. And quick. And since her only weak spot was that dirty dead husband of hers, that's where he'd have to start.

* * *

Hillary stopped off at HQ on her way back from the station, even though she suspected that she'd be about as welcome as a flea circus at a cat show. Her hip was playing her up after her day in London, and the first person she saw as she limped through into the big open-plan office was Frank, sitting at his desk.

Typical.

'Frank,' she said dryly, and raised an eyebrow as he jumped like a scalded cat, spilling coffee down his shirt front before turning to look at her.

'Oh, hello, guv,' he muttered. Something about the lack of a sneer made her give him a distinct double-take. He looked terrible. Well, even more terrible than usual. His tie had even more food stains on it, and his chubby cheeks had an even darker depth of stubble. Bags were gathering under his eyes, and he looked as if he hadn't changed out of his shirt for a week. But it was more than that. Along with the shambolic outer appearance, there had always been a miasma of ill will surrounding her husband's old friend and her greatest critic that was now oddly missing. For some reason, it scared her. It made her world feel out of kilter somehow. The sky was grey, her car needed exchanging for a newer model, England always lost at cricket, and Frank Ross was a right pain in the arse. And if any one of these details changed, it left her feeling wrong-footed somehow.

'You all right, Frank?' she asked sharply.

The fat shoulders shrugged. He had his back to her now, and didn't look around. Worse yet, there was no sarcastic comeback. What the hell was eating him? It surely couldn't all be put down to the fact that Janine Tyler had been put in working charge of the Malcolm Dale case.

As if thinking about her had summoned her up, Janine Tyler's voice suddenly cut through the air as she entered the office. She was talking to Tommy. 'I think we'll have to get McNamara back in. He's . . . Oh, hello, guv,' she added, with a distinct lack of enthusiasm as she spotted Hillary sitting in her old place. A look of panic crossed her face and Hillary quickly held up a hand in appeasement.

'Just touching base. I'm off home in a minute,' she reassured her quickly.

'You shouldn't be here at all,' Mel added, poking his head out of his cubicle. 'How the hell are you supposed to heal if you keep dragging your sorry carcase in here?'

Hillary's lips twisted into a smile. It was so nice to be home.

# CHAPTER TWELVE

'Thanks for the welcome wagon,' Hillary said wryly, eyeing her boss and old friend warily. He looked as if he hadn't slept properly for a week. She turned her attention to Janine, and lifted an eyebrow. 'You were saying about McNamara?'

'This isn't your case anymore, Hill,' Mel said, before Janine could speak. 'Why don't you go home and get some rest. You look like hell.'

'You say the nicest things to me. But you know I'll sleep easier if I get to hear all the latest first, so be nice.'

Mel rolled his eyes, but shrugged.

Janine, not looking best pleased, heaved a massive sigh, seeing the writing on the wall. Why couldn't DI Greene keep her big nose out of it? This was *her* case now! Reluctantly, the young blonde woman tossed her bag on her chair and sighed. 'I was just saying, with the mad shoe salesman out of it—' she managed to say this without gritting her teeth or blushing, '—I think we should take a closer look at McNamara. I was talking to one of those Tory biddies this morning, and they think McNamara's chances of getting the nomination to run as their candidate have skyrocketed since Dale's death. They even expect him to win the seat itself, since, according to their polls or whatever, they're almost certain to get a "sympathy"

162

vibe going. Apparently, when someone dies in the saddle, so to speak, it brings out the loyalty in voters. Or so she said.'

Hillary sighed. 'It seems a bit far-fetched to me. It's not as if McNamara was overly ambitious. Or at least, he didn't come across that way to me.'

Janine shrugged, unconvinced. Now that she'd had to rule out her prime suspect, she wanted another lead to follow, and fast. She could feel the case stagnating underneath her, and she was damned if it was going to happen on her watch. She needed a result, dammit. 'Well, there's not much else to go on, guv,' Janine said mutinously, shooting a poisonous look at Mel as she did so, fully expecting him to back her up. She'd moved out most of her stuff from his place yesterday, and was feeling the loss keenly. The bastard owed her!

Already the small semi she shared with her three friends seemed awfully cramped. So Mel could bloody well help her out at work.

'The wife inherits under the will, but she's got such a rich and doting daddy, I just can't see that going across to a jury as a believable motive,' Janine continued, holding out her hand and ticking off her fingers one by one. 'For another thing, the final reports are through on the autopsy, and they think that there's no way she could have bumped him off and still be placed at the scene where she had her flat tyre. Even taking the time she arrived at the bridge party as a final indicator, they still think he died later. So she's out of it. He has no obvious enemies that we've been able to find, no hidden vices that might have led him astray, and house-to-house have come up with squat. So what's left?'

'Any word on his business?' Hillary asked, without much hope. She'd have heard if there had been.

'No,' Janine said flatly, glowering at Hillary. 'Fraud have taken a look at his books and finances. Squeaky clean. Also, he has no business rivals to speak of — let's face it, the world of sporting equipment isn't exactly cut-throat.'

'There's still the GP girlfriend,' Tommy put in, 'and her hubby.'

Hillary nodded. 'How did you get on with them?'

Janine opened her mouth to object, then closed it again, knowing it would be pointless. When Hillary Greene got the bit between her teeth, there was no stopping her. It was a quality Janine respected, except when it trampled all over her! Instead, she contented herself with tapping her foot impatiently but loudly as Tommy brought Hillary up to date on his findings.

No one had seen Larry Knowles at his local pub on the night of the murder, so it seemed Gemma Knowles had got it wrong when she said that she thought he'd been out that night. It made collusion between them less likely, in Hillary's opinion. People who plotted murder together usually got their stories and alibis down pat.

Unfortunately, Tommy went on, nobody saw either of the Knowleses' cars in Lower Heyford on the night in question, or either of the Knowleses themselves. Furthermore, the fingerprints found in the Dales' kitchen and still unaccounted for belonged to neither of them. Janine had had them both fingerprinted yesterday.

'Which is why I think we should concentrate on McNamara,' Janine reiterated stubbornly. 'And get him printed right away.'

'He's a solicitor, right?' Mel said warily. 'He could turn shirty, stand on his rights.'

'Solicitors aren't exempt,' Janine snapped.

'Never said they were,' Mel said, with the air of a man getting used to practising his long-suffering patience. 'Just tread carefully is all I'm saying, and explain that we need them for elimination purposes only. And if he still refuses to be printed, or calls in a brief, then we'll start looking at him with a more beady eye.'

'Right, guv,' Janine said, and glanced significantly once more at Hillary. The sentiment *'Are you still here?'* couldn't have been made more plain if she'd spoken it out loud. Hillary smiled mirthlessly and got to her feet.

\* \* \*

She'd made herself some scrambled egg on toast for her tea, and was sitting in the boat's only armchair, the tray balanced on her lap, when she suddenly noticed it.

The Dick Francis book wasn't on the shelf with all the other paperbacks. A mouthful of food seemed to stick in her throat, and she had to force herself to swallow hard to get it down. Slowly, telling herself not to panic, that it had probably fallen on to the floor when a passing craft had gone by too fast and rocked the boat, Hillary slid forward and got on to her knees, setting the tray to one side. The wound in her hip twinged painfully as she did so.

Carefully, she scanned the meagre rows of books, wondering if she could have moved it from its usual place without realising it. But none of the other well-read classics were out of place. She quickly glanced behind the small radiator, then on the floor all around. No book.

It was definitely gone.

Shaking now, she levered herself back on to the chair. Her hands felt cold. Then she got up and grabbed her keys from the hook by the sink and made her way up the narrow corridor to the prow of the boat.

Outside, the wind had got up, and dusk was falling. She had to be careful how she picked her way along the dark towpath, watching out for the ropes of moored craft that could often trip the unwary.

Puff the Tragic Wagon started first go, but as she pulled out of the tiny village of Thrupp on to the main road, she felt curiously disembodied; she couldn't quite feel her feet on the pedals of the car and the noise of traffic sounded muted, as if she'd succumbed to a head cold. Travelling into Oxford, she was going against the rush-hour traffic that was streaming out, and so made good time. Soon she was parked in a rapidly emptying St Giles, and making her way to her favourite internet café.

She had memorized the numbers to her husband's hidden bank account many months ago now, and once seated inside with a cup of cappuccino, had no trouble logging on.

As she did so, she thought of Frank Ross and his strange behaviour and gave a mental head-shake.

Ross had known and been friends with Ronnie Greene long before Hillary met him and married him, and nobody doubted that Ross, to a very much lesser degree, had benefited from Ronnie's illegal animal parts smuggling operation. Was it possible the poisonous little git had finally found his old friend's hidden stash?

As she manipulated the keyboard and waited, heart pounding, for the bank's logo to pop up on the screen, Hillary felt slightly sick. If Frank *had* found Ronnie's hidden bank account, he wouldn't have looked scared, would he? Or at least not subdued, not worried. He'd be over the moon, gloating and full of beans, surely?

The screen asked for Ronnie's password, one that she'd been able to guess from the fake quotation, supposedly written by herself, on the paperback's inside page. She typed it in quickly, made a mistake, and forced herself to take a deep breath and do it again. Then she waited, her heart pounding.

The screen went blank, then popped up with all the details of the account. All those noughts. The money was still there. Hillary wasn't aware that she'd been holding her breath until she felt it rush out of her in a wave of relief. Or was it relief? All at once, she had a sudden insight that, sitting there in the aromatic warmth of the café, part of her had been hoping it would be gone. At least then the question of what to do with it wouldn't still be hanging over her.

Although she had never touched a penny of it since discovering it, and the mere thought of spending any of it had made her feel sick, she was only human after all, and the knowledge that she had access to over a million quid had been a satisfying one. The thought that she'd have money 'just in case' had made her feel secure. Even so, on more than one occasion she'd almost convinced herself to give the whole lot away to some charity or other. Once, she'd almost told Mel that she thought she might have discovered where her crooked late husband's ill-gotten gains might be stashed, and asked him to let the brass take over. But she'd never done it.

Now, sitting in the café, staring at the screen and thinking about the missing book, she knew that this was it; the luxury of prevarication was finally over. It was crunch time.

Someone had been on her boat. Someone had taken the book. Maybe Frank, but probably not. If he'd found it, surely he'd be on his way to Acapulco by now.

Maybe Gary, her stepson, had taken the Dick Francis book. It had been Gary who'd given it to her in the first place. What if he'd got around to thinking about it more deeply and realised its true significance? After all, he knew his father well, and knew how he'd thought, the same as Hillary.

Her finger hovered over the keys. It would be so easy to simply press a few buttons and transfer it all — to set up her own numbered account in the same bank and use a different password. The money would be safe then, and who'd know?

Except then, of course, she'd be as dirty as her husband had been. Right now, she was a righteous copper. OK, so she'd found the money and hadn't yet reported it, which didn't exactly put her on the side of the angels. But that was not the same thing as actively seeking to keep it.

What the hell was she going to do?

Then a very nasty thought suddenly hit her. What if it wasn't Frank or Gary who'd found it. What if it was Paul Danvers?

Slowly, Hillary leaned back in her chair. When Ronnie had died in a car crash, and evidence about his illegal activities had come to light, York had sent down two detectives to investigate the corruption. Danvers and another, even more experienced officer, who'd made it his life's work to catch bent coppers. They'd quickly uncovered evidence of Ronnie's guilt all right, but hadn't found a scrap of evidence against her, simply because there hadn't been any. She and Ronnie had been estranged for years, and she would have turned the bastard in herself if she'd known what he'd been up to. Frank Ross had been lucky to escape going down too.

Ronnie simply hadn't trusted him enough to allow him to be implicated, which is why the investigation hadn't been able to officially link Ross to Ronnie's schemes. But everybody knew Ronnie had bunged dosh Ross's way from time to time.

After the inquiry had been wound up, Danvers had transferred from his York HQ down to Thames Valley — ostensibly in search of promotion. But he'd tried to keep close to Hillary, even inviting her out, before she'd made it plain that that simply wasn't going to happen. Once or twice she'd wondered if the operation to find Ronnie's loot was still going on — only this time undercover. It had always seemed too much of a coincidence that Danvers should turn up at her own nick, only months after the investigation had supposedly been concluded.

So far she'd been half-convinced that it was just paranoia on her part. But what if it wasn't? What if undercover officers from another force were even now watching her, waiting for her to make her move? Just the thought of it brought her out in a cold, cold sweat.

She glanced around the café, but saw only students, kids playing games, and some more serious-looking older men and women, probably doing projects that were work-related. But barring the kids, any one of them could be undercover.

Hillary almost laughed out loud. It was no good. If she felt this guilty just sitting here looking at evidence of her husband's greed, what the hell would she feel like if she actually touched the money — even if only to transfer it? In her heart of hearts, she didn't really think Danvers or any team was watching her. She thought her radar would have let her know.

But even so, they *might* be. And she simply couldn't go to jail. Cops in jail didn't live long — or if they did, they came out as twisted as corkscrews.

Suddenly Hillary felt extremely stupid. Just what the hell was she doing here? This wasn't her. This fear, this guilt, this indecision. What did any of this have to do with her, or with her life?

With a grunt, she came out of the website and pushed her chair back. She had better things to do — like find Dale's killer and discover just what the hell her super was up to.

* * *

When she got back to the boat, a visitor was waiting. For just a second, as a dark shape moved out of the shadows lining the towpath and stepped in front of her, she half-expected to hear Paul Danvers' voice arresting her on suspicion of profiteering. Instead, Mike Regis's voice sounded calm and warm and blessedly normal in the dark night.

'At last! I was thinking of giving up and going home.'

Hillary swallowed the bile back down, swore viciously and then laughed just a shade hysterically. 'Sorry — bad night,' she said, as she sensed Regis's surprise. 'Come on in — I've got a bottle of wine in the fridge.' That and a tub of margarine and a head of lettuce going brown. But who was going to offer him dinner?

'Sounds good to me.'

He duck-walked under the low door and followed her down the length of the boat, glancing around as he did so. He'd been on her boat before, and it still felt as claustrophobic now as it had then. 'Take the good chair,' Hillary said, indicating the armchair. 'There's a deckchair under the foldaway table. I'll have that.'

But when she returned with two glasses of Chardonnay, he was sitting in the deckchair. 'Injured heroes get priority,' he said, accepting the glass.

Hillary sat with a shrug. 'So, what's up?'

'They found a secret exit,' Regis said, taking a sip and wincing. He was a red-wine man himself.

'Huh?' Hillary said blankly.

'At the farm. Fletcher's place. In the kitchen, there was a secret door — a real Heath Robinson affair hidden behind an Aga. The Aga doesn't work, obviously, but a section of the brick wall behind it swings out enough to let someone get

169

into the barn next door. SOCO found it not long ago. The fact that the Aga seemed so movable gave it away, apparently.'

Hillary sipped her wine, thinking it through rapidly. 'So they think someone got away that night, out the bolt-hole? Shot Fletcher and legged it, while our attention was on good old Brian Conroy outside, shooting me?'

Regis shrugged. 'It's a possibility.'

Hillary snorted. 'Not much of one. How'd he get out of the barn without being seen? And didn't the Tactical Unit have somebody under guard in there?'

'The Scouse driver,' Regis agreed. 'But he was in the second barn along.'

'Still,' Hillary said. 'Are they really saying that someone shot Fletcher, got out of the kitchen through the secret door, and then somehow magically slipped away into the night without anyone — us or Tactical — seeing him legging it? Do me a favour.'

'Then there's the question of the missing gun,' Regis said, and filled her in on that too. 'So the bullet that killed Fletcher didn't match any gun there,' Regis concluded, 'be it a cop's gun or that of a gang member, or one of the Scouse drug runners. So unless someone did manage to get away, taking the gun with him, I don't know how the hell else it *could* have happened,' the Vice man said.

Hillary stared at Regis for a long time in silence. This was a night for shocks. First of all the missing book, now this. 'Something's off,' she said finally.

Regis sipped some more of his wine before finally agreeing. 'It was a bit of a dog's dinner,' he said, reluctant to admit that she was right. 'But the result was good. There'll be no squaddie on the streets of Oxford, or at least not just yet,' he qualified, with typical Vice pessimism, 'and Fletcher, the bastard, is as dead as the proverbial doornail. So what's wrong with that?'

Hillary shook her head. There was nothing wrong with that. Any of that. Except that something was off. And she'd been shot, dammit.

* * *

Next morning she couldn't resist going in to work again before heading back to London. Janine and Tommy were out, presumably rousting McNamara for his fingerprints, and Mel came out as soon as she walked in, shaking his head. 'Just can't leave the place alone, huh?'

Hillary shrugged. 'I'm only staying a minute. Besides, I had a visit from Vice last night,' she said, following him back into his office, and quickly told him the latest. Mel, who wasn't on the investigation team into the Fletcher shootout, and wished like hell that he was, listened avidly. When she'd finished, he too was sceptical.

'I don't get it. How could someone shoot Fletcher and then leg it without us seeing him? But if there was a hidden way out of the kitchen . . . I suppose, when you were shot and we were all gathered around you someone could just have managed it if he . . . Oh, hell, here's trouble,' he added, looking over her shoulder as the door opened.

Hillary didn't bother turning her head to look. She knew who it must be. 'Guv,' Frank Ross said. 'Looks as if the Fletcher thing is sorted at last. About time too, if you ask me. You'd think somebody had shot the prime minister instead of some bloody dealer, the fuss they've been making.'

'Come in, Frank, and shut the door,' Mel sighed, and Hillary watched as the fat sergeant walked in and flung himself cheerfully into a chair. He looked almost hyper now, and so damned pleased with himself that Hillary felt sick. What was with the dipstick? Down as a sick dog one day, and looking like he'd won the bloody lottery the next.

'Yeah, I heard about the secret door. Behind the Aga, wasn't it?' Mel said, happy to see the sergeant's face fall. He mightn't be in on the investigation, but it didn't hurt Ross to know that he had eyes and ears everywhere.

'The super says they'll be wrapping things up now,' Frank muttered, shooting Hillary the usual gimlet eye. He even managed to put some sneer into it.

Nice to have some things back to normal.

'Well, since you've finished fooling about upstairs, you can get back to some real work,' Mel snapped. 'Anti-hunting lobby. Anybody have it in for Malcolm Dale?'

'Not in particular, guv,' Frank whined. 'I think it's a blind alley. I mean, if they didn't pop off fox hunters when it was legal, why bother bopping them off now?'

Mel sighed, secretly thinking the same thing. 'Well, get out there and see if Dale had any specific run-ins with any of them when he *was* hunting, then. And check with records — see if any particularly violent animal libbers have just got out of jail. It could be he pissed someone off, and they only now had the opportunity to get some payback.'

Frank Ross hauled himself to his feet and went off, muttering under his breath.

'He seems chipper again, don't he?' Mel said dryly, doing his atrocious Bugs Bunny impersonation. 'Seems to put a lot of store in his new best pal, Superintendent Raleigh. Hill, what the hell gives there? Can you figure it?'

Hillary automatically shook her head, but, in truth, it was possible that she might have a glimmering of an idea why Raleigh seemed so pally with the office leper. The only trouble was, the more she thought about it, the less she liked it.

\* \* \*

As she walked slowly across the reception on her way out, heading towards the large glass external doors, Hillary felt the hairs go up on the back of her neck, and quickly looked around. Then she relaxed. Walking towards her, smiling a greeting, was Marcus Donleavy.

'Hillary, surely you're not back to work yet?'

Hillary smiled wryly. 'Not officially, guv, no. But the Malcolm Dale case seems stalled.'

Donleavy nodded. That was the thing about coppers like Hillary — the best ones were always relentless. 'Any ideas?' He had a vague overview of all the prominent cases in his remit, and he was glad Hillary was still working on this one. Even if she was doing it on the sly.

'Not really, sir,' she said. 'I've been distracted.'

'Oh?'

For a second, Hillary was tempted to confide in him. It would be easy enough to go for a coffee somewhere and drop some gentle hints about what was bothering her. She knew Donleavy was a good cop, and trusted him — up to a point. But at the last moment, innate caution got the better of her. After all, what did she really have to go on? Frank Ross's odd behaviour, cock-ups that shouldn't have happened in the Fletcher bust, and evidence that just didn't make sense? She needed more than that.

'Oh, nothing specific, sir,' she lied. 'I guess the shooting took more out of me than I thought.'

Marcus nodded, not believing it for a second, and walked with her to her car. It was a nice morning and the sun had some real warmth to it at last, but as Chief Superintendent Donleavy watched one of his favourite detectives drive away, he was not a happy man.

Something was bothering Hillary Greene and it didn't take a genius to guess what it was. Something reeked about the Fletcher bust, but none of his superiors were too interested in finding out what. And although nothing was official yet, with the finding by SOCO of the secret door into the barn, the writing was on the wall. Fletcher was killed by a gang member who then absconded, taking the murder weapon with him.

He supposed it could have happened that way. But he guessed that Hillary Greene was being kept in the know about the bust, which in itself wasn't unusual. Coppers who got shot during a raid were entitled to know what was happening, and one way or another, they tended to be told.

And if she wasn't happy with it, then it bore watching.

# CHAPTER THIRTEEN

If Geraldine Brewer was surprised to see her visitor back again so soon, she showed no signs of it when she opened the door and smiled a welcome. 'Oh, it's you back again, dear. Come on in, I've just made a Victoria sponge.'

Hillary followed the old lady into her home, and accepted the delicious offering without a second thought. Well, maybe just one thought — namely, that if she forgot about lunch, perhaps it wouldn't be so bad.

'I still haven't remembered the name of Sylvia's daughter-in-law,' Geraldine warned her the moment they were both seated and sipping tea. 'Well, not strictly her daughter-in-law, since they never married, but nowadays, it amounts to the same thing, doesn't it?'

Hillary sighed and nodded. It was no more than she expected, of course, but perseverance was something she'd come to rely on during her years in the force, and there was always room for yet more persistence.

'So, tell me what you do remember about her,' Hillary said brightly. 'For instance, was she younger than Jerome, do you think?'

'Oh, not much. Not so's you'd notice. I reckon they were much the same age.'

Hillary nodded. 'And was she pretty in your opinion?' She didn't really need to know any of this, but once a witness was relaxed and got in the habit of talking, it was surprising what you could pick up.

'Well, I always thought she was too skinny for my taste. Blonde, though, and blue eyes. Men always seem to fall for that, don't they?'

Hillary, thinking of her philandering husband, grunted. 'Don't they just,' she murmured.

During the night, she'd had one or two thoughts about how she might track down Jerome Raleigh's secret family, and now she smiled and took a big bite of cake, eyes narrowing in bliss. Just how was it that old ladies could always get sponges so nice and fluffy, but whenever she tried it, they came out like doorstops? 'So, where did the little girl — Elizabeth, I think you said her name was — go to school? Was it the primary school around here?'

'Oh no, dear, I don't think so. She'd have gone to whatever school was nearest to her mother's place, I expect. Jerome and the mother never lived together, you see, far as I know.'

Damn, Hillary thought. Bang goes that avenue.

'And do you remember if Elizabeth's mother met another man? Was that why they split up?'

'Don't think so, dear. It was the job, like I said, made her move up north.'

'So you don't remember the name of any man Sylvia might have mentioned. You know, the man who finally ended up with her son's girl, that kind of thing?'

'No, but I do have some photos. I've been thinking about it, ever since yesterday. Would you like to see?'

Hillary would, but it turned out that the only relevant photograph Geraldine had was of her friend, Sylvia Raleigh, holding her granddaughter as a baby. It had the slightly faded quality of old photographs — even though it had only been taken in the late eighties, early nineties. Hillary studied the snapshot carefully. The old lady, Jerome's mother, was framed in what looked like a stone arched doorway. A church, maybe? Yes, come to think of it, the baby was dressed in a flowing white shawl, far too intricate for everyday wear. She felt her heart give a sudden leap. 'Was this taken at her christening, by any chance?' she asked casually.

'Yes, yes, it was, now I think about it,' Geraldine said, looking at the photograph again. 'I took this snapshot with an old camera of mine, after all the official photographs had been taken. Not that I'm much good with a camera, really.'

'Can you remember the name of the church?' Hillary asked, and saw the old lady's face fall.

'Sorry, I can't. It wasn't our local church, you see, St Thomas's, but the mother's local church. It was over in Islington somewhere, I think. Or was it . . . no, I'm pretty sure it was Islington.'

Which meant it was probably in Notting Hill, Hillary thought wryly. This was not good. She needed either the name of a specific church, or the surname of mother or child. 'She looks very proud,' Hillary murmured, smiling down at Sylvia Raleigh's faded face. 'Who were the godparents, do you know?' she asked, without much hope.

Geraldine suddenly laughed. 'You know, it's funny you asking me that! I don't remember the name of the godfather — I think it was an uncle of the mother's family or something — but the name of the godmother stuck in my mind because it was so unusual. Ophelia Gosling. Can you imagine?'

Hillary laughed. 'No wonder you remember it,' she agreed, and now that she had something solid to work with, accepted a second slice of cake and another cup of tea in celebration.

* * *

If Ophelia Gosling had married since being godmother to Jerome's baby daughter, Hillary knew her chances of finding her were remote. But sometimes luck smiled down on her, and the first O Gosling in the Islington phone book was answered by a woman, who did indeed answer to the name of Ophelia. Intrigued by Hillary's polite but circumspect request to meet, she chose a small café nearby, and Hillary agreed to be there within the hour. She took the Tube and found the café easily, but had to wait a nerve-wracking quarter of an hour before a middle-aged woman, dressed in a silver and maroon caftan, walked in.

Hillary had no doubt, after one look at the wild orange hair and chunky silver and amber jewellery, that this was Ms Gosling. She half rose, catching the woman's eye, and smiled as she walked across the small room. She was the kind of large woman who immediately drew the eye, and she was obviously well known in the small café, for the waitress nodded, and mouthed something to her. Ophelia Gosling nodded, then sat down opposite Hillary, eyeing her openly.

'Can't say I get many mysterious phone calls asking for meetings nowadays,' she said by way of greeting, seating herself into a chair that groaned under her weight. 'You a copper?'

The question came out sharply, and Hillary smiled. So much for keeping up the journalist fiction. Women like this could spot the law a mile off. 'Let me guess,' Hillary mused, eyeing her thoughtfully. 'Greenham Common or USAF Upper Heyford?' She had the look of one of those women who protested against nuclear-armed fighter planes on British soil. Or maybe she was a tree-hugger and by-pass saboteur.

'Both, actually,' Ophelia Gosling said coolly.

Hillary nodded. 'Well, the Yanks are gone from Upper Heyford,' she said, tacitly admitting that she was, indeed, a copper. Though she'd never had to police the CND marches or protesters of the eighties.

'But not from Lakenheath,' Ophelia shot back, then grinned. 'Still, I like you. You've got a good aura. Strong.'

Hillary blinked. Oh goody. One of those. 'Thank you.'

The waitress came to the table with a tray laden with some kind of muesli bars, a dish of dried apricots soaking in water, and a big carafe of what smelt like very dodgy herbal tea. Hillary gave a silent prayer of thanks for Geraldine Brewer's sponge cake, and declined all offers to partake of the tray.

Ophelia poured herself a large glass of the tea and took an apricot to nibble. 'So, what can the plod want with me? I'm not wanted for anything — well, not last time I looked anyway.'

Hillary grinned. 'Nothing like that. I just need a bit of information.'

'I'm not a grass.'

'Never thought you were. And like I said, I'm not after anybody. I'm just trying to trace a missing child.'

'Ah, well, that's different,' Ophelia said at once. 'Who, and how do you think I can help?'

And with those simple but genuine words, Hillary suddenly found herself liking this woman very much. 'Can you cast your mind back to the late seventies, early eighties? You were godmother to a baby girl called Elizabeth.'

'Lizzie Burns? Good grief you're right. Haven't thought of her in — oh, ten, twelve years. Just shows what an irresponsible godmother I turned out to be. Typical of Alicia for asking me. Wonderful girl, but a rotten judge of character.'

Hillary smiled. 'Elizabeth Burns. Her father was Jerome Raleigh, right?'

'Right. Another copper. Don't know what Alicia saw in him. Well, I do, he was tasty. But still the plod.' Her large blue eyes suddenly narrowed. 'Nothing's happened to Ally has it? Or little Liz?'

'Not that I know of,' Hillary said, truthfully enough. 'I just need to get in touch with them. I don't suppose you have an address where I could reach them?'

'Good grief, no,' Ophelia said. 'It's been yonks. And I don't think I'd give it to you, even if I had,' she added flatly. 'But I lost touch with Ally when she moved to Sunderland. Bloody awful place to move to, if you ask me, but she would go. I used to send Christmas cards for the first few years, but then she moved again, and I lost the address. You know how it is. Lizzie must be grown up now. I wonder how she turned out?'

Hillary wondered too. And wondered if Alicia Burns and her daughter had moved to Oxford any time recently.

'Well, thanks a lot. You've been most helpful,' Hillary said, starting to rise.

'Yes,' Ophelia Gosling said slowly. 'That's what I was afraid of.'

Hillary couldn't help but burst into laughter.

'Seriously, though, I haven't dropped them in it, have I?' Ophelia asked anxiously.

'Why do you think you might have?' Hillary asked, genuinely curious. 'Was your old friend Ally likely to get her collar felt by the plod?'

Ophelia snorted. 'Hell, no,' she laughed. 'Middle-class respectable through and through. The most daring thing she ever did was have a child out of wedlock. That was about as much of a rebel as it got with Ally.' Ophelia's blue eyes twinkled. 'So, why are you trying to find them?'

'I just need to ask them something relating to a recent inquiry. Nothing to worry about, I promise.'

Ophelia Gosling snorted, her large chest rising and falling with the effort, silver and amber jewellery clanking. 'Right! And we know how much a copper's word is worth.'

Hillary shrugged. 'About as much as a politician's,' she agreed cheerfully.

And this time, it was Ophelia who burst into laughter.

\* \* \*

It didn't take her long to track down the church where one Elizabeth Burns had been christened. The rector, a young man still eager to help, had gone through the records himself, and came up with date of birth and confirmation of the surname.

Hillary, resolutely ignoring lunch, found an internet café and trawled the public databases. Armed with both first name, surname and date of birth for Jerome Raleigh's daughter, she quickly pulled up her birth certificate. It did indeed name Jerome Raleigh as the father, and Alicia Margot Burns as the mother, so there had obviously never been any of this 'father unknown' business. Which seemed to confirm the honest and friendly nature of Jerome and Alicia's relationship.

While she was there, she trawled the database for the marriage registers, but Elizabeth Sylvia Burns had, so far, not married. She probably considered herself to be far too young, just yet. Hillary paused for a moment, then punched in the name of Alicia Burns. She had never married either. Surprising, that. Most women, even the wary, still tended to get married at least once in their lives. Perhaps Alicia Burns was one of those rare women who were able to learn by other people's mistakes.

Of course, she might have died. That would be one reason why she never married. It might also explain why Jerome Raleigh had moved to Oxford. Although she'd be fully grown now, Elizabeth would have felt the loss of a mother keenly if she had died, and might have contacted her father for some support and succour.

Hillary quickly tapped into the registry of deaths, but when she typed in Alicia's details, no record came up. More out of the habit of thoroughness than anything else, Hillary typed in Elizabeth's name next and almost spat out her mouthful of coffee all over the screen when it popped up with the relevant details.

Elizabeth Sylvia Burns had died on 13 March 2013, at the age of twenty.

Hillary stared at the screen, her mind racing. There might be more than one Elizabeth Burns in the world, of course, but surely not someone born on the same day as Jerome's daughter? With a hand that was shaking now, Hillary put her coffee cup back down and hit the keyboard to go through the procedure a second time.

But it was definitely the right Elizabeth Burns.

For a moment, Hillary simply sat there and stared. Twenty was an awfully young age to die. She called up the death certificate again, and turned her attention to cause of death.

The medical jargon was technical and brief, but it was one that was very familiar to Hillary, since it was one that she'd seen on many a teenager's death certificate.

Elizabeth Burns had died of an accidental overdose of cocaine.

\* \* \*

Back in Kidlington, Frank Ross ordered a second pint of beer and watched his quarry do the same. Nelson Bonnington, a lanky tree-hugger with delusions of grandeur, was the only animal rights activist that he'd found so far who might have been daft enough to kill Dale. His elder brother ran a wildlife sanctuary that specialized in rescuing foxes and grey squirrels, both vermin under law. Nelson was local, and had been inside once before for beating up a master of hounds at a local hunt. What's more, he had the reputation for favouring violence over peaceful demonstration.

Frank took his pint to the darkest corner of the pub and watched and waited. He wanted to see if the pillock met up with any of his buddies. If so, he might have boasted to them about doing Dale and they might just be persuaded to turn him in. In Ross's opinion, all crooks were stupid. But do-gooding crooks were the most stupid of the lot.

As he pondered buying a pork pie and a packet of crisps for his lunch, Frank hoped that it was true that the investigation into the Fletcher killing was now winding down. Rumour had it that they were about to present their findings, and certainly the boss thought so. It would be good to have the thing over and done with.

Somewhat to his surprise, Frank found himself breaking out in a cold sweat when he thought about Superintendent Jerome Raleigh. Not that he was a bad bloke or anything.

He was hard, sure. Harder even than Ronnie Greene, and that was saying something. He knew how to treat scum all right. But Ross didn't mind hard, so long as the man in question was also trustworthy. And in his opinion, Raleigh was as straight as a die. He'd look after him. The boss might be tough, but that was because he was old school. And old school knew what loyalty meant. No, he had nothing to worry about there. So why was his stomach churning as if he'd got a bad case of galloping gut rot?

* * *

Tommy Lynch was sitting in a van on the outskirts of Banbury, watching a bookies shop. The van had a pest control logo on the side but was in fact one of many undercover vehicles used by the squad. They'd had a tip-off that the bookies were going to get raided that afternoon, and Janine had put him on it, even though they were both sure it was rubbish. More likely a rival bookie had phoned it in, hoping that punters would spot the police watching the place, and take their custom elsewhere. Still, if it *was* raided, and they'd done nothing, it wouldn't look good.

Tommy would be glad when Hillary got back. Janine was driving him up the wall — carping at Mel whenever she got the chance and giving him, Tommy, all the shitty assignments. He wasn't even working on the Dale case anymore. Since McNamara had proved negative on the fingerprint match, that investigation was going nowhere fast, and everyone knew it. Janine Tyler most of all.

He sighed, and reached for his thermos to pour a cup of lukewarm tar into the plastic cup. Tommy couldn't really blame her for being so pissed off. The truth was, Janine was more than half convinced that if Hillary came back, the case would somehow get miraculously solved.

And Mel probably thought the same.

Tommy just missed having Hillary around and would have wanted her back, no matter what. And what the hell was eating Ross? Granted, the horrible little git was always obnoxious, but now he was acting like a cat on a hot tin roof as well.

Oh well. None of it was his problem. He sighed heavily and settled down more comfortably in the van.

\* \* \*

Hillary typed in the words 'Elizabeth Burns,' 'tragic,' 'drugs overdose,' and 'fatal,' and waited for the search engine to do its thing. And tried to ignore a dark, nauseous sensation that had begun tugging at her stomach.

Within moments, she was in business. The first thing she clicked on to was a newspaper article, and she felt her heart leap as the familiar logo of the *Oxford Times* filled the screen.

So, Elizabeth did have an Oxford connection.

And, as she read on, it was the obvious connection as well. Elizabeth Burns had fulfilled her grandmother's ambition that she do well at school, and had earned herself a place at St Luke's College in Oxford, to read modern history. She'd done well in her prelims, earning a 2:1, and had looked set to do well in her finals.

According to friends interviewed after her tragic death, Elizabeth Burns had been a friendly, studious, thoroughly 'normal' girl, and the last one any of her friends thought might die as a result of illegal drugs use.

Wasn't that always the way, Hillary thought glumly.

What must her father have felt, back in London, getting the phone call from Alicia, telling him that their daughter was dead? Would he have identified the body? As a policeman, he'd have known the procedure. And as a policeman, he'd have known all about the statistics relating to students and drugs.

Had he warned Elizabeth repeatedly about the dangers? Had she rebelled? Did he feel as if it was all his fault? Perhaps he'd come to Thames Valley only to try and save other Oxford students from the same fate. Perhaps that was why he'd been so mad keen to see Luke Fletcher, Oxford's biggest drug dealer, put away.

Yeah. Right.

Hillary took another sip of coffee, but it went down like acid. She was looking disaster in the face and for once, coffee and cynicism wasn't going to cut it.

As she read on, it only got worse. Elizabeth had been one of four people to die of a drugs overdose that week. One other student — a Malaysian studying engineering, a barman at a Cowley pub, and a shop assistant in a local supermarket, had all died a similar death. Pathologists confirmed that all four had died as a result of injecting from the same contaminated batch.

Cocaine, as every copper knew, was 'cut' with all sorts of things by dealers — baby milk being one of the most popular, but the list was horrendous. In her time, Hillary had come across cocaine that had been cut with household detergent, baking soda, flour, even weedkiller. Anything to bulk out the precious white grains and inflate the profit for the dealer.

But in Elizabeth Burns's case, and that of the three others who died, this particular cut had proven to be lethal.

Feeling sick at heart, Hillary logged off and left for home, the slight niggling pain in her hip all but forgotten now.

* * *

Janine pulled up in front of Mel's house, and slammed the door of her Mini behind her. She walked up the crazy-paving pathway, ignoring the weeping willows grouped around the ornamental pond, their leaves now turning lime green with the first flush of spring growth, and turned her face resolutely away from the last of the snowdrops and the earliest of the daffodils that rampaged across the immaculate lawns.

She scrambled in her handbag for her set of keys, then opened the letterbox and pushed them through viciously, scratching her palm as she did so and making herself bleed.

'Bastard,' she muttered under her breath, as she turned and walked away. From now on, she wouldn't give the sad old man another thought.

* * *

Hillary got off the train, but instead of walking to her car, headed into town. Past Carfax, she headed towards the handsome towers of Christ Church, and on the road opposite, walked through the doors into St Aldates nick.

She'd once worked out of St Aldates for a short time, many moons ago now, while still a sergeant. Her old boss had been DI David Kenwick, long since retired. But her face was known, and the desk sergeant had been a uniformed DC when she'd left.

'DI Greene, as I live and breathe,' he greeted her cheerfully. 'Sorry to hear about the bullet. Things going OK?'

Hillary obliged by giving a blow-by-blow account of the incident, knowing a copper's love for villain-taking was only exceeded by his love for gossip. Besides, she needed his help and it wouldn't hurt to keep him sweet.

'So, I'm still officially on sick leave,' she concluded with a heavy sigh, 'but you know what that's like! I'm bored out of my skull, so I snaffled some cold cases to keep the old brain lubricated.' She tapped her head. 'Which is what brings me here. Tell me, is DI Wallace still here?'

'Wally Wallace? Not hardly — left, must be six, seven years ago now. Retired.'

Hillary knew that. Wally Wallace had lived up to his nickname well, and was probably the last person she'd ever want to speak to. But she sighed heavily. 'Damn, I wanted to pick his brains over this cold case of mine. Don't suppose I could check with records? Who's the dragon guarding the sacred files nowadays? Do I know him?'

'Jack Findlayson,' the desk sergeant said with a grin. 'Hold on, I'll phone down, let him know you're coming. I'll put in a good word.'

Hillary smiled a thanks. Most cops had cold cases that they worried at periodically when times were slow, so she didn't think she'd be arousing too much suspicion in nosing around at another nick. But she'd have to be careful.

From her research, she knew that the initial investigation into Elizabeth Burns's death had begun right here. Later, when the exact nature and scale of the crime had come to light, Vice had got in on the act. But she was reluctant to ask Mike Regis for a favour, especially now. Besides, the last thing she wanted was to involve another department. Even though she was sure that she could trust Regis to keep his mouth shut, he was too good a copper not to put two and two together if she suddenly started nosing around one of Vice's old cases, and Hillary wanted to keep this strictly in-house.

After all he'd gone through, and no matter what the outcome, Jerome Raleigh was entitled to do his grieving in private.

'Go right on down — remember the way?' The desk sergeant hung up and pointed a finger through a dingy green door. 'Black Hole of Calcutta,' he muttered darkly, although Hillary knew he was exaggerating.

Back in the old days, when she'd first started, old records really were kept in station house cellars and were crammed full of folders of damp paper mouldering away and decomposing out of sight. Nowadays, Records was a well-lit office full of computers.

A uniformed PC stood up as she walked in, but he was silver-haired and tired-looking, the kind of copper who was content to be safe and warm and work regular hours, in exchange for a PC's salary. Hillary had nothing against such men, though she knew the likes of Janine and Tommy probably scorned them. But it was people like this who kept the whole damned machinery running, as far as she could tell.

'Constable Findlayson? DI Greene,' she introduced herself and held out her hand. 'Thanks for helping me out. The sarge explained?'

'Cold cases, yeah. Help yourself.' He nodded to one of the computers, and Hillary took a seat. 'You'll have to sign out any papers, and initial photocopies in the book, ma'am,' he pointed out, and Hillary nodded. In truth, she had no intention of leaving a paper trail behind her. If things turned out as she was beginning to dread they would, the less evidence of her activities she left behind her, the more she'd like it. No, she wanted to get in and out and wrap it up, and put the whole sorry mess behind her.

She wanted to find out that she was wrong about everything; that the dark suspicions that had been eating at her ever since she'd learned how Elizabeth Burns had died were nothing more than the results of her nasty mind. And then she wanted to be able to go home and curl up by the fire, with nothing more strenuous to worry her than what to cook for dinner.

That's what she wanted.

It wasn't what she got.

# CHAPTER FOURTEEN

Hillary studied the files for a long, long time. At first, she'd automatically started off taking notes, but she'd quickly realised that she was going to have to take Xerox copies after all. Lots of them. But that would mean signing for them.

Which probably wouldn't do her career much good at all.

Desperately, she reread the files again, looking for a way out. For anything that could allow her to read the facts differently. For any scrap that could prove she'd got it all wrong. But she couldn't see one.

Superintendent Jerome Raleigh had set up Fletcher to kill him. Not to arrest him, or have the satisfaction of being the one to send him to jail. But to kill him. To outright assassinate the son of a bitch. And now that she knew it, she had to do something about it.

She reread the file yet again, looking for inspiration, knowing that she wouldn't find it.

Elizabeth's story was a common one, but no less heartbreaking for that. For a start, she wasn't a regular drug user, and was not one of those raddled, down-and-out street dwellers that most members of the public thought of when they read of drugs abuse. She'd been smart, pretty, and seemed to have it all together. In point of fact, the investigating officers had found very little signs of drug use in the young girl's life at all. No track marks on her body, no heavy stashes hidden in her college room. And from talking to her friends and peers, it became evident that Elizabeth had exhibited none of the signs or personality changes associated with long-term, seriously hooked users.

So, she'd been a so-called 'social' user then. Nothing to worry about. Everybody did it. Hillary knew that kind of thinking well. She'd probably started off down the road that eventually killed her by taking the odd E tablet at parties. Went on to try the odd line of coke or two at a private residence now and then, just dabbling here and there. She'd probably told herself that she could take it or leave it. She was young, she was at college, fun was what it was all about. And maybe she'd even have got away with it, too, Hillary thought sadly. Lots did. She might never have become seriously addicted, or fallen foul of any of the other physical risks associated with the habit, or got caught or arrested, or been expelled from college. She might have sailed free and clear, except for one night, when she'd got hold of a 'bad' dose. A casual party in another college student's rooms perhaps. A night that had probably started off as all other party nights had started off — some booze, some dancing, some pairing off. Except that for Elizabeth Burns it had ended in sickness, fitting, and, twelve hours later in the John Radcliffe hospital, death.

And three others, similarly unlucky, had joined her in death over the next week — victims of the same bad dose.

Vice had been able to track the bad batch down to a small-time dealer called Johnny 'Buster' Smithers. One of Luke Fletcher's army of boys.

Now that she thought about it, Hillary vaguely recalled this incident. Although Vice wasn't her beat, she knew a lot of her fellow officers at HQ had been particularly angry about it. Smithers had been sent down for life, and was later knifed to death in prison in a territory dispute, but Fletcher, naturally, hadn't even been hauled into court.

And now Fletcher was dead. Shot dead, in odd circumstances, by a gun nobody could find, by a perp nobody could find, while Elizabeth Burns's father had been heading the raid.

Oh yes, she was going to have to take photocopies. Put it all together and tie it all up in a neat ribbon. Proof of Elizabeth Burns's identity, the whole shebang.

But she was damned if she was going to leave a trail. Apart from anything else, after being married to Ronnie bloody Greene, she was hardly in any position to point the finger at bent cops. Besides, why should she take the shit? She'd already been shot in the line of duty; she'd done her bit. Let someone else take the flak. Someone who had the rank and had been paid to do it.

She glanced across at Findlayson, who was busy tapping away on his own keyboard. He had a stack of files beside him and was going through them one by one, obviously entering old case files on to a database. A soul-destroying task if ever there was one. At some point, surely, he'd have to go to the toilet, or nip up to the cafeteria, or wander out to give his eyes a rest and have a gossip and a fag with someone. It was simply a case of waiting him out.

Hillary kept scribbling notes, feeling more and more sick as she did so. This was bad. As bad as she'd ever known it to get — on so many levels. Cops didn't grass on cops, that was a given. And what father wouldn't want to kill the man who'd poisoned his daughter to death? She hadn't joined the cops so that she could stand in judgement on people. This shouldn't be happening to her. Self-pity and anger raged, neither winning. For two pins, she could have got up and walked out. She might even have done so if, at that moment, the records clerk hadn't got up and walked instead.

Hillary couldn't help but twist her lips into a grim smile. Was that a sign, or what?

Never give a sucker an even break.

Quick as a flash, she selected the most relevant documents and headed for the photocopier.

When Findlayson came back a few minutes later, she was sitting at the terminal, scribbling notes. She kept at it for another twenty minutes, then sighed, folded her notebook, stretched and got up. 'Well, that's me finished,' she said, slinging her bag over her shoulder. 'Thanks.'

Findlayson nodded and watched her leave. He went to her terminal and checked that she'd logged off. She had. He typed in his code and was about to switch the computer off when the red flag appeared.

Findlayson silently whistled. He'd worked in records for ten years now, and only occasionally had he seen a red flag appear. He immediately clicked on the symbol.

Flags were put in place for many reasons, but mostly they were used on 'sensitive' or ongoing files and nearly always requested the records clerk to contact a certain officer if the files were ever opened. Sure enough, an instruction appeared on the screen, giving him the name of a superintendent at HQ, and a phone number.

Findlayson wondered what was so special about an old, solved drugs case, then shrugged. His was not to reason why. He lifted up the receiver and punched the outside number and got through to the switchboard in Kidlington.

'Hello? Can you put me through to Superintendent Jerome Raleigh, please?' he asked politely.

* * *

In his office, Jerome Raleigh listened to PC Findlayson, thanked him, and hung up. Then he got up and walked restlessly to the window. He'd hoped it wouldn't come to this. With the lucky find of that secret bolt-hole behind the Aga at Fletcher's farm, he'd been sure everything would work out just fine after all. He wouldn't need Ross as a fall guy, and nobody would be any the wiser to what had really gone down that night.

For some minutes he watched the comings and goings in the car park, the movement of squad cars, the groups of young uniformed constables chatting over their fag break, the civilians parking and walking into the building, distinguishable by their nervousness or curiosity. His world. His life. But not for much longer.

Would Hillary Greene have got on to him so fast if she hadn't been shot that night? Would she have been so curious if she'd still been working on a murder case and didn't find time hanging heavy on her hands? Perhaps not. Finding the killer of Malcolm Dale would have been her top priority, he was sure.

He sighed heavily. Well, it was no good standing here playing the game of 'what if.'

It was time he got cracking. He had things to do. He was glad now, after searching her boat, that he'd come up with such a good plan B.

It sure beat the hell out of his original plan A.

* * *

Hillary went back to the internet café in St Giles to write up the report. She wanted to leave no trace of it on her office computer, and she sure as hell didn't want it on her personal laptop.

As she ordered a latte and opened up a file, she was beginning to feel as if the café was becoming a second home. Certainly the waitresses were beginning to recognise her, as were some of the regulars.

How sad was that?

For a couple of hours she solidly typed, reread and rewrote until she was satisfied she'd included everything. She even made an index for the photocopied documents. She'd toyed with the idea of waiting until she could obtain her own official copies of Elizabeth Burns's birth and death certificates, but knew that she would just be putting off the inevitable. Instead she ran copies off the internet and added them to the index.

By the time she was finished, she had a neat, carefully itemized report that charted the whole sorry story from start to finish. Some of it was speculation. For instance, she didn't know who had helped Raleigh find out so much about Fletcher's network; she had no idea who his source was. And she was pretty sure that somewhere down the line, Raleigh must have had help from inside the force, but that was somewhere she was not about to go. And how had he come to be such a sure thing to get the superintendency here in Thames Valley? Again, not something she touched on.

Hillary stared at the dark blue folder she'd bought from WHSmith before coming in here and smiled grimly. Not even the stationery could lead back to her. Of course, once the investigation started, Geraldine Brewer might come to light, and give a description of the nice reporter who'd interviewed her. As would Marilyn Forbes. And if it came to an identification, she'd be in the shit. But at least Ophelia Gosling could be trusted to keep her mouth shut, and tell the plod nothing!

Hillary almost laughed out loud. Almost.

She was probably committing professional suicide. She knew it, and still she was going to do it. Why?

Was she really such a moralist? Or was she just so pissed off that she'd been shot in the arse — well, nearly — that she was out to get revenge? Did she really care that Fletcher was dead? Didn't he deserve it after all? And just what did she have against Jerome Raleigh exactly?

None of the answers to these questions helped her out. She simply knew, as she got up with the report clutched tightly in her hand, exactly what she was going to do with it. It was really quite simple.

It was a stick of dynamite, and what did any self-respecting DI do with a stick of dynamite?

She would toss it into some other poor bugger's lap. That's what.

* * *

She waited until the night shift was coming on, then went back to HQ. She let herself in, telling the desk sergeant she'd left her bag behind. The report was carefully tucked down the back of her knickers, and it rested warm and rustling in the nape of her spine as she took the lift, not wanting to crease it by walking up the stairs.

She was careful to go to her desk and bend down, as if looking for something. She knew that HQ was monitored by CTV cameras and didn't want to get caught out in any obvious lies. When she left the big, open-plan office, however, she took the lift all the way down to the bottom floor. The mail room was deserted, as she'd expected, and she stuffed the report, now in a plain brown envelope marked 'Chief Superintendent Marcus Donleavy. Personal and Confidential' into a pile of internal mail. First thing the next morning, it should find its way to Donleavy's desk.

When she got back to Puff the Tragic Wagon, she slipped off the cotton gloves she'd worn all that afternoon when making up the report, and stuffed them in her pocket.

Then she went back to the boat and got drunk.

It wasn't until she was on her fourth glass of wine that she noticed the Dick Francis book was back on her shelf.

She stared at it for a moment. Then thought about it a lot. Then said, 'Huh,' and poured another glass of wine.

\* \* \*

Next morning, complete with her first major hangover in years, Hillary saw the in-house police doctor. Dr Franks, as opposed to Doc Steven Partridge, was not trained as a pathologist, or in forensic medicine, and was mainly on call to attend to suspects who might be ill or came in from bar fights and pub crawls with the usual cuts and bruises. He was also on call for any officer who might need him. But as well as removing beer glass from faces, and stitching up constables who got on the wrong side of Millwall supporters, he was also in charge of overseeing the mandatory medical for serving officers.

The moment she walked into his office, he knew what she wanted, and began to shake his head. 'Oh, come on, DI

Greene, it hasn't even been a week yet! I've been taking bets with some of the lads on how long you'd last and had you down for early next week. I think it was PC Grover who said you'd be in today. The pot's nearly two hundred quid. Give me a break!'

Hillary grinned. 'Sorry, Sean. Look, I'm going mad. I'm walking fine and the district nurse said the last time she changed my dressing that I was healing fast. You wouldn't want me to go doolally just over a little nick in my hip, would you?'

'Oh, perish the thought,' he drawled with a sigh. He was a tall, thin man, with nine children and a wife who was always threatening to divorce him. 'Come on then, let's look at it.' Hillary quickly stripped off her skirt, and pulled her pair of very serviceable, very clean white Marks & Sparks knickers off her hip. Franks looked at the wound, doing the usual muttering doctors did under their breath, then re-attached the gauze. 'Well, she's right. You do heal fast.'

'Good hardy peasant stock,' Hillary said. Her father had always healed fast too. 'And look — I'm walking without a stick and everything. Have been for days.'

'You look terrible,' he said.

'Too much wine,' she shot back. 'Nothing to do with the hip. Come on, if I promise to stay tied to my desk with my feet up, and send my lackeys running hither and yon while I sip tea and read reports, can I come back? Just part-time?'

'Oh, all right,' Franks said. 'I hate to see a grown DI grovel.'

\* \* \*

Mel looked up as Hillary tapped on the door to his office and walked in, flourishing the doctor's get-out-of-jail-free card. Mel read it with a cynical smile. 'Turned on the famous Hillary Greene charm, huh?'

'Never fails,' Hillary said. Now that she'd put the whole Raleigh/Fletcher thing to bed, she was feeling better. It was probably only the calm before the storm, but what the hell? At least she wasn't agonizing anymore. 'Come on, Mel, don't say you don't need me. How's the Dale case going?' she asked slyly.

Mel grunted. 'You know damned well how the Dale case is going. It's going nowhere. You realise I'll have to put you back in charge? Janine will flip.'

'Not my problem,' Hillary said bluntly. 'And you were a prat ever to make it yours.'

'Nice to have you back, DI Greene,' Mel snapped right back.

Hillary slowly sank down into the chair opposite him. 'So it's all over between you two? Officially, finally and all that?'

'It is. She moved out the last of her stuff and gave me back my key. I only hope it'll all be worth it.'

Hillary shook her head. 'All men are bastards,' she said flatly, and when Mel shot her that look, shook her head again. 'Come on, we both know you would never have tossed her out of your bed if you didn't think Raleigh was on his way out, putting you in with a chance of his job. Again.'

Mel flushed a little, then shrugged. 'Yeah, well, it looks as if the joke's on me. Word has it they're about to wrap up the Fletcher case. Put the killing down to an unknown perp, and give our beloved super no more than a slap on the wrist for being a bit previous. What?' His eyes narrowed suddenly as he saw her tense. 'What do you know?'

Hillary widened her eyes innocently. 'Me? Why should I know anything? I'm out of the loop, remember?'

'Hell, Hill, you always know everything,' Mel said flatly. 'Besides, you're wearing your poker face. You never wear your poker face unless you're hiding something.'

'Like what?'

'How the hell should I know? You're wearing your poker face.'

They both laughed, but Hillary wouldn't be drawn, and got up. 'I need to get familiar with the Dale case again,' she said. 'See what Janine's been up to. I'll bet she's been working hard.'

'She has,' Mel said, wearing his own poker face.

'I suppose I'll have to break it to her that I'm back on the case? I thought so,' she added, as her old friend gave her his hangdog look. 'It's like I said. All men are bastards.'

* * *

When she got back to her desk, Frank Ross looked up. He seemed almost relieved to see her, which made her scowl.

'Frank.'

'You back then?'

'Yes.'

Ross nodded. 'Blondie should never have been put in charge,' he grunted. 'She's out interviewing the animal rights suspect I put her on to. She'll be mad as hell to see you back,' he said, and grinned happily.

That was better, Hillary thought sourly. 'Don't you ever get fed up with being universally hated, Frank?' she asked, pulling out her chair and sitting down with a small sigh of relief.

This was better too. Back in her own chair, surrounded by old friends and enemies.

'Never, guv,' Frank grunted, and looked at her. He opened his mouth, then closed it again. No, he'd be daft to talk to her. He didn't know why the hell he'd even want to. All he had to do was keep his mouth shut. The truth was, though, however galling, that he trusted her judgement. She might be a right pain in the arse, but when it came to it, Frank couldn't think of anyone he'd trust more.

Then he shook his head and turned away. Nah, it would be daft. Like the super said, all he had to do was keep it buttoned. With Raleigh owing him so big-time, he was in clover. He might even get promoted.

Still, he glanced across at Hillary Greene and found her staring at him. Quickly he hunched his shoulders against her, as if from physical attack, and picked his teeth with a fingernail.

Hillary watched him and shook her head helplessly. She had a good idea now what was eating him and he was right to be worried. Boy, was he ever right. Then a sudden thought hit her. Perhaps it was seeing Ross hunched over so defensively like that. Perhaps her subconscious had been eating away at her without her realising it. But suddenly she was back in Bicester, outside a garden supplies office, waiting for a gun raid to get under way. It seemed like a lifetime ago now. But it all came back. Finding the gun after Tactical had left, giving it to Ross and telling him to log it into the evidence locker.

Had he, in fact, done so?

'Frank, you stupid . . .' she began, realised she was talking out loud, and quickly snapped her lips shut. Ross heard her, of course, and shot her a look, but she was already up and walking away.

\* \* \*

The evidence locker comprised a big, steel-lined room in the basement of the building, and she approached the sergeant behind the steel mesh in the kiosk, and gave her ID and badge number.

'I need to check the register,' she said flatly, her mind counting back the days to the Bicester raid, and adding, 'for the week starting the eighteenth.'

'Hey, you're back. I thought you were still off sick?' The sergeant, a big woman who'd worked as a family liaison for many years before heading downstairs, handed over the large blue evidence book that covered the date in question.

'You know how it is,' Hillary said, running her finger down the line, half expecting to find nothing. She felt, therefore, a vast shiver of relief when she noticed Frank's signature. There, sure enough, was evidence of the gun being admitted. So she'd been wrong. She'd thought for a minute that the gun from Bicester had been the gun used to kill Fletcher. That somehow Raleigh had persuaded Ross to loan it to him.

For a second, she almost closed the register and forgot all about it. For a moment. And then she had another sudden thought. One that would explain why Raleigh, right from the start, had been so pally with Frank Ross.

She glanced across to the description of the article, flipped open her notebook and wrote down the serial number of the gun, thanked the evidence clerk, and left.

She was beginning to wish she'd stayed on sick leave.

* * *

Back at her desk, she pulled up the file on the Bicester gun raid on her computer. If memory served, the gardener-cum-gun runner, had kept meticulous records of all his transactions and stock.

For several minutes she checked his list of serial numbers against the one in her notebook — and couldn't find a match. She grunted, tried not to panic, and started again. After all, the eyes tended to go batty after looking at so many numbers in succession.

But it wasn't there.

It was easy enough to guess what had happened. Raleigh had either asked, or tricked, Frank Ross into logging a different gun into the evidence locker. And a simple check would prove that the gun now resting in evidence downstairs had never passed through the hands of their Bicester gun runner.

She closed the file and leaned back in her chair. Damn. Damn. *Damn!*

All this time, she'd been trying to keep a low profile, and now it turned out that the murder weapon that had killed Fletcher had actually been in her possession for a short time. If found, it would lead straight back to the Bicester gun raid, and to one DI Hillary Greene.

Hillary glared across at Ross. Of all the stupid, idiotic pricks! 'Frank,' Hillary hissed, then stopped as she saw Janine push through the door, Tommy right behind her. And the sight of her team, as yet unaware of the potential disaster staring them in the face, killed her fury stone-cold dead.

'Well, that was a waste of time, Ross,' Janine said, scowling at Hillary as she spoke. 'The suspect has an iron-clad alibi. Apparently he was out picketing a night-time angling match, or some damned thing, when Dale got it. Boss.' She nodded to Hillary, very much as a grudging afterthought.

'Carp,' Tommy said, trying not to grin. 'Apparently, they're most easily caught at night, with a torch and a tin of spam. The spam's for the bait, not for sandwiches.'

'Yes, thank you, Constable,' Janine snapped.

Hillary managed a rather sickly grin at Tommy, who quickly looked away when Janine shot him a killer glance.

'Well, I'm back. On desk duty,' Hillary said, before Janine could interrupt. 'So, I take it another lead just bit the dust?'

Janine could feel the blood draining from her face and quickly turned away, pulling out her chair and sitting down. 'Yes, boss,' she said. So Hillary was back heading the case. Perfect. Just bloody perfect. Angrily, she opened a file on her computer and began to type out her request for a transfer.

She'd had enough of this!

Hillary, even with her mind elsewhere, could easily guess what she was doing, but before she had a chance to say anything, her phone went. She picked it up, then froze as she recognised the voice of Marcus Donleavy's secretary on the other end.

'DI Greene? Can you spare a few moments for Chief Superintendent Donleavy? He'd like to see you right away.'

Hillary took a quick breath. Damn, that was quick! She'd needed time to mull over these latest developments. But it didn't look as if she was going to get it. 'Certainly, Mrs Oliver,' she said flatly.

Ross's head jerked up at the name of Donleavy's girl Friday, and a look of real fear crossed his face as Hillary got up to go. The look she gave him did nothing to relieve it.

Mel, who'd been coming out of his office to intercept Janine, sensing that a massacre might be in the offing, also caught the name. As he drew nearer, he gave her a reproachful look.

So something *was* up, and Hillary *was* in on it.

'Do you know what Donleavy wants?' he asked sharply, but Hillary shook her head.

'No idea, guv,' she lied carefully. But as she walked up the stairs to the chief super's desk, her legs felt as if they were made of water.

It didn't surprise her that Donleavy knew she was back at work. And it didn't really surprise her that he'd guessed at once who'd written the anonymous report.

But that didn't mean that she was looking forward to the next few minutes. And if the investigation team had found that bloody gun, she was well and truly up the Swanee with paddles in short supply.

# CHAPTER FIFTEEN

When Hillary knocked on the door to the chief super's office, her poker face could have cracked concrete. Donleavy's muffled voice called for her to come in, and she opened the door, trying not to give images of Daniel, lions and dens free rein. His office wasn't large, but it had a window with a view over some residential houses; the walls were plain and white and the hard-wearing carpet was a standard beige. Someone — his wife, perhaps — had given him some large greenery in pots to brighten the place up.

Donleavy pointed to the chair in front of his desk, and she sat. On his desk was a photograph of his family, the usual array of pens, desk diary, phone and pile of reports. And, sitting right in the middle and facing her, was an open copy of her report.

Hillary barely glanced at it. She knew it was arranged to draw her eye, and to deliberately not look at it would be a dead give-away.

'Sir?'

'I thought I'd give you an overview of where we stand in the Fletcher case,' Donleavy said casually, turning a pen, end over end, on top of the table. It was a casual gesture, but

Hillary knew Donleavy only ever did it when he was either agitated or thinking furiously. Or both.

'Thank you, sir.'

'Forensics are finally finished. There was evidence that Fletcher and Fletcher alone hid in the kitchen on the night of the shooting. He had a hiding space made to look like kitchen cupboards with a false back. It was next to the bolt-hole behind the Aga.' He paused, and Hillary waited. The silence lengthened. Then she got it. So this was how he was going to play it. Tit for tat — and see what turned up. Hillary cleared her throat, trying to pretend she couldn't hear her heartbeat thundering in her ears, and swallowed hard.

'I see, sir. You say there was evidence that Fletcher hid there.' Briefly she had a flashback to that night, and Jerome Raleigh making a brief phone call on his mobile just before setting off for the first checkpoint. Had it been to Fletcher, to warn him that he was about to be raided, and that he'd better hide, pronto? It made sense. His source must have told him where Fletcher's hiding place was, or how else would the super know just where to find him?

She gave a mental head-shake, and brought her mind back to the present. Donleavy was watching her like a hawk. 'Does that mean there was no evidence of any other suspect in there with him?'

Donleavy nodded, his level grey gaze fixed on her face. 'It does.'

Hillary kept her hands perfectly still, although, like Donleavy's compulsive pen manipulation, her nerves were screaming at her to fiddle with something. 'That seems to make a second shooter rather less likely,' she said neutrally.

'It does.'

Hillary nodded. 'You said that his hiding place was next to the bolt-hole?' Donleavy nodded. 'Was it accessible from Fletcher's hiding place?'

'It was.'

'So Fletcher chose to hide, rather than make a run for it?'

'It seems so.' Donleavy reached forward and pulled her report towards him. He turned it round, read a few lines, then looked up at her. 'There's something else about Fletcher's bolt-hole that isn't general knowledge yet.'

Hillary licked her lips, which felt as dry as sandpaper and said, 'Is there, sir?'

'Apparently, it's a bit of a fiddle to put the Aga back in place once you're inside.'

Hillary had to think about that for all of two seconds, then nodded. 'I see. It's hardly likely that a perp, having just shot Fletcher and wanting to make a quick getaway, would bolt down the hole, then stop to try and put the Aga back in place.'

'He'd have to have nerves of steel, I'd say,' Donleavy agreed. 'What with Tactical stamping around, voices out in the hallway, knowing he was surrounded. It would take a cool customer indeed to take the time to put the Aga back before legging it. Human instinct being what it is.'

Hillary watched him turn a page of her report and read it. She let her gaze wander to the window. The silence was almost deafening.

'Our enquiry into Fletcher's death was about to wrap up,' Marcus carried on, almost conversationally. 'The consensus of opinion is that Fletcher was shot by either one of his own, or a mole in Fletcher's gang, possibly loyal to the Scousers who were trying to peddle the squaddie, then slipped out via the bolt-hole when attention was focused on you. Do you think that's viable, DI Greene?'

'No, sir.'

Marcus nodded. He looked at her thoughtfully, then said quietly, 'Who else have you talked to about this?' As he spoke, his pen was casually tapping the top of the report.

She knew what he was asking, of course. He was asking if she'd told anyone about Raleigh, or made a copy of the original report. But the conversation was such that they could pretend they were talking about something else. If they ever needed to.

Hillary met his gaze calmly. 'No one, sir.'

Marcus Donleavy nodded. He pulled the folder closer to him, then slowly shut it. 'That'll be all, DI Greene.'

'Sir.'

Hillary got up on legs that felt distinctly iffy, and walked to the door. Outside, she managed a smile for Mrs Oliver, then walked through the small outer office and out into the corridor. There she leaned against a wall and took long, deep breaths. That had to qualify as one of the most surreal interviews of her life. But it had got the job done. Donleavy had learned that she'd kept it all to herself, and that, if asked, she would keep her mouth shut. And she'd learned that Donleavy had had doubts about the Fletcher killing long before her report had crossed his desk. What she didn't know, yet, was what Donleavy was going to do about it. Or, if he took the report higher, what those who were above Donleavy would do about it.

But Hillary suspected that most of the brass would argue that nothing at all be done. After all, Fletcher was off the streets, and there was very little real evidence that could convict Raleigh of murder in a court of law. Far better to let sleeping dogs lie.

\* \* \*

As she walked into the office, she was aware that many people were watching her. Janine with the usual resentment, of course, and Tommy with puzzlement. Mel looked a little put out, but then he knew that she knew something that he didn't, and wasn't going to tell him. And Frank looked positively terrified.

Just then the phone went on her desk and Janine reached across to answer it. She spoke a few words, then said, 'Frank, they want you in Donleavy's office.'

Mel shot a quick glance at Hillary and swore under his breath. She'd gone chalk-white and looked scared. Mel had seen her look scared before, of course, but never like this. Perhaps it was just as well he didn't know what was going on.

Ross, trying to look casual, shrugged and got up. He walked across the now very quiet open-plan office and Hillary reached out to take his arm as they passed. 'Keep your mouth shut,' she whispered. 'Play dumb.'

Frank nodded, looking a little less terrified, and walked on. He had no idea what was going on, what his DI knew or what was going to happen next, but he knew how to do both of those things all right.

* * *

Janine Tyler watched DI Hillary Greene take the seat behind her desk and noticed that her hands were shaking. She looked a little green around the gills too. Something was up. Very much up. And the only thing she knew of that Donleavy might want to talk to both Hillary and Ross about was the Fletcher killing. Was it possible that Jerome Raleigh was gonna take a fall after all? Now that would be something — for a start, it would mean Mel might get promoted to Raleigh's slot. And now he owed her big-time.

Casually, she reached across the desk for her letter requesting a transfer and ripped it up. When she straightened up from dumping the bits into the bin, she thought she saw Hillary Greene give a wry smile. But when she looked proper, her DI's face was as bland as milk.

'Right, I want a full report on what's been happening with the Dale case,' Hillary said crisply, and Tommy reached for his meticulously kept books. It was his first time keeping the Murder Book current, and he wasn't going to blow it.

Mel, after a long look their way, reluctantly went back to his office and closed the door.

* * *

When Frank came back, they were almost through with the file and Hillary was once more up to speed on the investigation. Janine had worked hard, and had doggedly followed every lead. It was not her fault that the mystery fingerprints in the Dales' kitchen had yet to be identified, or that no new witnesses had come forward, and that no viable prime suspect was in the frame.

Hillary looked up from reading Marcia Brock's second interview notes, and nodded to Ross. 'Frank, I want a word. Janine, I want you to go back to Gemma Knowles and her husband. Interview them both together this time, see if you can trip them up on anything. Don't be scared to shake them up a bit. Tommy, go back to McNamara. See if he's thought of anything new.'

She was getting them out of the way, of course, and they both knew it. Tommy, having picked up on the undercurrents as well, looked more concerned than anything, but Janine was merely resentful. When they were gone, she pulled up a chair right beside her, and patted it. 'Sit,' she said flatly.

'I ain't a bloody spaniel,' Frank snarled, but sat.

'A spaniel wouldn't give me half so much trouble,' Hillary spat back, then noticed several looks being sent their way.

Working in an open-plan office had its good points, but it also meant people were quick to pick up on it when something was going down. 'Let's take a walk, Frank,' Hillary said. As she walked across the office she heard Mel's door open, then shut. She could also feel the curious eyes watching her as she went. No doubt, when the shit hit the fan, the rumour would go around that Hillary Greene knew about it first. Which wouldn't hurt her rep any.

Outside, she walked around the exterior of the building, to a small paved courtyard, where the smokers hung out. She stood in front of a forsythia bush, rampant with sunshine colour, and stared at it, sighing heavily.

'OK, Frank, let me tell you a story,' she said, and gave him a brief version of Jerome Raleigh and his daughter. Long before she'd finished, Frank was white and cursing.

'Now, you tell me a story. It starts the moment you went inside the Fletcher farmhouse.'

Frank rubbed the side of his face, and looked around as a DC and a WPC turned the corner, both already lighting up. One scowl from Frank was all it took to make them scarper.

'Guv, I had no idea what he was gonna do,' Ross began, staring down at his shoes. 'Tactical gave us the all-clear to stay downstairs, and Raleigh went straight to the kitchen. I stayed in the corridor, then heard voices. I went to go into the kitchen, and then heard a shot as I was on the way. By the time I went in, Fletcher was on the floor and the super was putting something in his pocket. He looked up and told me to keep quiet, and let him do the talking. I was happy to, I can tell you! By then Tactical and Regis and everyone and their granny was coming in and swarming round, asking questions. The super said me and him had been in the room next door, heard the shot, come in and found Fletcher dead. I just went along with it. Later, the super told me to just keep schtum.'

'Did you see the gun he used?' Hillary asked flatly.

'No. Why? What's it matter? He'd have got rid of it the moment he left.'

'I doubt it,' Hillary said wryly. 'Tell me about the gun from the Bicester raid, Frank.'

Ross jerked his head up, stared at her, opened his mouth, then closed it again. She could see him thinking furiously, and then the colour drained from his flabby face, leaving his deep-set eyes standing out as the only dark spots in a sea of dough. 'Oh shit,' he whispered.

'Tell me, Frank,' Hillary grated. 'Why did you hand it over to him?'

'I didn't. I lost it!'

Hillary gaped at him. Then she laughed. 'Oh, come on, Frank. You lost it? *Sorry, m'lud, I had the gun, but then I lost it. Honest.* Come on, Frank, you can do better than that! Did he buy it off you, is that it? A couple of hundred backhander, no questions asked? And you thought it would be good office politics to have the super owe you one?'

'No, guv, no, I swear,' Ross pleaded desperately. 'When we left Bicester I had it in my pocket. I made sure it was safe first,' he said, flushing, as she shot him an incredulous look. 'I meant to take it down to evidence the moment we got in, but we had to go straight to Raleigh's office for a meeting. Remember?' he asked, his voice whining now for her to believe him.

Hillary's eyes narrowed as she thought back, then she nodded. He was right. They had gone straight to Raleigh's office. Suddenly it hit her. 'Oh, Frank, please don't tell me you told Raleigh you'd lost it?'

'Course I bloody didn't! I ain't thick!' Ross snapped. Then swallowed hard as Hillary gave him a flat stare. 'No, guv. I meant, after the meeting, when I realised it wasn't in my pocket, Raleigh caught me looking for it where I'd hung my coat. I tried to bluff it out, but it was as if . . .' Frank's voice trailed off as Hillary nodded knowingly.

'As if he knew you'd lost something,' Hillary finished for him, then exploded. 'Of course he bloody well knew it! He was the one who took it. What then? Did he tell you what kind of shit you were in? Ask if you had another gun nobody knew about, maybe, that you could put into evidence as a substitute?'

Miserably, Ross nodded.

'And of course, you hadn't got one,' Hillary snorted, then slapped her forehead. 'But wait a minute, what a relief, good old Superintendent Raleigh knew of an unregistered gun you could have? Is that how it went, Frank?' Hillary was almost shouting now, and made a conscious effort to lower her voice.

'Yeah. He had to go and get it, and come back with it. I waited in his office. Then I took it down to evidence and logged it in.' Ross looked at her with a slightly more cheerful look. 'So there's a gun in evidence, so we're clear, right? I mean, it can't come back to us.'

Hillary shook her head. 'Frank, what the hell are you using for brains? Of course it can come back on us! Remember our little gardening friend kept detailed records? Including serial numbers? If the gun Raleigh used to kill Fletcher turns up, all they'll have to do is run the serial number through the database, and up will pop our little Bicester friend. And the fact that that gun was supposedly retrieved by Tactical. Who will promptly remember that one gun was retrieved after they were gone. They'll check the evidence books for date and timeline and guess whose signature they'll find, logging in a rogue gun?'

Frank sat down abruptly on the raised bed nearest to him, crushing some pink and purple polyanthus under his fat backside. He looked as if he were about to cry — a sight that would be enough to unnerve anybody. 'He was going to set me up for it, wasn't he? If it all went pear-shaped?' Frank shook his head. 'The bastard.'

'Don't have kittens just yet, Frank,' Hillary said sourly. 'What exactly did Donleavy ask you just now?'

'Just the usual. Going over the night again. I told the same story Raleigh told. What does Donleavy know?'

'Enough to put Raleigh in the frame. And you too, if you stick to the same story. Which is why you're going to change it, right now. You're going to go upstairs, tell Donleavy me and you had a chat, and that I recommended that you tell the truth this time. Then you tell him that you weren't there when the shot was fired, but that Raleigh asked you to say you were. You agreed because he was your superior, and Raleigh gave you some cock-and-bull about how it would help speed up any investigation if you and he could back each other up.'

Frank swallowed hard. 'I'll be suspended. Almost certainly fired. I'll lose my pension for sure, maybe even be had up for aiding and abetting, and who the hell knows what else, if they charge Raleigh with it. Guv, I can't go inside!'

'I don't think it'll come to that,' Hillary said quietly, but with something so sure in her voice that Ross quickly looked up at her, sudden hope flooding his face.

'Guv? You think they'll cover it up?' Ross asked. Then went on before she could answer, 'Yeah, course they will. I mean, who cares that Fletcher's dead? They've got reasonable evidence that someone in his gang did it, right?'

Hillary turned away, feeling sick to her stomach. That Ross could also be so sure that their senior officers would be so quick to do a whitewash made her feel ill. She herself was almost convinced that Marcus Donleavy for one wouldn't let it happen without at least some sort of fight. And if he asked her to, she'd back him up. If she really had her back to the wall, she'd have no other option. She just didn't think it would come to it. But why tell Ross that, and let the miserable little worm off the hook just yet? Let him wriggle.

* * *

When she got back to her desk, she reread the Dale file from front to back for a second time, but it was hard to concentrate. Mel came out and started across towards her, but the look she gave him cut him off at the knees and he went back to his office again.

Ross, after speaking to Donleavy and amending his statement, had probably made tracks to the nearest pub, because he had the good sense not to show his face back in the office. Janine came back, with nothing to report on the GP and her husband, and within a quarter of an hour, Tommy too came back empty-handed. But then she hadn't really expected anything.

Hillary sighed and closed the file, glancing at her watch. Just another hour and then she could reasonably go home. Who knows, if she slept on it, she might dream who the killer of Malcolm Dale was. Wouldn't that be nice? Even though her conscious mind hadn't been able to pay much attention to the file when she'd been reading it, her subconscious mind might have been paying attention and miraculously come up with the answer.

It had happened before.

'I think we'd better . . .' Hillary heard herself say, then suddenly stopped. A queer feeling hit her at the back of her neck, then took the breath out of her lungs. 'Well, for Pete's sake,' she heard herself say and then laughed.

Because, suddenly, she did indeed know who had killed Malcolm Dale. And why. And she could probably make a good guess with what. It was, when you thought about it, so bloody obvious. So obvious, she simply hadn't seen it.

'Boss?' Janine said sharply.

Hillary slowly shook her head. 'I'm a bloody idiot. Tommy.' She looked across at him and told him who to bring in.

* * *

Rita Matthews watched and listened as Hillary set the tape running, going through the usual spiel. Beside her, Janine sat quiet and incredulous. Tommy, she knew, was watching through the one-way glass, as was Mel.

'Mrs Matthews, you have the right to speak to a solicitor,' Hillary said for a second time, even though she'd already read Rita her rights for the tape.

'I know that. Can't afford a solicitor.'

'One can be appointed for you,' Hillary said.

'We'll see,' the old woman said, glancing at her watch. 'Is this going to take long? Only, you know what my husband's like. I don't like leaving him alone.'

Hillary nodded. 'We'll try and make it quick,' she said enigmatically. She felt, at that moment, utterly calm.

'We know that on the night that Mr Dale was killed, your husband was at his usual poker night. But where were you, Rita?'

'At home. Watching telly, like always.'

Hillary nodded. 'But that isn't true, is it, Rita?'

Rita Matthews said nothing. Her greying hair was tied back in a typical old lady's bun, and she was wearing a grey skirt and a hand-knitted sky-blue jumper. She'd probably knitted it herself. Her large, red and work-roughened hands lay lightly clasped together in front of her on the table. She looked as relaxed as Hillary.

'Tell me about Wordsworth,' Hillary said.

Rita Matthews shrugged one bony shoulder. 'He was a cat. You ever had a cat?'

'My mother always had a cat, down the years. I remember one called Smudge best. He was black with a single white smudge on his nose.'

Rita Matthews nodded. 'You know one cat, you know them all.'

'So he was your husband's cat then, more than yours?'

'No, he weren't,' Rita said, just a shade testily. 'Oh, after he got killed, all the fuss he kicked up, folks probably thought that. But I was the one that fed him. I gave him his worm pills and cleaned up after the little bugger if he was sick. More often than not, it was my lap he used to curl up on. Percy could never sit still long enough. He always had to be up and about, fidgeting.'

Hillary nodded. 'So Wordsworth used to sit on your lap, right. When you were knitting, maybe?' She nodded at the jumper the old woman was wearing. 'That's cable stitch, isn't it?'

'Yes,' Rita Matthews agreed. 'He used to like batting my wool about. Not that I'd let him chew on it, of course.'

'Right.' Hillary smiled. 'And how old was he? Before the dogs got him, I mean.'

'Twelve,' Rita said shortly.

'You'd had him a long time then.'

'Yes.'

'They get to be like a member of the family, don't they, when you have them so long, especially?' Hillary said softly.

Rita Matthews said nothing. It was hard to tell if the old girl was rattled, or merely curious, or neither. She had that flat-faced kind of patience that could stymie many an interviewer.

Hillary merely nodded. 'So, you looked after the cat, and loved him the most. It must have broken your heart that day, when the hounds came, and you couldn't save him.' Her voice was quiet now, and genuinely sincere.

'It did, yes,' Rita Matthews said flatly.

'But you didn't get to grieve for him, did you?' Hillary mused. 'You didn't get to bury him, and mourn him, and then, after a while, forgive yourself for the way he died, and move on. You couldn't do that, because your husband wouldn't let you, would he?'

Rita Matthews sniffed, but said nothing. Her eyes went to Janine then back to Hillary.

'Because your husband became obsessed with Malcolm Dale, and what he'd done. It wasn't really about Wordsworth, was it, all that palaver he made? If it had been left up to him, I daresay you could have got another cat and it wouldn't have made any difference to him one way or the other. *You* were the one who loved Wordsworth. He was a good cat, wasn't he, affectionate, like? And your husband went on and on about the man responsible for killing him. Tell me, when did he first start talking about murdering Malcolm Dale, Mrs Matthews?'

'About a couple of weeks after it happened.'

Hillary nodded. 'And he went on and on about it, didn't he? Day after day, week after week, month after month. For years, even. Keeping Wordsworth's death alive and well, so to speak. Never letting you forget it.'

'Daft bugger,' Rita said, her voice just a bit shaky now.

'Until, finally, you'd had enough of it. Hadn't you, Rita? Enough of listening to your husband going on and on about Malcolm Dale, and how he was going to make him pay for killing Wordsworth — but never actually doing it. All that talk about how hard it was to kill someone and get away with it. All that endless research about brakes and how to fix a car so that it would crash. All that stuff about how hard it was to get hold of a gun. How impossible it was to kill a man.' Hillary sighed. 'But, in reality, it was easy wasn't it, Rita? What did it really amount to? You waited until your husband was at his poker night and then what? Grab your coat and the poker? Or maybe a walking stick with a nice knobbly end to it? A quiet stroll through the village, careful to get out of sight if a car came by? Then you knocked on the door. Dale answers, and you tell him you need to talk. He's reluctant, but he lets you in. He sees you in the kitchen, of course. He's not going to invite the working classes into his drawing room, is he, not someone like him. And then what? The moment he turns his back — WHAM — a quick bash on the head. Maybe another one or two to make sure, when he's down. Then stick the poker or whatever back under your coat and walk home. Wash up at the sink. Wait until hubby comes back, make some cocoa and off to bed. That simple, that easy. It wasn't hard at all was it? It went something like that, didn't it, Rita?'

Rita Matthews blinked, but said nothing. Her knuckles were white now, but her hands remained folded demurely in front of her. The room was deathly quiet, with only the faint hiss of the tape recorder as background.

Hillary looked at the old woman in front of her, looking for a way in. Searching for the crack that would open her up. Not the cat — that hurt too much and went too deep. She'd just clam up harder if she tried using the cat. The husband maybe. She must bitterly resent him, deep down. But then, she was his primary carer, and she'd been looking after him for years. Washing, cooking, putting up with his ways. No, not the husband. She'd just get defensive.

Her eyes wandered over her, thinking furiously. The clean but shabby clothing, the grey hair, held back in the bun. Her mind went back to her file. What did they know about her? She was the daughter of a farm labourer, and had done other people's domestic work for years. She and her family had probably thought of Percy Matthews as a real catch. Then her marriage, the little cottage, the raising of children. All as law-abiding and working-class as you could get.

And suddenly, Hillary knew the way in.

She sighed and leaned forward across the table. 'You know, Rita, we can't have people getting away with murder,' she said softly. 'I know, when you read the papers and watch the news, it seems as if people do get away with it all the time, but that's mostly just hype. Nine times out of ten, we police get the killers. And that's as it should be. Isn't it?'

Rita Matthews blinked, her lower lip wobbled a bit, then she sat up a bit straighter in the chair and said flatly, 'It was the rolling pin. Not the poker. The rolling pin wasn't so long and fit under my coat better.'

\* \* \*

The next morning, Hillary went in to check on the paperwork that would have been processed on Rita Matthews overnight. She'd left the formal arrest and charging to Janine, who'd deserved it, and gone home early, using an aching hip as an excuse to leave the mopping up to Mel. Personally, she hoped the Crown Prosecution Service could work out something for the old gal. Sure as hell, any decent QC could make out a case for diminished responsibility.

She hadn't sat down at her desk five minutes before a sergeant from two desks over rolled his chair across to her desk and asked her if she'd heard the latest. Apparently Superintendent Jerome Raleigh had gone AWOL. No one had seen him since yesterday lunchtime. His civilian secretary was in a bit of a tizzy, being unable to locate him, and they'd even sent some uniforms to his house to see if he was ill.

'But it looks as if he's just packed up and gone.' The sergeant, a lanky, sandy-haired man who preferred to work burglary, nodded sagely. 'Maud from Fraud is running a book. Odds-on favourite he's had some sort of breakdown and done a runner. Wild-card betting has it he's been bumped off and his body dumped by one of Fletcher's gang in retaliation. Fancy putting some money down?' he asked, eyeing her carefully.

Hillary felt abruptly sick, and just managed to shake her head and smile. Because suddenly she was remembering that missing Dick Francis book. When it had turned up again, she'd come to the conclusion that the only one who could have taken it was her stepson. Ronnie's boy by his first marriage. Frank wouldn't bother to return it: why should he? He'd like to think of her fretting over it. But Gary respected and liked her, and might not want her to realise that he'd figured out his father's hiding place. And she'd been prepared to let it slide. After all, it could be argued that the money was his inheritance. Moreover, it very neatly solved her problem of what to do with it. But now, with a hollow feeling that made her feel as if she'd suddenly shot several hundred feet up in the air, she knew that there was a second explanation for that book going missing so briefly.

She waited until her heart had stopped thumping, and she was sure she wasn't about to throw up, then got up and tapped on Mel's door, sticking her head around it without waiting for a summons. 'I'm just going out for a while. Everything OK on the Rita Matthews thing?'

'Yep. She's got a brief, and he's trying to get her confession thrown out, but it'll stand. Did you hear Raleigh's gone missing?'

'Yeah, I heard,' she said, and held out her hands. 'Don't know, don't care, don't ask me,' she said and closed the door hard on her way out.

She drove straight to the internet café and logged on. As the computer hummed and hawed, she felt like biting her nails. Part of her didn't want to know. If all that money was gone, she really didn't want to know.

But it made too much sense for it to read any other way. Raleigh could have found out that she was digging around about him, and would have wanted to get something on her in order to reciprocate. And he'd obviously concentrate on Ronnie, because he was her only weak point; and to an experienced investigator like Raleigh, that Dick Francis book would have stood out like a sore thumb on her bookshelves.

He probably never thought he'd have to make a run for it, either. He'd had it all so well planned, he must have felt confident of successfully pulling it off. And, if it hadn't been for her, he would in fact have got away with it and still be sitting at his desk right now. But since he did have to make a run for it, he'd need money. Lots of money. So why not take hers?

Now, as she punched in the keys to bring up the bank's website, she realised that Raleigh would have broken the code as easily as she had. Of course, she could be wrong about all this. He might not have taken the money and run for the nearest country with no extradition with Britain at all. He might just stroll into his office any minute and wonder what all the fuss was about.

But she didn't think so.

As she punched in the account numbers, her heart fluttered in a brief moment of hope. After all, it was over a million quid they were talking about, and who really wanted to know they'd let such a fortune slip away? She was only human, when all was said and done, and hope did spring eternal in the human breast.

Her fingers hovered over the final key. If the money was gone, it meant that she'd never have to worry about it again. It meant Jerome would be gone, and Donleavy and the others could wrap the Fletcher case up without any fallout. They'd simply put it out that Raleigh had resigned. It would mean Mel would almost certainly be appointed acting superintendent, and she herself could ask for, and probably get, the promotion to DCI Mel would leave vacant.

It would be a good deal for everybody.

Except that she'd be out of a million quid plus.

She pressed the button and looked at the screen.

The money, of course, was gone.

**THE END**

## ALSO BY FAITH MARTIN

### DI HILLARY GREENE SERIES

### JENNY STARLING SERIES

### MONICA NOBLE SERIES

Join our mailing list to be the first to hear about
Faith Martin's next mystery, coming soon!

www.joffebooks.com

Thank you for reading this book. If you enjoyed it please
leave feedback on Amazon or Goodreads, and if there is
anything we missed or you have a question about then
please get in touch. The author and publishing team
appreciate your feedback and time reading this book.